JUST BEA

DEBORAH KLÉE

ISBN: 978-1-8380804-3-3

First Printed, 2021

Published by Sherman House

Just Bea

by

DEBORAH KLÉE

Dedicated to those who are or have had experience of being homeless.

You matter.

1

TWENTY-NINE SHOPPING DAYS TO CHRISTMAS

If it wasn't for the flier that had glued itself to Bea's shoe, she might never have found out about Declan. It was one of the three Santas that had been dining at Bea's usual table who brought it to her attention. There were other tables in Hartleys's staff canteen but Bea was a creature of habit. She peeled the flier from the sole of her shoe. Damp and dirty, it stayed intact as though refusing to be ignored. Still she paid it no heed.

'Wait. You've a little speck of ketchup there.' Bea waggled an index finger at Santa's luxurious beard. The Santas employed by Hartleys were required to be impeccable in appearance at all times.

'Thank you. You will definitely have all of your wishes granted this Christmas.' Santa winked, and for a magical moment Bea imagined that he was the real Santa Claus. Then, the table was hers and she had thirty blissful minutes alone, a respite from having to think. Bea needed these breaks so that she could retreat into her own world. Like going backstage after a performance, shedding the costume and wiping away the face paint. Bea the stylish and competent sales assistant could become just Bea. It was exhausting being Bea.

The flier might have been cleared away by the catering staff, and she would never have known. But, it clung to the edge of the table. It was only as she gathered her things to leave that Bea saw the photograph of Declan with his impish face and dimpled grin. Bea detached the flier and sank back into a chair. *Missing. Declan Connor of no fixed abode, but known in the Kings Cross area. If you have any information on his whereabouts call this number...*

It couldn't be – not Declan. Declan, with his funny sayings and silly jokes. The photograph must have been taken before he became homeless, because he didn't look sad, or the way she thought homeless people would look. Starved and grey. The colour of pavements. How many times had she walked past a homeless person without even glancing at them? She could have walked past Declan. He would have called after her. Wouldn't he? Bea bit her lip to suppress feelings that she didn't understand: a lump in her throat and a prickling of tears. Of course she was sad, but this response was more than concern for a missing boy. There was something else, a dark demon, an emotion that threatened to engulf her. A recognition that she was responsible for this. Oh God, what had she done? Bea closed her eyes to try to block out the sights and sounds of the restaurant. She wanted to run away and hide, bury her head under her duvet. She took deep breaths; she couldn't fall apart here.

Bea pressed the heels of her hands into her eye sockets, but the images kept coming: Declan packing his bag. The way he looked at her before leaving. If only she could wind back time and do things differently. A chair scraped as someone sat down opposite her.

'Mrs Barone said I could go to lunch as you were due back.' It was Sophie, one of the junior sales assistants.

Bea uncovered her eyes and flinched at the brightness of the lights. Sophie rolled her eyes.

'A migraine,' Bea lied. She stood on shaky legs and attempted a smile. White Christmas, came around again on the playlist. 'I'd better be getting back then.'

She was responsible for Declan becoming homeless. When Bea discovered that he had been sleeping in the store overnight, she had told her manager. It seemed like the right thing to do, but evidently not, because she became even less popular than before. The junior sales girls and delivery boys talked about her, not bothering to lower their voices when she was in earshot. Following her allegation, Declan had lost his job and the temporary roof over his head. Bea had no idea that he would become homeless – that she had made him homeless.

And now he was missing. Anything could have happened to him and it was her fault. What had she done?

Mrs Barone's gravelly voice startled Bea. 'We have a VIP shopper this afternoon, Suki Dee. Miss Licious will be received in the Exclusive stylist suite with her assistant. I've asked Mrs Jackson to take a selection of undergarments to the suite when we get the call.'

'Thank you for informing me, Mrs Barone. I will make sure that all runs smoothly whilst Jemima is upstairs.'

'I know you will, Miss Stevens. Mr Evans has two excellent senior sales assistants from which to choose my successor.'

Head of department was what Bea had been working towards for the past three years. It was in her first year at

Hartleys that she had ratted on Declan. Blood rushed to her face as she remembered that day.

Mrs Barone frowned and Bea realised that something was expected from her. She felt sick and a little dizzy. It was important that she say the right thing. Bea closed her eyes to concentrate and then said, 'When do you think we will hear who he has chosen?'

'Well, it will have to be before Christmas when I retire.'

Pippa, who was waiting to ask Bea something, overheard and supplied the one thing that Bea should have said. 'Mrs Barone, nobody could replace you. We're going to miss you so much.'

'Nobody could…' Bea parroted, but Mrs Barone had turned away, her attention now on the boys in black, so called for their uniform of black T-shirt and jeans, who had arrived with armfuls of silk and lace garments held high above the floor to stop them trailing.

Somehow, she had to try to forget about Declan, at least until she finished work. Bea followed the boys in black to see that the supplies were displayed to their best advantage. Pippa was laughing and chatting with the boys.

'The hosiery shelves need restocking,' Bea told her.

Pippa flashed angry eyes at her, but Bea was too preoccupied to care. How had the flier come to be on her shoe? It couldn't be a coincidence that she lived in Kings Cross and… that's right. A man, a homeless man, had thrust a piece of paper at her outside the station. It must have fallen out of her bag when she retrieved her purse to pay for her lunch, and then she stepped on it.

'Miss Stevens?' Mrs Barone interrupted Bea's thoughts. 'Please could you take over from Mrs Jackson as she's wanted upstairs?'

Bea jumped to attention. 'Of course, Mrs Barone.'

Jemima was gathering a flurry of gowns: feather trim, satin and lace, a cloud of cream, white, and coral. She arranged them on a rail, waiting for the completion of her sale.

'Sorry, but you're wanted in the Exclusive stylist suite,' Bea said.

'I know. I'll just finish here.'

Jemima's party of Arab ladies had meandered away and were now looking at bra and panty sets. They both knew that customers needed time and could spend thousands more, so long as they weren't rushed.

'I'll look after them,' Bea said to Jemima with what she hoped was a reassuring smile.

An hour later, Bea rang up twenty-six thousand pounds on the till and took her commission of the sale. Jemima would be disappointed, but it wasn't Bea's fault. Sales staff were not allowed to interfere with the commission process. Whoever rung up the sale took the commission; it was Hartleys's rule. One of the junior sales girls was staring at her, making an ugly face. Was she meant to ignore the rules? Other people seemed to know when to bend them, but it didn't make sense. Why have rules if there was another set of unknown rules about when to ignore them? However hard she tried, she never seemed to get it right.

Mrs Barone left her station in the corner of the department and approached Bea with a frown. 'Could you go and help Mrs Jackson? Our VIP has a wardrobe malfunction.'

Bea took her department manager to one side. 'Could you be more specific?'

'Apparently, the bodysuit that Mrs Jackson thought would work under the dress that our VIP plans to wear at an awards ceremony is not to her liking. It gives the appearance of nudity in all the right places, but our VIP was hoping for a little more cleavage and lift.'

'Understood.' Bea selected a silicone skin cleavage enhancer and as a backup a voluptuous silicone lift bra in a double G.

Jemima sighed audibly when Bea arrived with the garments. They could hear Suki Dee's meltdown from the expansive consulting area out front. The dressing room was almost as big as Bea's entire flat – more like a penthouse suite, without a bed.

'I thought the U-plunge, backless body was perfect, but apparently it's not.'

'I know. Not enough cleavage. If you want to get back to the floor, I can take it from here,' Bea said.

Jemima's face lit up. 'Oh, would you? I was hoping to be quick.'

'Yes, go.' Bea hurried her away before realising that she might be hoping to complete her sale. 'Jemima, I'm sorry but...' Too late – the door had swung shut.

Bea handed both of the garments to Suki Dee's dresser with an explanation as to how they should be fitted. 'I think that the cleavage enhancer is the best solution, but if Suki Dee isn't comfortable wearing it, the bra might work.'

More wails and cries of despair. Then, the dresser reappeared red-faced. 'I can't seem to get the hang of these. Would you mind?'

Bea took the silicone mounds from her. 'Well, you sort of do this and this.' She demonstrated how the cups enclosed each breast and then the tape was adjusted to create cleavage. 'It's tricky to get a good grip; you have to kind of anchor it down and then pull it over –'

'I read the instructions but it's not working and Suki is going mad in there. *Please*.'

Bea went hot and then cold. She searched for someone –

anyone – to step in and offer to help. There was no way that she could fit silicone cups onto the celebrity's naked boobs.

'*Please.*'

Suki Dee was a customer and it was Bea's job to serve her.

'Okay.' Bea took a deep breath and prepared to enter the sacred chamber.

It wasn't hard when you knew how, and Bea had become something of an expert. Suki Dee was thrilled with the effect of the adjustments and Bea had to admit that she looked amazing in the backless and almost frontless dress. It had been a bit embarrassing coming into such close personal contact with the star, but she managed to complete the task sparing Suki Dee's dignity. And Bea noted she had gone a whole hour without thinking about Declan. Then she felt guilty for not thinking about him.

2

TWENTY-EIGHT SHOPPING DAYS TO CHRISTMAS

Bea's shift was midday until eight in the evening. Then, there was Mr Evans's Christmas reception for the fashion floor sales staff. On any other night anxiety about an impending social event would have kept her awake, but last night all she could think about was Declan.

Every day on her way to and from work, Bea had walked past the homeless people sprawled around the entrance to King's Cross Station, barely taking any notice. Overcome with chagrin, she had taken a good look last night. There were several, huddled in sleeping bags and cardboard boxes. One of the men had a pile of cases and bags strapped together with a bungee cord, and another, a woman, had carrier bags. Bea had taken peeks as she strolled by, searching for a man handing out fliers, as she had no other clue to his identity. It could have been any one of the men; she had paid him no attention at the time.

Bea squirmed as she reflected on her callous disregard for people like Declan. It wasn't Declan's fault he became homeless; she knew exactly where to lay the blame. This morning, on her way into work, she would ask about the man handing out fliers. If she was to find Declan and put right her wrong, this was the best place to start. But what would she say?

It was scary enough talking to any stranger but homeless strangers were on a different level.

Before stepping out of her door, Bea checked for the third time to make sure the notes she had made weeks ago were in her bag. If Evans announced the new head of department at his Christmas reception, she might be asked to make a speech. The thought both terrified and excited her. It was as well to be fully prepared. No surprises.

That morning, the sky was blue and the air crisp as Bea, in stiletto heels, navigated the icy pavement, as though walking a tightrope. On the days she had a late shift, it was her morning ritual to buy an Americano and skinny oats from Denny's and take them back home to enjoy with a magazine. She loved releasing a magazine from its cellophane wrap, the waft of fresh print, the slip and slide of gloss. The December issue of *Vogue* was waiting for this indulgence, but today it held no attraction.

As she approached the station, Bea's heart beat a little faster. The man was back, handing out his fliers. She had to speak to him to find out what had happened to Declan, but she couldn't; she was afraid. Maybe if she googled 'how to talk to homeless people'. The internet had come to her rescue before, when she had googled 'how to make small talk'. *Ask open-ended questions and show that you are interested in the person,* it had said. A homeless person was still a person and so that advice should be good. But how could she start a conversation about Declan?

Just say, *Hello, a bit frosty today.* No, that wasn't open-ended. Bea had walked straight past him. She couldn't do it. But she had to; this man was no different to Declan. Bea pirouetted with tiny shuffles and retraced her steps. Commuters passed him by, ignoring his outstretched hand. Couldn't they see he was handing out fliers, not begging?

The man looked straight at Bea and her stomach knotted. His gaze was bold and commanding, as though he knew all about her. She had to be brave; this was her opportunity to ask him about Declan. Bea took a deep breath and closed her eyes, willing herself to find the right words. But when she opened her eyes, he was still staring.

'Why are you looking at me?' That was the trouble. If she didn't prepare herself, the wrong things came out of her mouth.

The man dropped his gaze and shook his head. Now she had offended him. Bea tried again. 'What do you think of this weather?' She tilted her head and frowned slightly to show that she cared about his reply.

The man looked up through a fringe of matted hair, his face scrunched up. 'I think that if it gets much colder, it will freeze my…' He stopped himself from completing the sentence. 'Don't you have a pair of snow boots or something?'

Bea followed his gaze; he was staring at her Jimmy Choos. 'I do, but I always wear high heels to work.' So that's why he was staring at her.

He had an Irish accent just like Declan.

'Why are you handing out those fliers?' Her heart was beating too quickly.

'Ah, so you're going to be telling me I need a licence.' He shook his head and his eyes crinkled, but she couldn't see whether he was smiling or snarling beneath his beard.

'No. It's just… Well, why are you trying to find Declan? Do you know him?' It occurred to Bea that he could be giving out fliers on behalf of a charity to earn some money.

The man straightened his back, a look of expectation in his eyes. 'Do you know something? Have you seen him?'

Now, Bea felt stupid. There was nothing that she could say. To explain how she knew Declan, and why she was concerned for his well-being, would mean admitting to this stranger that she had made him homeless.

'No. You gave me a flier yesterday and I just wondered.'

'Wondered why it mattered that a homeless guy went missing, you mean?' He slumped back against the hoarding. 'Sorry, didn't mean to bite yer head off.'

'It's okay. I just wanted to help.'

The man sighed and went back to handing out fliers.

'I was just going to get a coffee. Would you like one?' That's what she should have said all along. Kind and compassionate and at the same time practical.

'No thanks.'

'Oh. Okay.' So that was that. But Bea was reluctant to walk away. This man was her link to Declan and somehow, she had to find him and put things right. 'What's your name?'

'Ryan O'Marley.' He grinned, exposing surprisingly white teeth.

'I'm Beatrice Stevens but people call me Bea.'

'Pleased to be meeting you, Bea,' he said.

There was something about his expression that Bea couldn't read. It was as though he was amused by her but she didn't know why. Feeling awkward and a little snubbed by his rejection of her kind offer, she continued on to Denny's, all the while sensing his eyes on her back.

When she arrived at work, the store was even busier than the day before. Mrs Barone called her over, just as she was going to take her break.

'Mr Evans wants to see you in his office.'

Bea studied Mrs Barone's face for a clue as to what this might be about. The tone of her voice had given nothing away. It was impossible, and so Bea asked, 'Do you know why?'

Mrs Barone smiled. 'I do not and neither will you unless you get up there.'

'Do you think it's about his decision on your successor?'

'I have no idea. Just go.' Mrs Barone dismissed Bea with a wave of her hand.

As Bea took the lift up to the fourth floor she imagined announcing her promotion to her family at Christmas. At last they would see that her obsession with fashion, as they called it, had paid off. She had a fifty percent chance of getting the job. Excellent attendance, always on time, and an exceptional sales record. But Jemima was more popular. She desperately wanted to believe that this was going to be good news but past experience filled her with self-doubt.

'Come in, Miss Stevens.'

He didn't look happy but neither did he look sad. Bea wasn't sure how to arrange her face. She settled for something between solemn and cheerful.

'You did an excellent job with our VIP yesterday, well done.' Mr Evans checked his computer screen. 'An impressive sales record too.'

Bea glowed from within. Her hands were sweaty.

'As you know, Mrs Barone is leaving us after many years of service.' He gently drummed his fingers on the desk. Bea wished he would speed things up, as she was finding it hard to remain calm. The expression on her face was feeling a bit tense and awkward.

'I've spent a long time giving due consideration to which of her senior sales staff should be promoted to head of lingerie and wanted to take the opportunity to give some feedback to each of you. A staff appraisal if you like. Tea?'

Bea had been concentrating so hard, the question threw her.

'Would you like tea or coffee?'

They were evidently going to be together for some time. Long enough to drink a cup of coffee. Did that mean that he wanted to prepare her for the new role? Surely, if he was going to let her down, he would come straight out with it.

'Coffee, please.'

Mr Evans reviewed his notes. 'Mrs Barone thinks highly of you. She has been impressed by your knowledge of the lingerie collections and your creativity in bringing together compatible products from across different departments to please our customers. Apparently, the lingerie buyers seek you out as you're well informed on what sells well, not just in Hartleys but in our competitors' stores.'

Mr Evans's PA distributed their drinks and Bea allowed herself to relax. This was all good; he was just building up to make his announcement. Words of acceptance formed in her head.

'These are admirable qualities, as are your dedication and commitment. Since joining Hartleys, you've exceeded our expectations.'

Bea smiled and her heart swelled with pride.

'However.' He paused and Bea held her breath. 'Head of department requires different skills and attributes, and I am sorry but I don't believe you have the capacity to excel in that role.'

The words she had prepared a few minutes ago felt like stones in her mouth. Her voice came out hoarse. 'I don't understand. Why don't you think I'm suitable for that position?'

She didn't say, *What about the hours I've spent learning Russian, the careful studying of competitors' displays and pricing, the researching of sales patterns, the keeping ahead of new trends?* Every day of her life, for the past three years, she had been working towards this goal and now he was telling her that she didn't have the skills and attributes required.

'What is it that I lack? What should I have done differently? Tell me. I'll learn.'

Mr Evans dropped a sugar cube into his tea and stirred. 'I don't think that you can learn these things.' He coughed. 'Um, maybe...' He picked up the teaspoon and put it down again. 'Perhaps you'd like to see our occupational health doctor, get some advice as it were? Maybe see a psychologist?'

Now Bea was angry. Really angry. This was how it had been at school. The constant referring to something considered missing. As if she needed to be 'fixed'. When she was younger, Bea found it hard to control the rage that this sparked, but now that she was older and wiser, she understood that it would do her no favours and she was better rising above his thoughtless remark.

'I appreciate that you are trying to help but an explanation of what you see lacking in me would be more beneficial.'

Mr Evans went a little pink and coughed. 'Of course. Yes, I see. Um. Let me put it this way, Mrs Jackson is a team player. She notices the little things, remembers our customers by name, even remembers some of our regulars' birthdays and the names of their children or grandchildren. The other staff work well with her; she knows how to motivate them. A leader. To be frank I don't think you can learn that, Bea.'

The change from Miss Stevens to Bea did not go unnoticed, but he wasn't going to soften her that easily. 'Thank you for being direct with me, Mr Evans. I don't necessarily agree that the attributes you mention can't be learnt and I will make every effort to develop skills where I am lacking.'

Having dropped this bombshell, Evans leaned back in his chair. 'Hartleys is a temple of retail. We have a reputation across the world for our customer care. Shopping at Hartleys is a luxury experience. One that is enjoyed by royalty and showbiz stars as well as the man in the street. Yes. It is all about our customers' experience.'

Bea knew all of that. She could have written the script. But whilst Evans spouted, it gave her the chance to think about what he had said and to try to regain a sense of calm.

When she returned to the shop floor, Bea couldn't look at Mrs Barone or Jemima. Had her failings been discussed with them? It was so humiliating. In a few hours there was the Christmas drinks reception where Mr Evans was bound to announce Jemima's promotion. She considered feigning a stomach bug but when the announcement was made everyone would guess the reason for her absence. No, she had to go. And hold her head high.

Bea was sipping a glass of champagne when Alastair from the PR department joined her.

'Thanks for sorting Suki Dee's wardrobe malfunction. Her PA was gushing about you. Anyone would think that you had brought about world peace.'

'Maybe it felt like that for her PA. Celebrities can't be easy people to work for.' Bea threw back the champagne and plucked another glass from a passing tray. She just had to stay long enough to hear Mr Evans's Christmas speech and then she could crawl away.

'Her publicist wants us to host a big charity event. Something that will link Suki's name with a good cause. She's going for an Angelina Jolie image to shake off the glamour girl one.'

'If that's the case, I wonder why she was so fussed about

her cleavage,' Bea said. Alastair chuckled, although she hadn't meant to be funny.

And then, the tapping of a glass brought them all to attention.

Bea smiled and clapped when the announcement was made and Jemima looked sheepish, like she didn't know it was coming, but Evans must have prewarned her. Bea imagined the conversation that Evans would have had with Jemima. The conversation that Bea had prepared for. When had Evans met with Jemima? Before Bea's meeting or after? She swiped another glass of champagne from the tray of a passing waiter. It was an automated response, as she tried to act as though she wasn't falling apart. But her head was beginning to swim and the drink tasted too acidic. There hadn't been any plates of food circulating for some time.

Bea lurched her way to the ladies' toilet. Oh dear, she felt a bit sick. It was having no food in her stomach. Sitting in a cubicle, head in her hands, Bea heard Pippa and Sophie talking about Jemima's promotion.

'Well, I'm not surprised Bea didn't get it. She may sell a lot of stuff but she's a bit self-centred. I don't think the management below stairs rate her; she doesn't have a good word for any of the delivery boys or the despatch staff and you have to get on with everyone as head of department. Bea's only interested in Bea.'

She waited until the door closed behind them and then sat awhile longer. Bea was fourteen again. That time it had been Hetty Chambers and Davinia Grayson laughing about the way the she wore her hair – with an Alice band – and the length of her dress, apparently it was too long and her shoes frumpy. So much had changed since then, her dress sense for a start. But still it wasn't enough. It was true that she was focused. Focused and determined to succeed. Not just for herself but for Hartleys. *Deep breaths. They don't matter. Be strong.*

But Mr Evans's opinion could not be so easily dismissed. Okay, if he wanted her to be more of a people person, she could do that too.

3

TWENTY-EIGHT SHOPPING DAYS TO CHRISTMAS

Bea stumbled out of King's Cross Station and into the scene from a Christmas card. Powder soft snow, already a few inches thick, coated everything. A scattering of footprints was fast disappearing as more snow fell. She saw Ryan, the man with the fliers, straight away; he was helping an old woman create some shelter out of cardboard boxes.

'You can't sleep out here,' Bea slurred as she carefully planted one foot in front of the other, her feet sinking into the new snow. Nobody should need to sleep on the street in this weather.

'Careful.' Ryan reached out his hand to Bea and she jolted away.

A heel skidded and she landed hard on her bottom. Cold, wet snow stung her calves and thighs.

'I saw you going, but I was too late.'

What was he talking about? If he hadn't tried to grab hold of her, she wouldn't have fallen and now she was sprawled, legs akimbo.

Ryan bent over her, as though *she* were the one in need of help. *Oh God, the humiliation.* 'It's okay,' Bea said as she struggled up.

'I told you it was snow boot weather.' Ryan held up one of Bea's shoes and in his other hand, the heel.

Bea used the railings to hoist herself up; the sting of ice on her shoeless foot was unbearable. How long did it take to get frostbite? She'd get chilblains, for sure. Bea slid back down the railings and landed on Ryan's sleeping bag.

'It's not fair. I work bloody hard. Nobody appreciates me. And now this!'

The old woman muttered something and then burrowed into her cardboard shelter.

'Life's shit. But you have to make the most of what you have and you –'

'Are a selfish cow. I know. Everyone thinks so.' Bea's throat clogged with tears.

Ryan was staring at her again – but maybe now he had cause to stare. She was making a spectacle of herself but Bea didn't have the energy or will to control her emotions. Losing the heel of one of her Jimmy Choos wasn't a catastrophe in itself but it felt like it on top of everything else she had endured that day. Then when she tried to be a good Samaritan – to show this man the compassion that she would have wanted Declan to experience – he bloody well threw it back in her face.

'Why didn't you let me buy you a coffee this morning?' she wailed.

'Because I don't drink caffeine.' Ryan spoke softly, a lilt to his voice.

Big flakes of snow that reminded Bea of ones she had cut from paper in school rested and then melted on her nose and eyelashes. They felt like tears, and maybe they were. Bea buried her face in her scarf, wishing that she could curl up and go to sleep right there. Let the snow bury her.

Ryan coughed. 'I don't want to seem inhospitable but you're sitting on my bed and it's getting late. Maybe you should go home and sleep it off.'

Her mother would be appalled. She was slumped on a homeless man's bedding at eleven thirty at night, on the street at King's Cross. *Bea* was appalled. She scrambled to her feet. The snow was falling thick and fast.

'I'll put something over the cardboard, Sal, make it waterproof,' Ryan said to the old woman.

It was almost impossible negotiating the snow with one heel missing, but Bea could not bear the feeling of ice on the sole of her foot. She headed for Denny's because that had been in her mind when she got off the train – to buy a strong coffee. But when she was at the counter, Bea had an idea. Hot chocolate. A hot chocolate would warm Ryan and Sal up and make amends for her bad manners. Hot chocolate didn't have caffeine. Then she would go home to bed.

When Bea returned balancing two large hot chocolates, Ryan was securing thick bin liners over the cardboard shelter. Triumphant in her act of generosity, Bea held up her offerings. 'I got you both a – ouch!' The lid slipped off one of the cups, scalding her hand, and Bea lost her grip. Almost in slow motion, she watched both cups tumble through the air. The brown liquid made an arc before landing on Ryan's sleeping bag.

'Jesus Christ!' He whipped up his bedding but it had already absorbed the hot, sticky drink.

'I'm so sorry.' Bea tried to help but he elbowed her away.

'What's the matter with you? Can't you just mind your own business like you usually do? Why pick on us?'

'What do you mean – like I usually do? You don't know me.'

'Maybe I don't, but once Declan pointed you out to me, I noticed you. Okay?'

Was he saying that Declan had sat outside this very station, watching her walk past every morning and evening? How could she have walked past without seeing him? It was official, she was a selfish bitch. 'No, it's not okay.' Her voice was a whisper.

'Ah not like that. Don't be getting any ideas, you're not my type. Or Declan's, for that matter.' He gave a half laugh. ''Twas just a game between us. Declan would make me laugh, trying to get you to notice us, but no – you always strutted past, nose in the air. Until today. Now why, I'm asking you, why all of a sudden can't you just let us be?' He shook out his sleeping bag. The stain was like a map of Kenya. Bea watched as the southernmost tip trickled downwards, like a river finding crevices in the folds of nylon.

Ryan didn't know. Declan hadn't told him how he knew Bea. Every day Declan had been waiting for her apology, for her to understand the consequences of her actions. Bea covered her face with her hands. 'Oh God. I'm sorry. How can I make this right?'

'It'll dry, to be sure. Don't be getting yerself worked up on my account.'

If he knew what she had done, he wouldn't be so kind. The map of Kenya was being rolled away as Ryan packed up his ruined bedding. 'Come on, I'll walk you home.'

'But where will you sleep? You'll freeze.'

'I'll be fine. I've a little hidey-hole that'll keep me dry. Here, lean on me.' He offered his arm and Bea took it, as she was finding it hard to balance with just one heel.

'Have you known Declan for long?' Bea asked as they

swayed across the square towards the welcoming glow of lights from her apartment block.

'A few years now. He's a rare one.' Ryan paused as though lost in thought.

Bea's foot slipped and Ryan caught her. They continued to meander at a slow but steady pace. 'I've never met anyone like Declan. He would do anything for anyone; there really isn't a bad bone in his body. That boy's like a brother to me.'

'Oh.' They had reached her apartment block. 'When did he go missing?'

Ryan looked into the distance and then dropped his head, as if the emotional weight of losing his friend was too great to carry. 'Eight days ago. Thursday, last week.'

'And you've no idea where he might be?' Bea felt the fug of alcohol lift a little. It could have been the effect of the freezing cold night or Ryan's unsaid words that something bad might have happened to Declan.

'I'll find him,' Ryan said.

It was time to thank Ryan and say goodbye, but Bea couldn't send him away into the night with a cold, wet sleeping bag. She had failed Declan, but she could show some compassion to his friend.

'Why don't you sleep in my spare bedroom tonight?' Bea blurted out and immediately regretted it. She didn't know anything about him. But he was a close friend of Declan, and she owed it to Declan. It was too cold for Ryan to sleep outside.

Ryan looked as though he too was surprised by her suggestion. 'Because you're a single girl. A slightly inebriated single girl. I've got a little sister, about your age. I would be telling her not to let a strange man into her home on any account – no matter what the circumstances.'

But he's not a stranger, Bea thought, and then she decided if

Declan trusted him, then so could she. 'Please. It would make me feel better about spilling hot chocolate on your sleeping bag. I could pop it in my washing machine and it'll be dry by the morning.'

'I'm not sure. This'll be the booze a talking. You'll wake up, forget you invited me in, and scream blue murder.'

They looked at each other, each weighing up the risks. The snow whirled in the light of a street lamp and Ryan pulled his jacket closer around him. 'I'd better be off. This isn't going to let up.'

'That settles it,' Bea said. 'Come inside before we both freeze to death.'

4

SEPTEMBER 1996

The cow flared its nostrils and Ryan struggled to step back but Da nudged him forward.

'She won't hurt you, lad. Give her nose a little stroke. There. Like that.' Da demonstrated and the cow shook her head free, her eyes fixed on Ryan.

He wanted to stroke her, to show his da that he wasn't afraid, but he couldn't. He was trapped between Da and the cow with its hot, smelly breath and mad eyes. She blew air through her nose, spraying Ryan's face.

'No. No.' He tried to wriggle free but Da grabbed his wrist. 'You have to let her get used to you. Show her who's boss.' He squashed Ryan's hand against the bristle of the cow's warm hide. Ryan shut his eyes, praying for it to be over.

'Moo cow.' Caitlin, Ryan's baby sister, let go of Ma's hand and ran to pet the cow. 'There's my princess,' Da said, lifting Caitlin into his arms. 'Caitlin's not scared of the cows, are you, angel?'

Ryan hung his head. The nightmare he had as a little kid of cows coming down the chimney still haunted him. The way they took over the farmhouse, filling every room, squashing him out. More and more of them kept coming down the chimney. There wasn't any room. He would suffocate!

'William, that's not fair. Give him time and he'll be grand with them. You can't force these things.'

Ma was trying to help but it made him feel more ashamed. He was seven and Caitlin three; he should have been the one helping Da. 'I'm not scared,' Ryan shouted and he ran from the barn.

As they walked home, Ma ignored his outburst and made cheery conversation about school.

'I made Da a mug in art class,' Ryan said as they approached the spot with the view, the place where they always stopped. 'It's got a cow on it.'

'He will be pleased,' Ma said.

Ryan hoped so. He couldn't seem to please Da no matter what he did. 'I'm sorry I didn't make you one too but I didn't have time.'

Ma put an arm around him and although Ryan knew he was too old for cuddles he leant into her and took comfort from the familiarity of her scent: a combination of baked bread, warm milk, and lavender soap.

'I'll make you a dish for your dressing table, like the one Siobhan Riley made her ma, but better.' He didn't have to try to please Ma; she was hardly ever cross, even when he and Caitlin buried all of the cutlery in the backyard pretending it was hidden treasure. They found most of it, eventually.

'Will you take a look at that view?' Ma said when they got to the top of the hill and looked out over the valley: their farm and Riordan's arable land which adjoined their pastures.

'One day, I'm going to build a house here like the Magic Faraway Tree.'

'You'll have the farm, you won't need to build a house,' Ma said.

Ryan thought about this. He wasn't sure he wanted to live with the cows when he grew up. 'But if I have a house of my own, all of my friends can live with me.'

'What about your wife and children?'

'They can live there too, and you can if you want to and Caitlin.'

'It'll have to be a big house,' Ma said and they continued on down the hill for their tea.

'And it will be a magic one,' Ryan said. 'Everyone who lives in my house will have their wishes come true.'

5

TWENTY-EIGHT SHOPPING DAYS TO CHRISTMAS

Dirt lined the creases around his eyes. Very dark eyes – brown, and they were darting around like a bluebottle taking everything in: the unopened post on her hallway table, the hats and accessories on her coat stand, the money that she had left out to pay the maintenance man.

Keeping her back to the front door – it was what the security firm had advised when they did the mandatory training on terrorist attacks, *keep your exits clear* – Bea said, 'Um, the spare room's there.'

Maybe she had been a bit reckless, but it was past midnight; in five or six hours she could send him on his way.

'If you're having second thoughts, it's okay. Maybe I should just leave you to it.' He hoisted his bag further up his arm.

'No. Here, give me your sleeping bag and I'll stick it in the machine.'

'You're sure? You won't wake up and accuse me of taking advantage or the like?'

'Well, if you're saying that you don't trust *me*,' Bea bridled.

'Okay, okay. If you hadn't thrown cocoa over my bed, there would be no reason for all of this.'

They were both tense, maybe both regretting the arrangement. He could be a bit more appreciative though, instead of acting as though it was *him* doing *her* a favour.

'Your sleeping bag?' she said.

Ryan dropped his holdall with a thud and then wriggled out of his rucksack. The sleeping bag was between the handles of his holdall, an imitation Armani bag. Declan had one just like it; she remembered being surprised to see the EA7 logo, when he was packing away his things and then she had realised it was imitation. Maybe it was Declan's bag.

'You have a lot to carry around,' Bea prompted, hoping to find out if she was right.

He shrugged and then dropped his bundle of bedding into Bea's arms. 'The spare room's in there you say?'

Bea pushed her bedside table against the door before climbing into bed fully clothed. Just a few hours' sleep and then she would wake Ryan and say goodbye. Next time they met, she would find out more about Declan's disappearance. There must be something she could do to find him. It wasn't true what the sales girls said; she wasn't self-centred. Bea remembered bringing home an injured cat when she was a child. It had been hit by a car and so she rolled its broken body in her school blazer.

Bea drifted into a muggy sleep. Declan was lying in the road; he would get run over, but Bea couldn't get to him. Lorries blared their horns as she tried to cross, cars swerved, people jeered and shouted at her. Then, she reached him and turned him over. '*No*,' Bea screamed and woke up. Declan's face was bloody, both of his eyes gauged out.

Her head ached and her mouth was dry. Bea stumbled out of bed and saw the bedside table had been moved. Then, she remembered Ryan and the misery of the day before.

Bang. The noise came from her living room. Bea froze. He was creeping around her flat. She had got it wrong – again. Her common sense impeded by too many glasses of champagne. 'Reckless' didn't begin to describe her error of judgement. She was alone in her flat with a complete stranger, a rough sleeper who was over six foot tall. If he murdered her, nobody would hear. She'd never met her neighbours, had no idea who lived in the flat downstairs or next door. She imagined *Crimewatch* images recounting her last steps. Was there a CCTV camera at King's Cross Station? Would they have seen her walk away with Ryan? Then, she thought of her parents hearing the news of her tragic death and Bea was furious for putting herself in this dangerous situation.

He was definitely sneaking around the living room. Bea grabbed one of her stilettos, the only potential weapon in her bedroom. *That must be why they called them killer heels,* she mused. The hall light was off, but a shaft of moonlight fell across the living room entrance. She always closed that door before going to bed. *Rattle. Rattle.* It came from within.

Keep your back to the door, Bea reminded herself. But wasn't there something about not cornering a crazed man? Something or someone moved near the window.

'Freeze,' she shouted. It was the first thing that came to mind.

'Curse-a Jaysus.' The man shifted into the moonlight, sucking on the side of his thumb. 'Bugger. I caught it.'

Bea dropped her shoe. 'What are you doing?'

'Didn't you hear the window a banging all night? You've left this top one open and the catch has broken. If you leave it like this, it'll freeze up by morning and you're wasting energy – losing warm air.'

Bea watched as Ryan fiddled with the catch.

'I've got some Gaffer tape in my bag. I'll make it good for tonight but you'll have to get it fixed.'

He returned with the tape and after a few minutes the window was secure. Now would be the time to say goodbye, if he hadn't been for the fact that he'd just done something nice for her.

'Have you slept at all?' Bea asked. He didn't look as though he had.

'I don't need a lot of sleep. You get used to making the most of a few minutes' kip when you can. Doesn't look as though you have either.' Ryan nodded at her appearance and Bea became conscious of her crumpled clothes and smeared make-up. Nobody saw her like this. But, he was a rough-sleeper and she wouldn't see him after today and so it didn't really matter.

'There was a lot of snow in the night,' Ryan said, turning his attention from Bea to outside where the distorted shapes of cars were silhouetted in the moonlight, as though packaged for delivery.

'Will your friend be alright?' Bea perched on the arm of a chair.

'The snow would've made a nice little igloo for her. Sal's okay. It's one of the safest spots at night.' He came away from the window to join her. 'Do you mind if I sit? My clothes may leave a mark.'

Bea switched on a lamp. 'No, of course not.'

He hesitated. 'Maybe I should just leave, let you get some sleep.'

Bea was tempted to accept. But it was still snowing and his sleeping bag wouldn't have dried. Besides it could have been

Declan – his accent, his courteous manner. That's why Declan was so popular. The gift of the gab. What did they say? *He'd kissed the Blarney Stone.*

'No. It's fine. Try and get a few hours' sleep.' She would have liked to do the same but was afraid to go back to sleep now that she was sober.

'Okay, if you're sure, but first light I'll be gone.'

6

TWENTY-SEVEN SHOPPING DAYS TO CHRISTMAS

Bea awoke to a police siren. Three years of living in London and Bea had not got used to the urban soundtrack. She fumbled for her phone on the side table. Nine thirty-five. Why was she lying on top of the bed wearing her Sandro jumpsuit? And then she remembered Ryan and how he fixed her window in the middle of the night.

Bea changed into jeans and a jumper – she would dress for work later – and hung up her jumpsuit, smoothing out the creases. Thankfully, she hadn't torn the fine mesh, but it would need a dry clean.

There was little light when Bea drew open her curtains. Snow framed the window and it felt as though the flat was cocooned in cotton wool. With any luck, Ryan would have gone. The flat was very quiet. *Please let him be gone,* she pleaded in her head.

She knocked on the door of the spare room and when there was no reply, Bea quietly turned the handle and peeked in. A musty, sour smell greeted her. Ryan wasn't in the bed but the duvet had gone. Her body relaxed; he was welcome to the duvet. At least she didn't have to try to make polite conversation.

'What's the time?' a voice came from the other side of the bed and Bea jumped.

Ryan was lying under the duvet on the floor.

'Nine forty-five. Why didn't you sleep in the bed?'

'You don't want a dirty tramp messing up your nice things. This was fine but I didn't mean to sleep so long.'

Unguarded and bleary-eyed, Ryan looked younger. If he were Declan, she would have wanted someone to show him kindness and compassion. It was true, he did smell a bit ripe, but that wasn't his fault.

'I was going to pop out to buy a coffee and skinny oats; I don't have to be in work until twelve. Why don't I get something for you and while I'm out, you can have a shower, if you like.' Bea blushed as soon as she had said it. Was it rude or patronising to suggest he bathe? It was crazy to leave him alone in her flat, but at least he could be dressed again by the time she returned and it was nothing to buy him breakfast. Mum would be apoplectic if she knew – all the more reason to do so.

'I don't want to take liberties. But it would be good to clean up.' He draped the duvet back over the bed.

'Help yourself to anything in the bathroom – shower gel, shampoo.'

In her bedroom, Bea found a big towel in the airing cupboard. Then, she stuffed her jewellery into the back pockets of her jeans. Best not leave temptation in his way.

'What will it be? A bacon sarnie?'

'If you don't mind, something cold. I can make it last a while longer.'

Bea cringed. She had no idea what life was like on the

street. 'Okay. And a hot chocolate or is there something else you'd prefer?'

'A camomile tea would be grand.'

'Okay, a camomile tea and something cold. Won't be long.'

A crisp wind chafed her cheeks and nipped at her nose. Maybe it would be a white Christmas. She was going to spend it with her family in Hampshire. Then, it hit her again – a wave of disappointment. Bea had pictured herself dropping the news into conversation at the dinner table. They would have to take her seriously then. Except they wouldn't, because she was still a sales assistant. It didn't matter to Mum and Dad that it was Hartleys, she might as well be serving at the pick and mix counter in Woolworths, just as her mum had once predicted – although the chain had long since disappeared from the high street.

At this hour, before the snow turned into sludge, Kings Cross was magical. Ryan was right, Sal's shelter did look like an igloo. Bea stomped across to the white dome. 'Hello? Sal?'

There was no reply; maybe she was asleep.

A few minutes later, Bea left a tea outside the igloo and returned to the flat with a bag of sandwiches, her skinny oats, and a couple more drinks balanced in a cardboard tray. Other footprints had joined hers, maybe a size nine and smaller prints – perhaps a child's. Paw prints too. Who were these people that flowed around her? She had never noticed before, wasn't interested, but Declan missing had made her think. Everyone had a story. They existed alongside one another, in separate worlds.

Bea lived precariously between two spheres – Hartleys, where she thought she had created an image of normality, and her own world where she could be herself. Last night, she had fallen through the cracks. Inviting a stranger into her home wasn't normal, she knew from her mother's reaction when she brought home the injured cat. Hurt by her colleagues' impression of her, maybe she had been trying to prove that she was caring. Her sense of self had been shattered and she was too weary and miserable to piece herself back together. She looked up at her flat, no longer a place of refuge, and then down at the footprints dissolving in the melting snow.

'I'm back,' Bea called from the front door – just in case he was naked. The money for the maintenance man was still on the table. It wasn't much, just fifteen pounds, but it confirmed that Ryan was trustworthy.

There was no reply and then the bathroom door opened bringing with it the scent of geranium. Bea ducked her head and was relieved to see Ryan's bare feet and denim clad legs. But when she looked up her heart bounced against her ribcage. He was different – so different that he seemed strange again and her old fears returned.

'You said to help myself to stuff in the bathroom. I used one of your disposable razors, hope that's okay.' He rubbed a hand across his cheek, the exposed skin endearingly pink like peeled fruit. His hair was blond, almost golden.

'Yes, of course.' Bea closed her mouth. 'I, um, bought a few things.'

'Here.' Ryan relieved Bea of her load and took it through to the kitchen.

'I'll fix your window before I go.' Ryan sat at her kitchen table, watching Bea as she fussed around with plates. In three years, the only visitors to her flat had been her parents when she first arrived. Her heart was beating a little too fast and she was hot. Bea went to take off her jumper but stopped. It was too intimate. And having this stranger in her personal space was way too intimate.

'No, it's okay. The maintenance man can do it. Here.' She pushed two packs of sandwiches across the table. 'I didn't know if you were a vegan or not, so I bought a meaty one and a veggie one.' Please let him just go and then she could forget this ever happened.

'I can't accept these if you won't let me pay my way. I may not have any money but I have these.' He presented two red callused palms.

And your dignity, Bea thought. She knew how important it was to feel that you mattered. 'Of course, I'm sorry. That's a kind offer, thank you.'

He was waiting for something more.

'I accept,' Bea said and eventually he relaxed and inspected the sandwiches.

He bit into the ham one. A little bite for a big man.

Bea gulped down some coffee, grateful for the caffeine.

'You should drink some water,' Ryan said.

Oh yes, the champagne. It was a hangover, something Bea hadn't experienced in a long while. 'Water, of course.'

'You seemed a little upset last night.' He had a soothing voice – a deep timbre. If she shut her eyes she could imagine he was a radio presenter. One who eased you into the day, with a familiar rhythm and lilt to his voice. Maybe that was why Bea told him about her meeting with Mr Evans. There was something comforting about sitting with this stranger in her own clothes, the ones she only wore when she was alone, the snow enveloping them.

'I did *everything* – everything I possibly could to prepare for that job. I don't understand why it wasn't enough. What does it even mean – *connecting with customers*?'

Ryan took his plate to the sink.

'It's okay, I'll put it in the dishwasher.' Too late, he was already rinsing it, his back to her.

'I don't suppose your Mr Evans knows the meaning of connecting any more than you do. Tricking them into handing over their money, pretending a friendship, hoodwinking them.'

Bea regretted moaning about her lot. It was insensitive given his situation.

'Why are you homeless?' she blurted out and then blushed.

He turned to face her. 'Not because I'm a junkie, although that's what you thought. Or a wino.'

'I didn't think that for one moment.' But she had.

'Or because I choose to live on the streets. That's the other one – they're happier there. Who in their right mind would want to sleep out in this crappy weather?' The window rattled in agreement. 'Have you got a tool box?' He raised his eyebrows as though guessing her response.

Bea shook her head.

'Thought not. Give me half an hour or so and I'll be back. You aren't going to work for a while yet?'

Snowflakes had settled on the window pane robbing the flat of light.

'Not until eleven-thirty.' Bea didn't want to go in, for the first time in three years. Her heart ached for the loss of that joy. She gave a wan smile, glad of his company as a distraction from her pain.

Ryan left, taking his holdall with him. Maybe it was just habit never to leave valuable possessions unguarded. Bea would have liked to have asked whether it was Declan's bag, but that would mean admitting she knew him. If Ryan knew that she had made Declan homeless and then walked past him twice a day without even seeing him, he would have a very poor opinion of her.

7

TWENTY-SEVEN SHOPPING DAYS TO CHRISTMAS

The room grew darker as snow formed a feathery cuff around the window, just like the sumptuous trim on the sleeves of the Jovani robes. Feathers, silk, and satin. She loved the touch of fine lingerie. Loved the tranquillity of their department: a hint of perfume, soft barely audible music, and the gentle glide of staff. Like the surface of a still pond. Shoppers were unaware of the scientific calculations that went into sales. The sharp eyes and wit of sales assistants ready to help them spend. Record sales this Christmas and yet the department had never once seemed rushed. Always an oasis of peace. She ought to be dressed and ready for work, not sitting there watching the oval of light in the window get smaller and smaller.

'Thanks, mate,' Ryan called to somebody as he pushed open the front door.

Bea jumped up, feeling guilty that she had not moved since he left. 'Who were you talking to?'

'Mike from flat F.'

Bea frowned. 'You know him?' She didn't know any of her

neighbours. Couldn't even recall their faces. There was a baby somewhere in the building because she had heard it cry, but there again, it could have been visiting.

Ryan dumped a screwdriver and a can of oil on the table. 'This shouldn't take long.'

Bea inspected the oil. 'This is only half full.'

'Yeah, Molly found it in her storeroom, bless her.'

'Who's Molly?' Yuck, she had oil on her fingers. It would ruin her jumper. Bea got up and washed her hands at the sink.

'How can you have lived here – what? Two or three years and not know Molly?'

Bea suppressed a sadness that threatened to engulf her. Did she have a missing part? Something everyone else had but her? She didn't even know what it looked like – just that she was missing something. Something that Evans thought was essential to being a head of department and she didn't know how or where to find this mysterious thing. This knowing everything about strangers – like their bloody birthdays! Ryan was staring at her again.

'How do you know how long I've lived here?' It came out like an accusation.

Ryan sat down and nodded at the other chair. When Bea had joined him, he said, 'For sure I didn't know. I knew you had lived here for eighteen months or so. Just guessed.'

They sat in silence watching the snow until the oval of light was the size of a saucer. 'I'd better fix this window, you'll be wanting to get to work.'

Bea sighed heavily. 'I don't want to go to Hartleys.'

'So, that's where you work in your fancy clothes.'

'You mean you didn't just know that by looking at me?' He thought she was teasing, but Bea wasn't. 'You didn't tell me how you knew Molly. Or Mike for that matter.'

Ryan stood up and wiped his hands on his trousers. 'Molly

is the cleaner for this block. She has a cubby hole on the ground floor, although she calls it a storeroom.'

'Okay. And Mike?'

'Mike came by when I was talking to Tom about West Ham.' He caught Bea's expression. 'Oh, Tom lent me his screwdriver.'

She really ought to be getting changed for work; it had gone eleven. But she had to know more. 'But why would Tom and Molly help you if you don't know them?'

'May I?' Ryan pulled a chair to the window. Bea nodded and he stood on it. 'Tom was wearing a Hammers hat and we got talking about the match. That's when Mike came by. Tom lent the screwdriver but didn't have any oil. Could you pass me a cloth or something to shift this snow?'

Bea found a pack of cloths under the sink.

'So…thanks.' He opened the window to a blast of freezing air. 'Mike suggested I ask Molly if she had some oil. Her grandson, Toby, sometimes leaves his bike in her storeroom.'

Bea shook her head in disbelief. He even knew the name of the cleaner's grandson.

'Do you know the date of his birthday?'

Ryan groaned. 'It doesn't hurt to take an interest in people, Bea.' Snow fell with a thud and the room became light. 'I might need a hairdryer to unfreeze this lock. Now, I know you'll have one of those.'

He offered an open palm and Bea handed him the screwdriver.

'Molly has arthritis in her knee. I suggested she try using knee supports. My da had a similar problem and they worked a treat for him. I don't think we'll need your hairdryer.'

'It's eleven twenty. I'm going to be late.'

'I'll be away in just a few minutes. There. It's fixed. Make sure you close the window in future, especially in this weather.'

Bea didn't budge. 'I don't want to go in. I *really, really* don't.'

'Then call in sick.' Ryan stepped down from the chair.

'I've never missed a shift in the three years that I've worked there.'

Ryan frowned. 'Really? Never? You must have done – everyone gets sick.'

'No. I've always loved my work.' That was an understatement; it was what she lived for. In fact, without Hartleys, life had no meaning. It sounded overly dramatic and she wouldn't voice that sentiment to Ryan but it was true. She felt as though the oars of her boat had been taken from her and she was at the mercy of the river's flow, with no control over her future. If not head of department – what? And then there were those girls. They hated her, talked about her behind her back. She thought that she had left that all behind but no – she was still the fourteen-year-old who didn't fit in.

'You will love it again,' Ryan said. 'You're sick today. Don't you have an almighty hangover? You were pretty tanked up last night.' He grinned and Bea blushed.

'Go on – play hooky. It's beautiful out there. A walk along the canal in the snow will clear your head and hot chocolate at Fandangle's Food barge.'

Bea laughed. It was impossible. *He* was impossible. How did he know more about her neighbourhood than she did? Bea hated to ask but she had to. 'I know that there's a canal but I've never heard of Fandangle's Food barge.'

'She knows that there's a canal!'

It sounded wonderful but she couldn't go out in company dressed as she was and yet it didn't feel right putting on make-up and stylish clothes when she was with Ryan.

'I can't. Not like this.'

'Like what? You look grand to me.'

'I'll put on some make-up and tidy myself up,' Bea said, thinking ahead, trying to remember what was recommended for a casual day – relaxed wear, maybe what people would wear in the country. But she was in London. It was too confusing. Best just say no.

'The folk who hang out at Fandangle's don't give a monkey's about make-up and fancy clothes. To be sure, you'll be fine as you are. Just wrap up warm. Haven't you got some snow boots or wellies?'

'No, but I have ankle boots. They've only got a three-inch heel.'

Ryan gave a look of exasperation. But Bea didn't mind. Today was a day like no other. Maybe she would go with Ryan to meet his friends.

8

SEPTEMBER 2005

Ryan slunk back to the farmhouse as the day crept up to greet him, the sun a milky outline already burning away the mist that rose in a ghostly veil. His feet were damp with dew and his heart heavy with resentment. His da should sell the bloody farm if he was too old to get up at five to milk the cows and too mean to pay someone else. What was he, slave labour? They didn't even pay him, said he would inherit the farm and so he was investing in his future. What future? If all there was to look forward to was a life like his parents' then he didn't want to get old.

At the top of the hill Ryan paused as he always did and swept his gaze across the horizon: sweet green meadows garnished with buttercups for grazing, the bleached bronze and faded gold of fields after the harvest, and queenly bales of hay awaiting collection. It was beautiful. And despite his determination to remain angry because it was justified, Ryan's mood lifted a little. He could understand why his da didn't want to part with the farm, but it wasn't fair to expect a sixteen-year-old to commit to a lifetime of dairy farming. He hated the cows, always had.

Da watched from outside the barn as Ryan made his way down the hill towards the farmhouse. He had been up early too, but his da had been rising at five every morning since he was fourteen years old, as he constantly reminded Ryan and his little sister, Caitlin. He struggled now at sixty-eight, but refused to make plans for the farm, expecting Ryan to continue the family tradition.

'All done?' he said.

The question didn't need a response and Ryan was in no mood to pass pleasantries.

'Your ma has made breakfast. Go and wash up, lad.'

What was he, nine years old? Ryan scowled and stomped past, his hands in his pockets, shoulders hunched.

'Tell your ma I'll be in the top field.'

The letter was propped against a bottle of brown sauce when Ryan sat down to a plate of eggs and bacon. His ma sat opposite, nursing a mug of tea. It was the same mug that she had used for eight years, a cow clumsily painted on its side. He had given the mug to Da but he barely acknowledged the gift and Ma had taken ownership with pride. She tucked her curly hair behind her ears, as though ensuring the best view of him.

'No sausage?' Ryan asked.

'Oh sorry, luv.' Ma fetched the frying pan and tipped two plump sausages onto his plate. And then she sat back down and waited, an expectant look on her face.

He hated disappointing her, but he couldn't risk blowing this. If Da got wind of his plans he could say goodbye to them forever. The letter taunted them both. Ryan found it difficult to swallow his bacon. What if he hadn't done enough? What if it was a no?

Ma gave up waiting and said, 'It came this morning, early post.'

Ryan nodded but kept his head down.

'Aren't you going to open it?'

Ryan snatched the envelope from the table and slipped it into his back pocket. 'Later.'

He knew that it was mean leaving Ma in suspense like that. Four years ago, she was the most important person in his life. He told her everything: day-by-day accounts on the progression of his tadpoles to froglets as they lost their tails and grew tiny limbs, his personal best at school cross country. Every time something exciting happened, Ma was the person he longed to tell. But now, weighed down by his deceit, he couldn't bear to look at his ma and see her reproach. Oh shit, she would be thinking it was from the agricultural college and then she would be telling Da.

'It's nothing. Just stuff about the school certificate, everyone's been sent one. A different curriculum or something.'

That seemed to satisfy her as she left Ryan to eat his breakfast and called up the stairs to Caitlin, 'Hurry up, sleepy head. I've made porridge.'

When Ryan was clear of the farmhouse he tore open the letter. Everything depended upon this – *please God let it be good news.*

9

TWENTY-SEVEN SHOPPING DAYS TO CHRISTMAS

It was as though the city were inside a glass bauble, the usual traffic sounds muffled by snow. How easy to pretend that she had stepped outside of time and had no responsibilities. A woman with rosy cheeks, just visible between hat and scarf, greeted them.

'Isn't it marvellous?'

Ryan's eyes were on Sal's igloo and Bea guessed what he must be thinking – this weather might be fun if you had a warm home to return to. So, Bea nodded at the woman before catching up with him.

'Sal's gone. I hope she accepted shelter from the church. She's independent – a tough old bean. But, she'll need somewhere to stay if this carries on.'

The polystyrene cup that Bea had left earlier jutted out of the snow. Bea retrieved it. 'I bought her a tea, but I don't know whether she drank it.'

Ryan shrugged and walked on.

'Where would you have gone if you hadn't stayed at my place last night?'

'Not here. I have somewhere to keep dry but it's no good for Sal with her dodgy joints.'

'Ryan, I want to help you find Declan,' Bea said, trying to keep the urgency from her voice.

'And how would you be doing that? Do you have secret powers, supersensory skills that will track him down?' he chuckled.

She had to be careful, not give herself away. 'No, of course not. But if you could tell me everything about his routine and what he did before he went missing, maybe we could find him together.'

'If only it were that simple. I appreciate your offer, but it's best you don't get involved.'

They crunched on through the snow. The sky was sky blue, still a popular shade for spring, although princess blue was the new trend. Sky blue, having tipped a heap of snow from the clouds. And the canal, a diamante belt or a glittery scarf as sun reflected off its icy surface.

What was she doing following the footprints of this tall stranger along the tow path when she should be at work? She hadn't even telephoned in with an excuse. Bea felt a little queasy – a hangover or guilt?

'So how far have you walked along here?' Ryan's breath was a wisp of white as he looked over his shoulder at Bea.

Bea hadn't. She'd noticed the canal, admired the council's efforts to make it more attractive with astroturf covering the wide concrete steps to create tiered seating for office workers and tourists, but she hadn't actually walked along it.

'Not far,' she replied.

Ryan made a funny noise. It could have been a snort of derision or maybe he was just clearing his throat. They walked in silence and Bea gave herself up to enjoying the moment. It was hard not to – the blinding whiteness of the snow contrasting with the jauntily painted narrow boats and barges.

'Some of them are clear of snow,' Bea observed.

'Wood burners. It'll be cosy inside. That's Fandangle's.' Ryan pointed ahead, but it could have been one of several boats moored side by side.

The crisp air and walk were invigorating, but Bea was looking forward to getting warm. It was then she realised that Ryan was wearing a denim jacket and had no hat or scarf. Yet again she had been selfish – thoughtless.

'I know it's a bit late, Ryan, but you can borrow my scarf. Sorry I didn't offer earlier – maybe on the way back?'

'It's okay. I'm used to being out in all weathers. I arrived here in the spring and didn't really pack much for the winter months.'

At last, he was sharing something about himself. Bea encouraged him. 'When was that?'

Ryan cocked his head as though thinking. 'It would be spring, last year.'

'Is that when you met Declan – spring last year?' It was like prising open a clamshell, getting Ryan to talk about himself or Declan.

'It was when we first met, but then we met again. Life had changed for both of us.' Before she could ask how life had changed, Ryan said, 'Now, are you ready for a bacon butty?'

Bea shuddered. She would never put something so laden with fat and carbohydrates in her mouth. 'I'd love a hot drink.'

'Well, here we are. Fandangle's Food.'

A white man with huge holes in stretched earlobes and dreadlocks tied back in a rag sat on the deck smoking a roll-up. Ryan and the man clasped hands, the man clutching Ryan's forearm in his other hand.

'I've brought my friend Bea to sample Fandangle's hot chocolate. The best in London.'

'Leila's just baked up a batch of brownies. You keeping warm, mate?'

A couple squeezed out of the barge doorway and Bea felt the heat from within before the door closed behind them. The couple stepped off the barge and walked away arm in arm, their breath visible in the cold air, like speech bubbles. Ryan was chatting to the man and seemed in no hurry to get warm. Bea considered going inside to wait.

She caught the tail end of a conversation as the man said to Ryan, 'You want any backup, just say the word.'

'Appreciate it, Roots, but after Declan...' He shrugged. 'I've got to do this myself.'

'How much did he have on them?' She couldn't hear any more as Roots had lowered his voice.

'Hail the gypsy queen!' Ryan stepped back as a woman with a tangled mane of black curls came through the door backwards, carrying a tray laden with brownies.

Bea's stomach rumbled, betraying her self-discipline. *If* she succumbed to a hot chocolate that would be enough sugar for one day.

'I thought I heard your voice, Ryan. We were worried about you in that snowstorm last night. Come into the warm, these are fresh from the stove.' The woman had an Irish accent. Ryan was right – with her long skirt and wild hair, she reminded Bea of the gypsy girl dancing with a tambourine in one of her childhood books.

Ryan said, 'Bea gave me a room for the night.'

'In that case, Bea, you must have a hot chocolate and a brownie on the house. Come in. Come in.' She passed the man, Roots, a mug of coffee.

'Why is he called Roots?' Bea whispered to Ryan as they

climbed down the steps into a pretty dining area with two bench seats and a long table. There were already six people squeezed into the space, drinking from an assortment of mugs. Frying bacon, roasted coffee beans, and the waft of brownies made Bea's mouth water despite herself.

'A nickname he got in prison.'

Bea didn't know anyone who had gone to prison and didn't want to. Had Ryan met Roots in prison? He said that when he met Declan again, that life had changed. Bea had a sense of foreboding. When Ryan was talking to Roots just now, she had seen another side to him – tougher, determined. Who did he think was responsible for Declan's disappearance? She had to find out.

'Were you ever in prison?' Bea said under her breath, trying not to sound judgemental.

Ryan laughed out loud, causing a couple farther along the bench to look up from fussing a pretty cockapoo dog to see what was amusing him.

'My life's not all that exciting, just a country boy from the green isle,' he played to his audience. They then exchanged pleasantries, until Leila arrived with a sausage for the dog and Ryan and Bea were forgotten.

'We'll be having a couple of bacon butties when you're ready, Leila,' Ryan said without consulting Bea.

'Just a coffee for me,' she whispered, hoping not to attract everyone's attention again.

Ryan gave a half smile and shook his head. Bea felt as though he was judging her. 'What's wrong with being careful about what I eat?' she hissed. 'You don't drink caffeine.'

'I didn't say anything.' Ryan held up his hands in surrender, just as Leila slid their plates of sandwiches along the table. They looked so good – soft white bread and beautifully crisp bacon peeking out the sides.

Bea watched Ryan take a big bite. 'Good for a hangover.'

He had eaten one half of his sandwich, before Bea gave in and took a bite of hers. It was absolutely delicious. The best thing she had tasted – ever. The bacon slightly salty and the bread warm and fresh.

Ryan didn't remark on Bea's change of heart, he was too busy eating. The old Bea didn't eat anything fattening; the old Bea didn't do social events or talk to strangers and would never take a day off work. The old Bea would be in Hartleys now, pretending to be a model sales assistant, watching everything that she said, afraid to let her façade slip to reveal who she really was. Bea licked warm, salty juices from her wrist and grinned at Ryan.

'I told you they were good,' he said.

'I baked the bread this morning,' Leila said, finding a space on the bench opposite Bea.

When Ryan stood up to greet a man with a shaven head and bushy beard, Bea finished her sandwich and gave a satisfied sigh. 'I love what you've done with this place. It's magical. So cosy and *that* was amazing.'

Leila beamed. 'Really? That makes me feel so proud. I dreamt of having my own café with home-baked bread and cakes but couldn't afford premises – not in London. Then I saw this old barge for rent and Roots helped me tart her up.'

Bea loved the girl's exuberance and the way that she seemed to accept her as she was – without make-up, wearing jeans and a snuggly jumper. She couldn't remember feeling so relaxed in the company of another woman who wasn't family.

Two large women sitting at the far end of the bench clambered down and squeezed past Bea with their bags. 'Thanks, Leila. We'll see you tomorrow for the Potato Heads.'

It was hard to believe that outside the temperature was

sub-zero. Through a little archway, Bea glimpsed a wood burner and cosy seating.

'I've never seen inside one of these little houseboats before.'

'Don't let Roots hear you calling this a houseboat – there's a difference apparently.'

'Is Roots your partner?' Bea asked.

'No – not in business nor love. I rent Fandangle's from Roots but he lives on another barge.' Leila got up and stretched. 'Now, I promised you a brownie.'

Ryan was deep in conversation and so Bea offered to help in the kitchen. She was curious to see where Leila prepared food in this miniature home.

They washed up the crockery together – Leila washing and Bea drying. Through a window, Bea saw a family of ducks nesting inside a snow-covered tyre that hung from the side of a barge, like an arty Christmas wreath. She could understand why Leila loved this little boat – it was warm and peaceful tucked away down here.

'Why did Roots go to prison?' she said and immediately regretted it. This was exactly the kind of thing Mr Evans was talking about – she always said the wrong thing. Opened her mouth and put her foot in it – foot and mouth disease, her sister, Lizzie, called it.

'For chaining himself to a tree in the nineties,' Leila said. 'Leave the rest of them to dry there and come and have a brownie. Ryan will wonder what I've done with you.'

Leila wasn't at all offended and Bea sighed with relief. 'Why did he do that? Chain himself to a tree?' It was a very odd thing to do.

'Demonstrating about climate change and the destruction of a woodland to make way for housing. That's what our event is for tomorrow afternoon – to raise money for Friends of the

Earth. The Potato Heads are performing on the top deck if it doesn't snow and we're having a garage sale along the tow path. You and Ryan must come.'

'Come where?' Ryan joined them, relieving Leila of a tray.

It was rash of Bea to agree that they would go. Later, when lying in bed going over the unusual events of that day, Bea put it down to her relief on hearing that Roots hadn't been in prison for rape or murder and therefore Ryan wasn't implicated by virtue of knowing a hardened criminal. Her reasoning for inviting Ryan to stay another night in the spare bedroom wasn't so easily explained away and so Bea didn't try. She tucked the duvet under her chin and thought about the little houseboat with the wood burner. It would be wonderful to lie in one of the bunks that Leila showed her, rocked to sleep by the flow of the river.

10

TWENTY-SIX SHOPPING DAYS TO CHRISTMAS

Ryan had gone for a run along the canal and Bea was rifling through her wardrobe weeding out clothes that she hardly wore, so that she could contribute to the garage sale, when her mobile rang. Sunday, nine-thirty – it would be Mum. Bea took her phone through to the spare bedroom to find the list that she made in advance of Mum's weekly call. It was on her desk beneath her notebook for studying Russian. That's what she should be doing on a Sunday. Bea felt a pang of regret, as though by missing this ritual she was taking a step further away from her goal. The reminder that her chances of becoming a head of department before she was thirty had diminished, regardless of her study, was a kick in the gut.

Mum greeted Bea with her usual enthusiasm. The ritual was for Mum to go first with news of her week and then it was Bea's turn. Bea jotted down anything that happened in the week so that she had something to say. As her mother talked about Lizzie's cold and her nephew Ollie's school nativity play, Bea cast her eyes around the room. There was nothing to suggest that she had a guest staying; Ryan was very tidy. She had persuaded him the night before to use her washing machine and so most of his clothes were now drying in the bathroom.

'So how was your week, love?'

Bea consulted her list. 'Good. I was asked to help a celebrity, Suki Dee Licious, shop for underwear.'

That was strange. Ryan had left his rucksack the other side of the bed but not the Armani bag. It must be in the bathroom or by the washing machine. She had been hoping to have a little peek inside to see if there were any clues that might help her to find Declan.

Her mum sighed. 'Really, Bea, it's time you got a proper job. Whoever this celebrity is, surely she can buy her own knickers. I get mine from Marks – they do every kind.'

'She wants to buy them from Hartleys. That's my job, to sell beautiful lingerie to people who can afford it.'

Her mum harrumphed and changed the subject. 'Now, about Christmas, when are you arriving? Lizzie and Tristan are joining us on Christmas morning so that Ollie can open his presents at home.'

Bea glanced into the bathroom. Ryan's clothes were almost dry but no bag. 'I don't know, it depends on work and the trains.'

'I hope you're looking for new accommodation, Bea. You know we have to sell the flat early in the new year to pay for our retirement and we want to put some in a trust fund for Ollie's education. Aunt Fiona, God rest her soul, would have wanted that.'

It wasn't by the washing machine either. Maybe he hadn't gone on a run; maybe she had misheard.

Mum was always going on about selling the flat. Why did her family assume that everything Bea did was a whim? That she would settle down and find a job that they approved of in Hampshire? Bea gritted her teeth. 'Don't worry about me. I'll make other arrangements when you're ready to sell.'

The front door banged; Ryan was back. Bea poked her head out of the kitchen to see if he was carrying his bag. He wasn't, but it did look as though he'd been running.

'Okay, I have to go now, Mum. No, I'm not hanging around other department stores all day. For your information, my friend Ryan and I are going to see the Potato Heads on Fandangle's Food barge.'

'You look happy,' Ryan said. He used his T-shirt to wipe sweat from his brow and Bea caught a glimpse of his hollow belly and bony ribs. She should try to find a way of fattening him up. 'I'm guessing that wasn't work.'

'No, my mum, but I did call in yesterday and explained that I had overslept because I was so ill.'

'You're a wicked girl for sure,' Ryan quipped and then he ducked into the bathroom for a shower.

Bea had intended to make her excuses and send Ryan to the charity thing with her donation of clothes and accessories. The idea of a band and lots of people overwhelmed Bea. She didn't do social events – only work ones and that was because she had to. And yet, telling Mum of her intentions had made her feel proud – more normal. Yesterday had been fun and Bea did have a yearning to curl up on the old sofa that she had spied next to the wood burner. She could imagine herself sipping hot chocolate with Leila when all the visitors had gone, sharing news and observations from the day. Bea had never had a special friend – just her sister, Lizzie. Leila and Ryan were both so easy to be with – they seemed to accept Bea without her having to try to be someone else. Before she could talk herself out of it, Bea gave her face the lightest touch of make-up and changed her jeans for a calf-length pleated skirt in a sheer fabric. *It would be suitable for dancing.* Had she really thought that? Bea's heart skipped in delight.

The snow had melted, with only a grubby collar remaining where the wall shaded it from the sun and the trampling of feet. The weekend was almost over too; tomorrow Bea would have to go back to work. It was the first time in three years that the prospect did not excite her and Bea felt a physical pain at the loss of that joy.

'What do you do during the day, apart from running?' she asked Ryan.

'I keep busy,' he said.

Bea couldn't imagine what it was Ryan did to keep busy but decided it was rude to ask. Instead she said, 'What did you do before you came to England?'

'I come from a long line of farmers and so growing up that's all I knew – the family farm. But it's not what I wanted for myself.'

He didn't elaborate and so Bea encouraged him. 'What did you want? Why did you leave Ireland?'

'I ask myself the same question. Sometimes you take a wrong turn and it's hard to find a way back.'

Bea sighed. 'I used to love my job, but now I don't know how I feel. It's like the end of a love affair, or at least the way people describe breaking up. Does that sound stupid?'

'Well then, it is the end of a love affair, of sorts.'

'It's the disappointment. I thought I knew where I was going. I was absolutely sure that I was going to get that promotion. But what they want me to do – how they want me to be – I don't know if I can do that.

'I'm a good saleswoman, one of the best on the floor. But I don't think that the others like me and maybe that counts more than I realised.' She swallowed hard, willing herself not to cry.

'It shouldn't,' Ryan said.

'I can ignore them and go on working as I am now. I earn good commission. But I need more security than that.' Her voice wavered.

Ryan stopped walking and turned Bea to face him. 'You're awesome, Bea Stevens.'

Bea felt a bit shaky, like she'd drunk too much caffeine. Ryan was wrong. He'd believed what she'd wanted him to but it was phoney, she was fake. He didn't know how hopeless she really was – nobody did, because she hid it well.

'It's true. I've watched you marching back and forth to the station every day. Now, there's a girl with a purpose, I said to myself. Didn't you tell me yourself that you've never had a day off sick? You're not afraid of going after what you want. I saw all of those exercise books in your spare room. I would've been impressed if you were studying French, but Russian? They don't even use the same alphabet. For sure, stop your dwelling on the things that you're not and be proud of who you are.'

The thought of Declan sitting with Ryan and remarking on her as she strode past with her head held high shamed Bea, despite Ryan's kind words.

'There must be something I can do to help you find your friend Declan.'

Ryan turned away and then continued to walk. 'You are helping to keep my mind off worrying, and that is a help to be sure. You are grand, Bea. Just grand. Don't you forget that.'

It took a while for Ryan's words to settle in her heart. She wanted them to; they were wonderful words, but out of habit, she questioned them – turned them over and over, looking for the flaw, the secret meaning. It was what she told herself every morning: *You can do this, Bea. Go after your dream.* But it was a mantra. A way of convincing herself that she wasn't a failure. If she allowed herself to reflect on her shortcomings then she would give in, and she had promised herself as a teenager that she would overcome any obstacles to prove that she was strong and independent.

Despite her guilt for making Declan homeless, Bea felt lighter than she had for days and she did a little skip to catch up with Ryan who was stalking ahead. 'Thanks, Ryan. Now I'm actually looking forward to going back to work tomorrow.'

'That's my girl. Now, have you got your dancing shoes on? I'm going to show you how to dance the Irish way.'

Buoyed up by Ryan's words of encouragement, Bea applied herself to the art of Irish dancing and discovered to her amazement that not only did she enjoy it but according to Leila was a natural. The Potato Heads were playing on the deck, an Irish band with an unusual assortment of instruments: a washboard, accordion, ukulele, banjo, and harmonica, but they could play a good tune and below deck Bea gave herself up to the music, oblivious to all else.

The band had paused for some refreshment and Leila, who had been dancing with Bea, was now in the galley kitchen. The wood burning stove that had seemed so appealing to Bea that morning was not so welcome now as her body had its own heat. Desperate to cool off, Bea climbed onto the deck. It was only mid-afternoon but already it was getting dark. In the summer months their party would only just be getting started. The sales stalls on the tow path were being packed away and Bea headed over to see whether the clothes she donated had sold.

Ryan was walking towards the *Fandangle* with Declan's bag slung over his shoulder, a younger man with dark skin and closely cropped hair at his side. She wondered where Ryan had been to collect his bag; she hadn't even noticed his absence. The two men stopped to face one another, and Bea caught snatches of conversation as she absently trailed her fingers through a basket of scarfs.

'You should have told me. Stopped him.' Ryan sounded angry.

'You know Declan…' The other man's words were lost to Bea as a woman asked the price of a faux fur stole.

'Why wait until now?' Ryan was still talking, but as women closed in around Bea foraging for a bargain amongst the belts, bags, and vintage clothes, she could no longer hear him.

A few minutes later the man strode past Bea, his hands in his pockets. He looked as if he was in his early twenties; a good-looking man, possibly Asian. She waited a little longer, before slipping back onto the barge to find Ryan saying his goodbyes.

On their trek back, the almost affectionate camaraderie that lightened Bea's mood on their walk to Fandangle's had been replaced with a weighty silence. Ryan slumped his shoulders and kicked anything in his path, a can and then a take-away carton. A few chords of a Christmas song as the door of a café swung open and then closed. The cry of a duck on the canal.

'I didn't notice you pop out to collect your bag,' Bea said. Ryan grunted and hoisted the bag up his shoulder. She wanted to say more: *Was that a friend of Declan's you were talking to? What did he say that made you so angry?* But she sensed that her questions would be unwelcome and instead of opening up, Ryan would become more guarded. Instead, she tried to engage him in trivial conversation, hoping he would relax and tell her what had upset him. 'The snow's melted,' she said

'Yes. I'll collect my stuff from your flat.'

That wasn't what she meant, but maybe it was a good idea. The weekend was over.

'I'll be going into work early tomorrow, so…' Bea trailed off.

Ryan nodded. And apart from saying goodbye and thank you, that was the end of it.

11

TWENTY-SIX SHOPPING DAYS TO CHRISTMAS

Ryan had come and gone with the snow, but unlike the snow of which there was now no trace, Ryan had left his mark. Bea sat at her dresser to apply her make-up. It was a ritual that she usually enjoyed – applying foundation to create a flawless finish, and then the rouge for a strawberries and cream complexion. With each layer the real Bea was camouflaged until she resembled the other sales assistants on the fashion floor at Hartleys. It was a requirement to wear full make-up; the strict dress code had appealed to Bea when she first applied for the job – no ambiguity about what was expected. Glamorous and fashionable.

But when Bea danced at Fandangle's she had pleased herself. Her eyes sparkled when she remembered the joy of that day. Leila, Roots, and Ryan accepted her as she was – they even liked her. Ryan had called her 'awesome'. Bea's hand, which had been poised to apply eyeliner, fell back onto the dresser.

The man Ryan had been talking to was a friend of Declan. *Should have stopped him from doing what?* Why was Ryan so opposed to her helping him find his friend? She wanted to help him, and not just because she felt guilty about Declan, but because she cared about Ryan and hated to see him so unhappy.

Bea flicked mascara over her lashes. She *would* help Ryan to find Declan, but not today. Today, she had a chance to prove that she was a caring sales assistant who could connect with customers. There would be other head of department posts and Bea was determined that she would be the next in line. Mr Evans would be sorry that he had underestimated her. She was *awesome.* Remembering Ryan's words, Bea smiled at her reflection.

The old Bea would have pounced on Mrs Carmichael, a regular customer, as soon as she approached the luxury night-gowns, but today Bea hung back to watch Jemima. Studying other people, learning how to be popular was once second nature to Bea, but she had become complacent, and that was what had let her down. Just as the snipe about her appearance had triggered fourteen-year-old Bea on a mission to transform herself, so did Mr Evans's more subtle observations.

'Veronica.' Jemima greeted Mrs Carmichael as though they had met up in a country club. Bea edged closer to listen.

'You must be excited, with the wedding so close.'

Veronica Carmichael clasped her hands to her breast. 'Excited doesn't begin to describe it. But Daisy could have picked a better time of year to get married. The weather in the Bahamas is perfect but with us leaving on the 27th it doesn't leave much time for Christmas preparations and packing.'

Bea wondered when Jemima would get around to promoting the silk charmeuse nightgowns. By now she would have completed a sale.

'Let me guess, you're looking for a special present for Daisy.'

Veronica Carmichael smiled. 'Yes!'

How did Jemima surmise that from their short conversation?

'We've paid for the wedding and some glassware as a present for them both, but I wanted something special to give Daisy from me.'

'Well, if you were thinking luxury nightwear, let me show you our gorgeous silk charmeuse sets. They have only just come in and are exquisite.' This was whispered as though Jemima was suggesting Mrs Carmichael take a peek at the Crown Jewels. But it worked – half an hour later Jemima was ringing up a couple of hundred pounds in sales.

Pippa and Alice were rearranging the lingerie display, their heads bent close together as they spoke softly. They were doing more talking than working, but Bea resisted the temptation to intervene. Instead, she pretended to be checking the robes and listened. If she could pick up a clue as to what interested them then she would be able to spark a conversation, just as Ryan had in befriending her neighbours. The truth was, she knew nothing about their lives. Junior sales assistants came and went; they were very much like one another given the dress code and Hartleys's selection process.

'So, he's invited his two daughters to spend Christmas with us, whilst his ex goes on a skiing holiday. It's going to be a nightmare. They don't even like me and you know how teenagers are.' Pippa had raised her voice and Bea checked that there were no customers in earshot.

'They can't be much younger than you. I bet his wife's doing it on purpose to mess up your cosy Christmas.'

Out of the corner of her eye, Bea glimpsed a customer, Patsy Lovell, who was once known for being a member of a popular eighties dance troupe. Before approaching Patsy, Bea reminded the girls to finish the job as quickly as possible. Mrs Barone and Jemima were in a meeting but if they returned they would be horrified to see lingerie spread across the floor. She helped them by hanging up a gossamer bra so fine it resembled a spider's web.

'Good job, girls, thank you.'

Alice stared at Bea as though she had spoken in an alien tongue.

Undeterred, Bea persevered. 'My school went on a skiing trip once.'

There was complete silence and Bea saw the girls exchange a look.

'O-kay.' Pippa made a ridiculous face, backing away and widening her eyes. This seemed to amuse Alice, as she stifled a laugh.

Bea knew that they were laughing at her but she didn't understand why. Her attempt to bond with them hadn't worked but she could try a new approach with Patsy. Remembering customers' birthdays was apparently a good thing and so Bea googled Patsy Lovell. Patsy was admiring the Charmel collection.

'Those cami-knickers are made from silk charmeuse, that's why they feel so soft and silky. We have some nightgowns in the same collection,' Bea said.

Patsy hummed through her smile, almost a purr. 'They really are divine.'

'With your sixtieth in January, you should treat yourself to an early birthday present.' Bea thought that she had got it right, until she saw the faces around her. When did the store get so busy? They were all looking at Bea and Patsy with dropped jaws. Bea wanted to run and hide – it was her worst nightmare. Like being naked at work.

The clothes rail rattled as Patsy swung away and then she stormed out of the department almost colliding with Mrs Barone. Bea knew that she would have some explaining to do.

'Miss Stevens?' Mrs Barone didn't waste any time. Bea's stomach churned as she tried to think of an explanation for Patsy's behaviour that would satisfy her boss. 'Mr Evans would like you to meet with Alastair from PR in marketing in half an hour's time.'

A reprieve, some time to think up an excuse for her disastrous sales encounter. The old Bea would never have behaved so rashly. She was always calm, efficient, and professional. Personal comments had always been a no-no for her and that was why. If she hadn't tried so hard then Bea would have made a good sale. Instead she had offended one of the store's valued customers. Bea hoped that Patsy wouldn't complain to Mr Evans.

'Come into my office and I'll arrange coffee,' Alastair said, leading the way into his glass partitioned cubicle within the open plan office. Bea felt like a fly being invited into a spider's web.

'I told you that you made an impression on Suki Dee,' Alastair said.

A secretary placed a mug of coffee in front of Bea. When she had left them Alastair continued, 'Suki wants Hartleys to host a big charity event in her name. Something original that will capture media attention and show Suki's humanitarian side. So, Mr Evans suggested that this would be a project that you could throw yourself into – an opportunity.'

Bea tingled with anticipation and excitement. Maybe Ryan was right and she did have more potential than she realised. 'What exactly does Mr Evans want me to do?'

Alastair's face contorted, as though he was reluctant to say what he thought. 'If you don't mind me being frank, Bea?'

She should have known better; here was the let-down.

'I think you're being given this, um, *opportunity* to show Evans what you're capable of apart from sales.'

Did everyone know that Evans thought her uncaring and unable to connect with people? It was tempting to tell Alastair where to stick his bloody opportunity and walk out of Hartleys never to return. If Bea did that then she would have proved her family right and the past three years would be written off as something Bea had to get out of her system before doing what her parents thought best for her – letting them run her life.

'I'll do it,' she said.

'Great. It has to be before Christmas.'

'But there are only –' Bea caught sight of the store's calendar reminder on Alastair's desk '– twenty-six shopping days left.'

'If you don't think you're up to the challenge, say so now.'

Did she detect a smirk on his face? *You are awesome, Bea Stevens,* she said in her head. 'Please tell Mr Evans that I am grateful for this opportunity and he won't be disappointed in choosing me to lead on this important event.'

'You'll have to work to me. I'm in charge of PR,' Alastair blustered, as though taken aback by Bea's newly found confidence. She was a bit impressed herself at this self-assured Bea taking command of the situation.

It was only later, when the reality sank in, that she felt as though she had jumped from a plane only to find that she had no parachute. How on earth could she put something of that magnitude together in just twenty-six days?

12

SEPTEMBER 2007

Ryan turned up the radio and sang along to 'Summer Breeze' as his truck bumped over the track up to the farm. Having a set of wheels had made life easier for him, although Da's motive was to reduce time spent travelling to and from school, to give more time to the farm. *School.* That was a distant memory. Now that he had the truck, Ryan had a secret place to stash his tools and keep a change of clothes. He still got up at five to milk the cows and Da would have jobs for him on the farm until sunset, but that was okay; he was in control of his own destiny. Since receiving the letter from Hennessey, a local builder, accepting him as an apprentice carpenter, Ryan had gone on to apply for a carpentry and joinery course and was accepted. He just had to complete the four-year apprenticeship and save enough to fund college.

Caitlin was at a downstairs window – the boot room – waving her hands wildly, miming something. Ryan screwed up his face. *Crazy sister.* Then he opened the back door, the one that took him into the kitchen, and there, instead of the welcoming smell of freshly baked bread that usually greeted him, the air felt chilled. Rage radiated from Da as he faced Ryan like a sumo wrestler, his bulky arms impersonating the Incredible Hulk. Ma's eyes were red and she clutched a balled tissue.

'William,' she cautioned, but Da's jaw tightened and fists clenched.

They knew. It had to happen sooner or later. Fine. He was eighteen; if they didn't like it he would leave the farm altogether. Ryan dropped his bag and mirrored his da, the two of them posturing like a couple of elks ready to lock antlers.

'William. Ryan. Sit down, the pair of you. We need to be talking, not fighting.'

Let him try and fight me, Ryan thought. *A seventy-year-old man.* And then he felt ashamed, because however much he hated him right now, this was his da. But, he wasn't going to sit down and neither it seemed was Da.

'What have you got to say for yourself, lad? I can't believe that you've been lying to your ma and me for the past two years. It's, it's...' He sought for a word to do justice to the terrible sin and then spat out, 'It's a betrayal of our trust. How dare you treat your ma like that, can't you see what this has done to her?' He was trembling now, his face so red Ryan imagined blood vessels popping.

'A betrayal? What do you call raising a son for the sole purpose of running a farm? You bred me like a fucking cow. What did you think? I'm fifty, it's about time I bred an heir to take over the work? Well, I got news for you – I ain't going to be a fucking farmer.'

Da held up his fists and Ryan was ready for him.

'Stop! Stop! Stop it, the both of you.'

The sight of his ma in tears shamed Ryan and he dropped his fists. As soon as he did, Da grabbed hold of his arm and threw him across the room, where he fell bashing his head against the side of the kitchen dresser.

'William!' Ma screamed and his da flew out of the door into the yard.

Ryan clambered up, rubbing his arm. 'I'm sorry, Ma, I shouldn't have lied to you.' He was crying now and hated himself for his weakness.

'Oh Ryan, come here.' She opened her arms but he couldn't. He wasn't a kid.

He sank into a chair and held his head in his hands. 'I tried to tell him that I didn't want to farm but he wouldn't listen. What else could I do?'

'I know. I told your da that you would end up resenting him. That he had to let you make your own choices, but his da and his grandda had this farm and generations before them. To give it up would be like giving away his family.'

'I get that, but it doesn't mean I should feel the same. I don't, Ma. I love the farm as a place, but not farming.'

'I know. I know.' She soothed in the same voice that Ryan remembered from being a child, her hand stroking his hair after a long crying bout. It brought a lump to his throat.

'I didn't mean to hurt you, Ma.'

'You didn't. I should have stood up for you years ago. Ryan.' She took his hand in both of hers. 'It was me who wanted to start a family when I met your da. He was against it, said we were too old, but I was only forty and I desperately wanted to be a mum. You and Caitlin have brought me so much joy. If we hadn't had you, if we hadn't met and married, then your da would have had to sell the farm. He shouldn't have expected you to take it on, it was naïve, but since the day you were born he had such plans for you. He loves the farm so much he doesn't understand how you could feel differently.'

'He loves it more than me,' Ryan said, but he knew that he was being childish.

Ma kissed the top of his head. 'Are you going to tell me your plans now? I'd love to hear about what you've been doing these past two years. I miss our chats. You and I have always been friends, Ryan.'

The emotion in her voice was too much for Ryan. 'I will, Ma. Let me go and wash up and we'll talk later, okay? I promise,' he croaked.

13

TWENTY-SIX SHOPPING DAYS TO CHRISTMAS

As Bea travelled home from work she mentally replayed her meeting with Alastair. A big charity event that would capture media attention and show Suki Dee's humanitarian side. Before Christmas. There were twenty-six shopping days to Christmas. Twenty-six. Less than four weeks, and she had no idea how she was going to do this. Mr Evans thought she was capable, that was a positive. He was giving her an opportunity to prove herself. She had to make a success of this; she was being given a second chance. *Think, Bea. Think.*

When she got off at King's Cross the Salvation Army were playing 'Good King Wenceslas'. There was no sign of Ryan or his friend Sal, although a couple of homeless men were helping to collect money for the band. The trombone and tambourine were irritatingly cheerful and Bea wanted to shout at them that it wasn't nearly Christmas, not yet. Deep in thought she tried to hurry past but a woman with soft grey curls beneath her Sally Army bonnet disarmed Bea with a smile. It was a real smile, one that seemed to say *I know you* and *I care.* Bea was reminded of Ryan. She fumbled in her purse and dropped a couple of pound coins into a collection box. She just had to keep calm and believe in herself. An idea would come to her. It would.

Bea turned her key in the lock and leaned against the door. As it opened, Bea knew that she was not alone. Somebody was in her flat. The air felt charged with energy and her skin prickled. 'Who's there?'

She kicked open the living room door, hanging back ready to make her escape. A soft light flickered near the window, and then wafts of candle wax, garlic, and herbs. Homely, comforting scents, but those of a different place. She froze. Distracted by her thoughts, she must have entered the wrong flat. Any minute now, she would be found out.

'Surprise.' Ryan waved a wooden spoon as he stepped from the open plan kitchen into the glow of the candlelight.

It was a surprise, and Bea wasn't at all sure that she liked it. Everything that was solid in her life was falling away – her job and now her sanctuary, her fortress. Terrified of the commitment she had rashly made to Alastair and Evans, Bea needed more than ever to shut her front door and turn away from the outside world. Was Ryan assuming that because she had let him stay a couple of nights that she had invited him to share her home? Had she given the wrong message? She was always doing that, or so boys had told her in the past. That was why she avoided relationships, but she thought Ryan was different.

Bea switched on the light. 'How did you get in, Ryan?'

'Ah Molly, bless her. I was telling her that I wanted to do something special for you.'

'You had no right. This is my home. You had no right.'

Ryan held up his hands, a look of bewilderment on his face. 'Bea, I'm sorry. I got it wrong. You're right, I shouldn't have.'

She continued to glare at him. He had no right to invade her personal space uninvited. Molly shouldn't have let him in. It was all wrong. And yet the sounds and smells of something bubbling in the kitchen, and the warmth of his presence, comforted her. The flat felt different. It felt like a home.

'I'm going. There's a stew on the stove and some garlic bread in the oven. A dessert in the fridge and a bottle of wine – red. I hope that's okay.'

He opened the front door a fraction. 'I just wanted to thank you.'

'Don't go.' Bea was overwhelmed with emotion. The shock of seeing him there, her distress, and then gratitude. He had done something so kind. She didn't want him to leave.

Ryan had one foot out of the door. His shoulders slumped as though he was folding himself up. 'I'm an eejit. What was I thinking?'

'It's okay. Please come back in.'

'If you're sure?'

Bea wiped away a tear. Molly shouldn't have let him in, but his thoughtfulness undid her.

'Hey. I didn't mean to make you cry.'

'It's not that. It's just that it's been a strange day, and then with you being so kind.'

Ryan pressed his hands on her shoulders and Bea felt as though he was replanting her – helping her to find her roots. 'Okay?'

She took a deep breath and nodded.

'I moved your kitchen table into the living room. Sorry they're not fancy candles. If you go and sit yourself down, I'll serve you.'

There was only one place set at the table. As a rule, Bea preferred to eat alone but it felt awkward, Ryan waiting on her.

He brought in a bottle of wine and poured her a glass.

'Aren't you going to join me?' she said.

Ryan frowned. 'I did this to say thank you for everything, not because I was trying it on with you.'

Bea had no idea what he was talking about and said as much. 'Let's just sit down together and eat. It smells delicious.'

Any reservations about sharing her personal space melted away in Ryan's company. He was so easy to be with and Bea found herself telling him about her day. She started with her disastrous sales encounter with Patsy Lovell.

Ryan ate slowly, serving himself a smaller portion than Bea. There had barely been enough for the two of them and Bea knew that he would have to go without food after spending what little money he had on the meal. It made her feel ashamed for grumbling, but Ryan hung on every word. He wiped a piece of bread around his plate and popped it in his mouth.

'What made you think that it was a good idea to copy the way Jemima Puddle-Duck served customers?'

Bea laughed. 'I call her that in my head! I loved Beatrix Potter as a child, with my name being Beatrice.'

'So, this Patsy woman was a bit arsed with you telling everyone that she was about to collect her pension?'

Remembering her face, Bea got the giggles. 'She was a bit.'

It could have been the wine or hysteria but once she started Bea couldn't stop.

Ryan was laughing with her. 'It's you,' he said. 'Seeing you laugh like that, it sets me off.'

Eventually they calmed down and wiped the tears from their eyes with the kitchen towel Ryan had provided as napkins. Bea felt spent, as though she had had a good long cry.

'Bea, you don't need to model yourself on anyone else. I told you that you're awesome and I meant it.'

'But you're the only person who thinks that.'

'The only person who matters is you. If you believe in yourself it doesn't matter what anyone else thinks.' Ryan looked right at her and for once Bea didn't mind having eye contact.

'There's something else.' She was reluctant to tell Ryan about Evans's challenge. It had been good to forget about it for a while, and she was afraid that he would think her ridiculous for agreeing to what now seemed an impossible request.

'Go on,' Ryan said in his soft lilting voice.

Bea outlined the conversation with Alastair. Ryan's face gave no clue as to what he was thinking.

'I've been set up, haven't I? It's impossible. I shouldn't have agreed. I was too cocky. Too confident.' Bea covered her face with her hands. When she looked up, Ryan met her gaze.

'I'm proud of you, Bea.' Then he got up and started to clear away the plates.

Bea wasn't sure whether he was being sarcastic. Was he shocked at her audaciousness? She followed him to the sink, carrying the bread basket. 'But I can't do it. It's impossible, and if I fail then I'll never get another opportunity. Leave the dishes there. I'll put them in the dishwasher later.'

Ryan leaned back against the worktop. 'Okay. What do you need to succeed at this?'

'More time,' Bea wailed.

'Could you do it in twenty-six days if you had nothing else to do?'

'Yes, but Alastair said before Christmas. Twenty-six days takes us up to Christmas Eve and I still have to work on the shop floor. I don't know how much time they'll give me away from sales at this time of the year.' Bea spoke all in one breath. She felt as though she was having palpitations.

'So, you set the terms. Go to the big boss and tell him what you need to get this done. Then get him to make a commitment. What will he give you if you succeed?'

'Yes! That's it. I'll tell him I have to do this full-time. I'll need a budget. And I'll need to have control –'

'Sorry, Bea, I'm going to have to leave you.' Ryan was looking out of the window. Bea followed his gaze and saw a figure move from the lamplight into the shadows. 'What is it, Ryan? Who have you seen out there?'

Ryan's face had clouded over. 'It's a friend of Declan's. He told me something important on Sunday that he should have told me before. Sorry I can't help with the washing up.'

'Ryan. You can tell me. I want to help you. You have helped me so much.'

'I know, but trust me you are best to keep out of this business. Promise me you'll see the boss man tomorrow and tell him what's what?'

Bea nodded and Ryan, like a cat escaping domesticity, slipped out into the night.

14

TWENTY-FIVE SHOPPING DAYS TO CHRISTMAS

Sal was perched on a plastic crate wearing a jaunty hat when Bea returned from Denny's with her breakfast that morning. Sal was wearing so many layers of clothing that Bea wondered at the size of her frame when unwrapped. There was no sign of Ryan or his bags.

'Hi, Sal,' Bea said.

Sal tilted her head and peered up at Bea.

'Here, have these.' Bea passed Sal a couple of croissants she had bought in the hope of meeting Ryan.

Sal took the offering and after inspecting the contents of the bag, stuffed it inside her tweed coat. 'You won't find Ryan today.'

'Oh.' Bea had assumed that she would at least see him later and was disappointed. 'Why's that?'

'Won't see him for some time, I reckon.'

Bea dropped to her knees, a hollow feeling in her stomach. Had he come to harm or gone missing like Declan? 'What's happened to him, Sal?'

The old woman shrugged and then dug around in her coat

pockets before producing a tobacco tin. Bea waited whilst she opened the tin and fiddled with a cigarette paper. Eventually Sal said, 'He'll be back.'

Relieved he hadn't come to any harm, Bea relaxed. 'When?'

Sal shrugged her shoulders again. 'A nice cuppa tea would go down a treat.'

By the time Bea had bought Sal a drink, it was after ten and she still had to get changed for work. The cup of tea had not coaxed any more information out of Sal but at least Ryan was safe.

It was twelve-thirty when Bea arrived at work that day. There was no time to compose herself in the staff room and so she had to face the department feeling unprotected and a bit dishevelled after the rush.

'You're thirty minutes late.' Jemima was wearing a red carnation.

Bea gaped. 'You're not the head of department yet.'

Jemima raised her eyebrows at someone behind Bea, and she spun around to see Pippa wearing a white carnation, the same as Bea.

'Mrs Barone had some leave owing and so she left sooner than expected. Pippa's been promoted to senior sales assistant. You missed the morning briefing – basically we're not expecting any VIP visits but with Christmas fast approaching, I expect you to work hard and achieve at least what we did this time last year. Now, you'd better get going to make up for lost time.'

Bea's heart sank – so this was what it was going to be like working with Jemima now that she was in charge. She had none of Mrs Barone's grace and gravitas – an ugly Puddle-Duckling compared to Barone's serene swan. Last week she and Jemima were equals and now Bea felt as though she had been demoted to the same level as Pippa. Except Pippa hadn't been entrusted with a special project by the floor manager. Ryan's words came back to her: *Go to the big boss and tell him what you need to get this done.* He was right. She had to take control of the situation and give herself the best possible chance of success.

When the floor was quiet Bea made a call. 'If Mr Evans could spare me a few minutes –'

'He's available now if you want to come straight up,' Evans's PA interrupted Bea. She hadn't expected that and wasn't prepared.

With Jemima's permission, Bea took the lift up two floors mentally going through her list of conditions. *I'll have to work full-time on the project. I'll expect to be paid what I would have earned on the shop floor, including commissions. If it is a success then I want to be considered for a promotion. No, I would like to be guaranteed a promotion – a head of department. It could be anywhere in the store – haberdashery, stationery.* Her stomach was tight with nerves. The lift doors opened. She couldn't do this. She would just say that she wanted to thank him in person for the opportunity. That he wouldn't be disappointed – that sort of thing.

'Go on in. Mr Evans was going to do a walk around the floor but said that he would see you instead.' For some reason that Bea didn't understand, his PA winked at her, as though they shared a secret.

'Miss Stevens. Twice in one week. To what do I owe this pleasure? I understand that Alastair has told you about Suki Dee Licious's charity event.'

Bea remembered the last time she was in this office and squirmed in her seat. *Do not have what it takes,* he had said then. She would show him. She wasn't a difficult employee who needed the attentions of a clinical psychologist – she was awesome. *Believe in yourself,* Ryan had said. Bea drew herself up and expanded her chest. She looked directly at Evans, with what she hoped was an *I'm taking no nonsense* face. 'He has and that's why I am here.'

Evans nodded his head up and down quickly, as though once set in motion it had to slow of its own accord. 'Of course. Of course.'

Bea wished that she had brought a notebook and pen so that she could look more businesslike. She planted her hands on the table and took a deep breath. She could do this. 'What you are asking me to do is, um. Well, it's a big ask.'

Evans sighed. 'Maybe I was expecting too much –'

'But not impossible,' Bea continued. 'There are twenty-five shopping days to Christmas. If you want me to organise a spectacular event that meets all of Suki Dee's criteria then I must work on this project full-time.' *There*. It was out. A bit garbled; she hadn't paused for breath.

Mr Evans cup rattled as he thrust it into the saucer, tea slopping over the sides. 'That's impossible – not at this time of the year.'

Bea hadn't really expected him to accept any conditions. Ryan didn't understand how the hierarchy worked at Hartleys. In fact, she had probably messed up any chance of promotion after being so demanding. She would just apologise and exit as quickly as possible. Evans rocked back and forth in his seat as though planning what he would say next and Bea prepared herself for the worst.

'If you are released to do this full-time then we would have to find another senior sales assistant to cover for you.' Evans frowned and looked as though he was thinking this through.

Relieved that he hadn't dismissed her request after all, Bea threw in another, before she lost her nerve. 'I would need a budget and complete control over the project.'

'Okay. Stop right there.' Evans held up his palms. She had gone too far. *Now* he would show her the door. But he didn't. 'Here's my counterproposal. I replace you in lingerie with a permanent senior sales assistant. There's a lass I have in mind. I've been trying to find a senior position for her. You will be responsible to me for delivering this project successfully, but you will report to Alastair on a daily basis keeping him abreast of developments. That includes potential risks and how you will resolve them.'

Bea's heart was pounding. There was too much information to process. Evans was talking too quickly and Bea felt as though she was in a runaway car with no brake. Before she could say anything, he continued, 'Alastair will control the budget. If you need to exceed the allocated fund, you will have to present your case to me. I think that is all, Miss Stevens.' Evans squared the papers on his desk and then looked at his watch.

Bea tried to make sense of what he had said. 'But my job? Where will I work after Christmas if I can't go back to my current post?'

Evans stood up as if to indicate that Bea had outstayed her welcome. 'If this event is a success, and I stress *if*, then you will have a rewarding career at Hartleys.'

'And if it's not?' Bea had a sickening feeling that she knew where he was going with this.

'Miss Stevens, I am giving you an opportunity to demonstrate that you have skills that are of value to Hartleys. I know that you are ambitious but as I said before, I'm not convinced that you are best suited to sales. However, there are other senior roles in Hartleys. Let's just wait and see how you get on, shall we?'

The back of her neck tingled. 'You didn't answer my question. What happens if I fail?' Bea swallowed hard.

'I'm afraid we will have to part company. But you will succeed. I have every confidence in you.'

Bea didn't share his confidence – not really, not deep down. She could act as though she was brave and bold but she was terrified. If Evans was setting her up to fail he was going to be disappointed because she was determined to succeed. He wouldn't get rid of her that easily.

'In that case,' Bea said, standing up so that she was on the same level as Evans, 'we need to agree exactly what success would look like. It can't be subjective. And if I do meet those requirements – then I need a guarantee that I will receive a –' she thought quickly '– a fifty per cent pay rise and a suitable position within the organisation.'

'Thirty per cent,' Evans said.

They settled on thirty-five per cent and Evans said that he would get personnel to prepare a contract the same day to seal their agreement.

Bea was heady with the implications of her daring as she took the Tube home. She tried to imagine herself at the charity event accepting everyone's praise – maybe holding a bouquet of flowers presented to her by Evans. Suki Dee mentioning her in a press release. In a couple of years, she may even be senior to Jemima – a lingerie buyer, travelling the world to find the finest silks and lace. She just had to plan something amazing that met all of Suki Dee's requirements. It couldn't be that hard. It was just one event. She couldn't wait to tell Ryan about her meeting with the 'Big Boss'.

'You're popular all of a sudden,' Molly, the cleaner, greeted Bea as she stepped into the lobby. The first time she had acknowledged Bea, let alone greeted her.

It was Ryan! She could tell him her news. Bea grinned.

'Thank you for letting Ryan in yesterday, it was a wonderful surprise.'

'He's a grand lad that one.' Molly ducked back inside her store room.

Bea was imagining Ryan outside her flat door. He knew what time she got home and must have been waiting. *You'll never guess what happened at work today,* she rehearsed in her head, breaking into a smile, as though she was already talking to him.

But when Bea reached her landing she saw two men in suits and one of them was slotting a key into the lock of her door.

'Hey! What do you think you're doing?'

The man with the key jumped and threw his hands up as though scalded.

'Miss Stevens?'

Bea nodded. Were they bailiffs? Mum kept saying that they were short on income but surely it hadn't come to that.

'Mrs Stevens thought that you might be at work and told me in that event to use the key.'

'My mother told you to let yourself into my flat?' He had to be lying. Why would Mum suggest something so outrageous? It was like when she was ten and a man offered her a lift home from school saying that her mum had asked him to. Bea believed him and got in his car but then she saw her mum across the road. *Never, never get in a stranger's car no matter what they say,* her mum had said.

'Stanley Larkin, Larkin and Dunstable Estate Agents.'

'If this is a bad time?' The other man in a suit shuffled back and forth. He looked at his watch. 'I can come by another day.'

Great, Mum had already put the flat on the market without telling Bea. 'No, it's okay. I wasn't expecting you and it was a bit of a surprise.' That was an understatement.

Stanley Larkin was expounding the benefits of living in a gentrified area just a few metres from a major rail station, when Bea phoned her mum from the spare room.

'There's a bloody estate agent in my flat and he has a key!' she hissed.

'Bea darling, we've discussed this nearly every Sunday for the past six months. You always knew that you had three years in the flat before we sold it.'

'But how could you tell him to use a key to let himself in? What if I'd been naked? I thought you were worried about me being *vulnerable* living in London. Great – then why not hand out keys and invite every weirdo in the city to let themselves in and have a peek? Oh – maybe you're going to let my spare room to a stranger. Have a look in the lonely-hearts column and find a crazy.' Bea paused for breath. The irony of what she had accused her mum of sinking in.

'Sweetheart, if you look at your phone you'll see that I told you Mr Larkin wanted to show a prospective buyer around the flat.'

The door opened and Mr Larkin gave a meek smile.

'Hold on, they need to look in here.' As Bea moved into her bedroom she checked her messages. There was one from Mum sent yesterday morning. It explained everything but Bea had been distracted by the challenge and then Ryan surprised her and today had been a bit of a whirlwind too.

She sighed and hated herself for sounding like an adolescent. Mum always did that to her. 'Okay. Fine.'

'Don't worry, darling. If you haven't made any arrangements you can come back home. You always have a room here.'

Bea pictured the box room where she had lain awake at night dreaming of a different future. Her parents loved her but their concern was stifling. To go back would be to rewind her life as though the past three years hadn't happened, her independent life in the centre of London.

'It's okay, Mum. I appreciate it but I've made arrangements. I hadn't read your message and Mr Larkin trying to let himself in just took me by surprise.'

When Bea had hung up and seen the estate agent and his client out of her flat, she collapsed on the sofa. How could life have changed so much in just a few days? Last week she had a secure job as senior sales assistant and expected a promotion to head of department. If Mum had mentioned selling the flat, Bea hadn't taken her seriously. She honestly thought that once she got a promotion and offered to pay decent rent, she could live there for as long as she wanted. The life she had created for herself in the city had felt secure but now it was all crumbling around her. Her dream of working her way up to an executive position in Hartleys had been her guiding star for so long, it had become who she was – what she lived for. With all of her heart, Bea wanted to succeed at this challenge. To fail was unthinkable. No job, no flat. She felt as though she was drowning – if only Ryan was there to bolster her confidence. If not for Ryan, she would never have marched into Evans's office making all of those demands. Now she had had time to think it over, she regretted the confrontation. It was too much of a gamble, especially now she had to find somewhere else to live, but the signed contract was in her bag and there was no going back.

15

TWENTY-FOUR SHOPPING DAYS TO CHRISTMAS

Last week Bea knew exactly what to do on her day off: the same thing that she always did – a tour of Hartleys's competitor stores, lunch at Roberto's – seafood linguine – and then four hours improving her Russian. Like an athlete in training, Bea felt invigorated by the discipline of these rituals as she inched closer towards her goal. Now she was playing Evans's game and the goal posts might as well have had moved to a different planet. She had to come up with a brilliant idea, but her mind was completely blank – paralysed by the enormity of what this meant to her. Bea buried herself under the weight of her duvet until a text from her mum had her reaching for her phone.

As it is your day off I have arranged for more viewings. Please stay in if you don't want Mr Larkin showing buyers around in your absence. There was no way that she was going to waste her day waiting in for an estate agent.

Standing outside her apartment block, the crisp air biting her cheeks, Bea felt disorientated, as though the world had tilted and she was upside down in a snow globe. There was no time for a day off; she had to come up with an idea for the charity event and a plan of action by the end of the day. Fortified by this resolution, Bea strode along the tow path of the canal hoping for inspiration.

As she walked she began to feel calmer. It was restful watching the few ducks that had not flown south skimming across the water. Truthfully, she hoped to see Ryan and her heart lifted every time a runner came into view, but he was not to be found.

'Hey there.' A man with a bald head and fulsome beard called to Bea from the deck of his boat.

Unused to anyone greeting her, Bea assumed he was talking to someone else.

'What did you think of the band?'

There was nobody close by on the tow path and she couldn't see anyone else on his boat, *No Worries*. Maybe he was talking to someone below deck.

'We met on Sunday at Fandangle's. You're a friend of Ryan's, right?'

Hearing his name brought Ryan a little closer and Bea realised how much she needed him. Anything felt possible with Ryan at her side.

'Do you know where he is?' she asked the man.

'No. You know Ryan. He'll be gone for months and then just turn up as if he's never been away. Are you off to Fandangle's?'

Bea hadn't known that she was, but now that he suggested it, it felt as if that was where she had been heading all along. 'Yes. Thought I'd have a coffee and a bite of breakfast.'

'Say hi to Leila from me. I'd join you but I've an engine to fix.'

Bea had walked away a few metres before remembering that she didn't know his name.

'Mouse,' he called in response to her question. Nobody could have been less like a mouse, with his broad girth and booming voice.

An invigorating walk had not stimulated any ideas for the Suki Dee event and neither had the coffee and bacon sarnie that disappeared from her plate. If it wasn't for the lingering taste she might have denied having eaten it.

'You look deep in thought,' Leila said, joining her at the table.

Bea sighed. Her mind had been whirring like an over-wound watch, too panicked to think through anything rationally. 'I do seem to have a lot on my mind.'

'Wait there. I've got something that will make you forget your troubles.'

Through an archway, Bea spied Leila tumbling steaming muffins into a basket. She really shouldn't, not after eating a calorie-laden sandwich, but to refuse would be rude, and Leila's friendship was much more important to Bea than worrying about her figure.

A scrawny-looking man with a goatee beard, and beneath a parka jacket, jeans that seemed to be slipping down to his knees, shuffled past Bea and found a seat at another table. Fandangle's visitors tended to crowd together on the long table that stretched the length of the cabin, but there was another smaller table opposite covered in maps of the canal, tourist information, and newspapers, and this was where the man with the goatee beard sat. Leila served him a coffee and when he grunted in response to her small talk about the weather and the ducks, she left him to enjoy his coffee in peace and joined Bea.

The scent of baking powder and butter infused the air as

Leila and Bea sat plucking apart their muffins. 'Didn't I tell you that these would work their magic? Now tell me your worries. A problem shared...'

Bea told Leila that she needed to find somewhere else to live and asked about the cost of rent in London in the hope that Leila might know of someone looking for a flatmate.

'I couldn't afford to rent somewhere big enough to live and work. I was really lucky finding the *Fandangle* because I only pay Roots for the mooring and maintenance. It's much cheaper to live here than on land.'

That was an option that Bea hadn't considered, living on a houseboat. For a few seconds she felt a glimmer of hope and possibility. 'Maybe Roots knows of someone who might rent me a houseboat?'

She was imagining living on the water in a cute little boat with a log burner and pots of geraniums on the deck in the summer, when Leila brought her back down to earth with a jolt.

'No chance. As I said I was lucky. You might find a bedsit in Bexley for, say one thousand, two hundred a month. Are you using a room finder app?'

Bea didn't even know there was such a thing. She really ought to have done some research; a couple of thousand a month was way more than she had expected.

'And then there's the deposit,' Leila continued.

'Deposit?' Bea's mouth was dry.

'Usually two months in advance.'

'Oh,' was all that she could say.

How was she going to find somewhere to live at the same time as arranging the event? After Christmas. She would worry about finding somewhere to live after Christmas. Mum would understand. All of her attention had to be focused on the Suki Dee challenge. When she got a promotion, she would be able to afford somewhere close to the canal.

Leila stood up to clear away their plates. 'I hope you don't mind, but those clothes you donated to the sale were far too good to put out on a stall. I thought I would sell them on eBay to make more for the charity.'

Bea helped her by stacking their plates. 'No, that's what they were for. I haven't worn any of them for at least a year and so it was time to throw them out.'

'Really? Wow. But they have Hartleys labels and must have cost a bomb. Sorry, am I being indiscreet? It's just that with you being a friend of Ryan's I assumed well…I knew that you weren't homeless but…'

'Oh, I get a big discount and some of those things were already in the sale,' she improvised.

'Ryan said that you worked in a shop but I didn't know it was Hartleys.'

Bea's heart swelled with pride. She couldn't imagine not working at the world-famous store. Maybe she had been too hasty in making demands of Evans. A senior sales assistant was better than no job at all. If only she had saved some of her salary instead of spending it all on clothes, she might have had enough for the deposit on a flat. Bea had an idea. 'How much do you think those clothes will fetch on eBay?' she said.

A sharp intake of breath, then Leila said, 'Do you want them back?'

The cabin darkened as Roots filled the doorway. 'Hiya, Leila. Bea.' He made himself comfortable on the bench.

'I was just checking with Bea if she was okay with us selling those clothes on eBay for Friends of the Earth.'

'Yes, of course you can,' Bea said. 'I just wondered how much they might go for.'

'I'll let you know,' Leila said with a wink.

Bea left Leila and Roots discussing business and with a full belly, the warm glow of friendship, and at least one positive plan – to sell her clothes – she turned in the direction of home.

'You looking for a place to live?' A low, deep voice startled Bea. She hadn't been aware of the man with a goatee, who had crept up behind her.

'No.' He had scared her. Then Bea collected herself. 'I might be. Why?'

The man shrugged and made some distance between them. 'Just heard you talking. You might want to check out this site.' He handed her a flier.

Bea felt stupid for being so suspicious; he was just trying to help her. This man was probably a friend of Leila and Ryan. She should have learnt not to judge people by their appearance. 'Thank you. That's very kind of you,' she said and slipped the flier into her bag to read later.

The man with the goatee was on the other side of the tow path, when a young man walked between them. As Bea made room for him to pass, she thought that there was something familiar about him. Maybe he was one of Hartleys's delivery boys, the boys in black.

A mobile phone rang from somewhere in Goatee's parka and as he took his phone to huddle in conversation, Bea followed the young man along the tow path searching her memory. She really ought to take more notice of the people around her. Then, it came to her. It was the same man that Ryan had talked to outside the *Fandangle*. The man who had given Ryan important information. He was a friend of Declan. Bea increased her pace. She had to catch him up so that she could talk to him.

16

SEPTEMBER 2009

Caitlin was sixteen when Ryan's college course started. He had managed to keep up the milking routine and work as Hennessey's apprentice, building timber frames for houses and working on building projects. In two more years he would have enough experience to start the NVQ in carpentry and joinery.

'Don't expect me to be paying your fees, lad,' his da had said. 'The farm barely makes enough to keep us and I'll have to pay for labour when you're away.'

'I don't need you to provide me with anything.' Ryan glowered. 'I've earned enough to pay for the course and can support myself.'

'*Yourself.* That's all you think about. Never mind your ma and me, scraping to make ends meet, paying for labour because our son is too selfish to help out.'

'Enough. Enough.' Ma covered her ears. 'We've hired help and between us we'll manage fine.'

'I like doing the milking. I want to go to agricultural

college. Nobody says, well done, Caitlin! Nobody thanks *me* for my work on the farm.'

'I've told you, farming is no occupation for a woman. That's what sons are for. My da wouldn't have passed the farm to my sister, it's unthinkable, a woman running a farm.'

'Arrgh.' Caitlin stormed out of the room.

'Unbelievable.' Ryan shook his head.

Ma glared at him and he followed Caitlin upstairs. He found her in her room, lying with her eyes closed, ear pods connecting her to her phone. Ryan sat on the edge of the bed and she opened her eyes, then shifted up to make room for him.

He tugged an ear pod free. 'Do you really want to farm or are you saying that out of a sense of duty?'

Caitlin pulled out the other ear pod and sat up. 'Why wouldn't I want to farm? It's in my blood. I can't imagine not living on this farm, I even love getting up at five to milk. Have you ever stood at the top of the hill as the sun rises? I look across the valley, at our farm, and sometimes I feel like I can't breathe, it's so beautiful.'

Ryan pushed a teddy in her face, like he did when she was a tot. It was hard to think of her as a young woman. 'What about the cow shit? The freezing fog that cracks your knuckles in the winter? Getting stomped on the foot?'

'I know all that, but I still love it. Why do you and Da always have to fight? It upsets Ma. I've seen her cry after you two have been at each other.'

Ryan had too and he hated himself for hurting her, but he and Da had never got on; the sooner he moved out the better. He would miss Ma and Caitlin – the farm too – but finally he would be in control of his life. He was going to train as a carpenter and work his way through college, working on building sites. Hennessey had given him an excellent reference and he had found a house share near the college at student rates. Ryan vowed never to ask his parents for a penny. He didn't want to inherit the farm; they could leave it to Caitlin for all he cared. That's if his bigoted da ever trusted her to make a go of it. From here on, he was independent and would make his own way in the world.

17

TWENTY-FOUR SHOPPING DAYS TO CHRISTMAS

A group of young tourists, maybe Germans, meandered together on the path and Bea lost sight of the man for a minute. When they had passed, she scanned the way ahead. A man selling hot chestnuts, and two women with pushchairs and young children. If he was still on the tow path, Bea couldn't see him.

The sleet had evaporated and the air was heavy like a sodden blanket. The light was already beginning to fade and Bea felt resentment for the shortened day and gloom of winter. The promise of Christmas in a few weeks did not lighten her mood, unlike the two young mums who were joyfully singing a song about Santa getting stuck up the chimney.

The man had passed Granary Square, where Bea would have left the canal to thread her way through sightseers back to her flat. He was far ahead and she didn't really expect to catch him up but neither did she want to return home. It had always been a place of solitude. Just as work had been a playground of possibility. Now, work felt like a scary big dipper ride and strangers were poking around in her flat talking about its market potential. Instead of feeling comfort from the familiarity of these safe places Bea felt rejected – kicked out, like a bird thrown from its nest. At least the walk had a calming effect; it slowed her thoughts as she watched life on the canal.

Bea paused awhile to watch the cascade of water from a lock. A train rattled by the other side of the canal and an announcement boomed from the station. It felt different this side of the square, as though she was in new territory – the sounds more urban. Dusk turned to dark and Bea made her way up the steep incline alongside the lock. How easy it would be to slip and fall on an icy day in the dark. She checked that nobody was following her and was both relieved and a little afraid to find that she was quite alone apart from Ryan and Declan's friend, who was now a few metres ahead.

There was a housing estate to the right and menacing graffiti on the wall that led to a long tunnel. A skull with burning bright eyes and a purple hat. The man had disappeared into the tunnel and Bea hesitated. What on earth was she going to say to this stranger? Ryan had asked her not to get involved. Maybe now was the time to turn back. The tunnel was long and dark. What if she came across someone else lurking in the shadows? A train screeched and then rumbled and Bea shivered.

Fired by adrenaline, curiosity, and determination, Bea continued through the tunnel. On the other side, there was only one barge in sight. Even in the moonlight, she could see that it was a wreck. Irregular shapes jutted out of the deck, giving the impression of a floating junkyard. There wasn't much else to see this side of the bridge and the man she was following had disappeared. Possibly up the steps that led from the canal where signage pointed to Camden.

It was time to go home. The estate agent should be gone by now and the damp air was starting to seep into her bones. As Bea began to turn, she was startled by a thump. A man had jumped from the old barge, and as he straightened up Bea recognised him as the man she had been following. If he had walked back the way he had come, she might have finally caught him, but instead he continued along the canal. It was getting colder and danker. Bea felt as though she were breathing in the murky waters of the canal as her lungs filled with night dew. Bea let him go. Even if she had the energy to chase after him, she didn't know what she would say. The escapade had been a complete waste of time, unless – Bea wondered at her daring – unless, she peeked inside the dilapidated barge that the man had just visited. There might be a clue that could help her to find Declan. This man knew more about Declan's last movements than Ryan. Maybe they had been together.

The old barge rocked gently with the current. If she had a name, it was no longer visible on the faded blue paint that cloaked her disintegrating body. As Bea planted a foot on deck the barge tilted to one side and she nearly lost her balance. The ramshackle of oddments jutting from the deck formed a makeshift cabin. The sides had been reinforced with hardboard and extended with an old door, a window, and planks of wood. A very different home to the cosy *Fandangle* but it looked as though it had been used by someone as a shelter.

Bea slid back the hardboard and peeked into the cabin. The smell of petrol and seaweed hit her first and then a musty, bitter tang that grazed her throat. Bea twisted her head and took a gulp of untainted air before venturing in.

There wasn't much to see, just a rusty oil lamp, newspapers, and a scattering of envelopes. Bea bent down to retrieve these from the soggy cardboard floor covering. They were addressed to the owner of *Moby*. So that was her name. One day, long ago, she would have been brand new, the name inspiring growth and opportunity. What became of the owner? Was it the man she had followed? She doubted it; he didn't look as though he had once been affluent, but would strangers have known that Declan was once carefree? Bea was learning not to make assumptions about people. She had been wrong about Ryan, labelling him as homeless instead of seeing the man. A kind, funny, and thoughtful man who seemed to see the best in her.

It was immoral to open someone else's mail but the letters must have been lying there for months if not years. Eighteen months, according to one of the postmarks. Nobody was looking and so Bea worried open an envelope. It was an official letter with a warning that the owner had to pay his licence or the houseboat would be removed from the waterway.

'Poor old thing,' she muttered. 'You're for the knacker's yard.'

A cupboard door had been used to create an entrance to the cabin. Bea crawled through its narrow opening. The underlying scent was thicker and more putrid here. Bea wrapped her scarf tightly around her nose and mouth. An old baking tray had once been used as a barbecue. Bea wondered what had been made edible over the driftwood that was blackened and white. Squirrel? Duck? Bluebottles buzzed in the confined space. A can of baked beans, a tin of sardines, and a box of camomile teabags sat forlornly on a hardboard shelf. Bea picked up the teabags and her heart contracted. *Ryan*. So, this was where he hid out. The man she followed must have been looking for Ryan. She wanted to fill the shelves with food, an early visit from Santa.

A scratching and rustling behind her. Bea twisted to see the glint of sharp teeth. A ginormous water rat. She screamed, shrinking back, and the rat stared at her with unblinking eyes. He was not more afraid of her. This rat considered himself king and this his kingdom.

'Go away. Go away. Shoo, shoo,' Bea yelled, trying to assert her authority. The rat scurried past her and Bea flinched. There was a clatter as it knocked over a box of rubbish and then it thankfully disappeared. She should have left then but thinking of Ryan Bea stooped to tidy away the rubbish, old cans, and packaging. Then, her hand found something soft and slimy. The fat bottom, scrawny legs, and wormlike tail of a dead rat protruded from a can of corn beef. Urgh! She threw her hands up and watched in horror as the can hit the deck. A maggot clung to her wrist and she screamed, knocking it free. She wouldn't use her hands again *ever*. Not until they had been disinfected and scrubbed. Oh God, this couldn't be where Ryan hung out. It was disgusting.

Back in the fresh air, Bea held her hands away from her, afraid that she might forget where they had been and touch her face. Oh, to go home and scrub herself clean in a hot shower. Then, Bea's foot went straight through the soggy cardboard floor. Her thigh and forearm hit the deck. Bea yelped. *That bloody hurt.*

She lay still, checking that nothing was seriously injured, before scrambling to her feet. The cardboard had been used to cover rotten floorboards. Bea tore it away gingerly, afraid now of uncovering more dead rats. But, it was a safety hazard; children might play on the wreck. No wonder the authorities wanted to tow her away.

Whatever Bea thought she might find it wasn't this. In the exposed cavity was Declan's bag. The one that Ryan had been carrying when she first met him. It might as well have been a bomb the way Bea's hands shook. She fumbled with a front pocket, afraid that Ryan would appear from nowhere and catch her in the act. Inside was a driving license for Declan Connor. Bea cradled his sweet face in the palm of her hand. *Where are you, Declan?*

18

TWENTY-THREE SHOPPING DAYS TO CHRISTMAS

Bea regretted stealing Declan's bag. It had been hard to sleep, knowing that it was in the top of her wardrobe. It was as though Declan was in her bedroom, whispering accusations into her dreams. She awoke, more determined than ever to solve the mystery of Declan's disappearance. His bag was unlikely to offer any clues; she had opened it last night and recoiled at the damp and musty smell, reminiscent of the school changing rooms for PE – stale sweat and old trainers. It brought back memories of Davinia Grayson and Hettie Chambers giggling and whispering as Bea used an inadequate towel to hide her folds of fat. She had closed the bag and hidden it from view. There must be another way to find Declan. He had been popular with the boys in black when he worked at Hartleys; maybe one of them had kept in touch with him. That's what she would do. She would talk to the delivery boys to find out more about Declan. Her mission to find Declan had started as a way to atone for her guilt in making him homeless but now it was also about Ryan. Ryan had done so much for her and she wanted to help him. He would be heartbroken if anything happened to Declan, and she suspected that Ryan already feared the worst.

'You might as well go and see Alastair now,' Jemima sighed. 'I said after your break at four, but if you're going to hang around the desk ignoring customers you might as well go and do something useful.'

Bea was jolted from her thoughts. She wasn't aware that she had ignored anyone, but now she noticed all of the other assistants were busy serving and last time she looked there was nobody there to serve.

'Sorry, Jemima. I've just got a lot on my mind. I'll work a bit later if it helps.'

Jemima waved her away. 'Just make sure you kick into gear when you get upstairs. I'll be glad when your replacement arrives, someone who has a bit of motivation.'

Bea resisted the temptation to remind Jemima that as peers, their sales records had been neck and neck. Nonetheless, Bea did a few positive mantras and prepared herself before knocking on Alastair's door. It was only Alastair – not so long ago he was an intern.

'Excite me!' Alastair pronounced leaning back in his executive swivel chair, hands linked above his head. They bizarrely resembled a cock's comb.

Bea wasn't sure what to do in response to this command. Shout boo. Flash him. Start a fire.

'Ideas. Have you brought an idea for discussion? Some outline plans we can throw around?'

If he had warned her she would have come with some notes to discuss. Who was she kidding? Bea had tried hard to think of something amazing to astound Alastair and Evans with her creative genius. Her flat was littered with scribbled notes – each new page a possibility, before it was discarded with ideas crossed out and angry scribbles. As though afraid of the spotlight, her creativity had deserted her. If it was cowering somewhere in the furthest reaches of her brain, she wished it would come out and show itself.

Alastair raised his eyebrows in expectation.

'Of course I have,' Bea said and then regretted sounding so confident when she had nothing to offer. Not a single idea. *Think. Think.*

He was waiting. Legs splayed as he rocked back and forth on the chair, a kid on a seesaw.

'Well, the obvious choices are a fashion show or a charity ball.' She played for time, hoping inspiration would strike.

'As you said, the obvious choices. We have to do something sensational for Suki.'

'The timescale is very tight, Alastair. How are we going to organise something worthwhile before Christmas?'

'That's what you're going to show me. To get on in Hartleys you need to be exceptional, to pull off the impossible. Suki Dee insisted that you were involved and although I personally don't share her faith in you, Mr Evans obviously does.'

Bea didn't know that Suki Dee had asked for her by name. It gave her confidence, that she *was* up to the challenge. She had let worries about the flat and finding Declan distract her. Of course she could do this. This was her chance to shine and Bea couldn't afford to let anything get in her way. It might be her last chance to prove herself. 'Well, if you want sensational then stand back and get ready to be amazed. I have a brilliant idea. Suki Dee will love it.'

Alastair went a little pale and sat up in his seat. 'What is it? You have to tell me because I'm your PR contact. It may not be an appropriate idea. In fact, I forbid you to do anything without passing it by me first. The reputation of Hartleys can't be compromised.'

Bea forced a smile. 'Don't worry, I'll follow protocol. I just need to check a few things out first.'

A few minutes later Bea sailed out of the marketing department on a bit of a high – Suki Dee had asked for her by name. It wasn't until she was back in the lingerie department that she remembered she didn't actually have an idea.

'I hope you know what you're doing, Bea,' Jemima greeted Bea on her return to lingerie. 'That's Millie, your replacement.' She nodded in the direction of a pretty blonde girl who was hovering close to Patsy, the customer Bea offended, waiting to pounce.

Bea wasn't at all sure that she did know what she was doing. Yesterday, she had considered asking Evans to tear up the contract, that she would happily remain a sales assistant and forget about a promotion, but she knew that it would only be a matter of time before Evans found a reason to 'move her on'. Her face didn't fit. She was a square peg in a round hole. The clichés reflected Bea's place in the world – she didn't fit in. It was surprising that she had lasted three years at Hartleys without being found out.

'Bea. *Miss Stevens*,' Jemima hissed at Bea. There was a customer who needed serving. The middle-aged man was admiring the Agent Provocateur playsuits, his fingers toying with the fine gold chains which, when strategically strewn around the body, formed a garment.

'I can see that you appreciate the craftsmanship in these unique garments,' Bea spoke quietly, as she stood close enough to the man for private conversation but not too close to intimidate him. Jemima nodded her head in approval and then turned her attention to the new stock that was being wheeled in by the boys in black.

The man dipped his head and Bea noticed a blush creep up his neck. She hoped that he wasn't just window shopping for thrills. It wouldn't be the first male customer to ask one of the girls to model the garment.

'This one is nine carat gold, and the other one you looked at is of course encrusted with real diamonds. We have more in the stockroom. Perhaps you could tell me what you're looking for?'

'I don't know. Maybe this wasn't such a good idea. I can buy these online, right?'

Bea's pride wouldn't let her lose this sale. 'You can, but with these garments being so valuable, it is perhaps prudent to buy in person. Especially around Christmas when packages may get lost in transit. At least let me help you to select a playsuit and then, if you want to order online, you will know what to look for.'

The man seemed to have relaxed with Bea's calm and professional approach. He was now examining a leather playsuit with gold chains and studs.

'We have a suede in that style. And another which is similar but with more chains and less leather.'

'Could I try this one on?'

Bea gulped. He was a bit on the large size. This was a women's lingerie department and although they catered for transgender and transvestite in some of the lines, she didn't know whether the playsuits came in extra large.

'We supply a body stocking for customers trying these on,' Bea said.

'If you could also bring me the one with more gold than leather and perhaps this one too?' He pointed to the delicate playsuit with fine gold chains and Bea winced. It wouldn't fit; the chains would snap.

Anxious not to offend the man Bea found the biggest body stocking that they had and took it to him in the changing room.

'I'm not sure exactly how to wear this. Could you come back and help me?' he said.

Bea left him with an extra-large leather and gold playsuit as it was the most robust and, after promising to return once he had put on the body stocking, she checked the computer for sizes. She would order one made to measure, if he could afford it.

Bea was making her way back to the changing room to impart this information when she saw two of the boys in black slip out of the department through one of the doors that led to the hidden part of Hartleys. Like a cruise ship with its hull beneath the sea, there were almost as many floors beneath the ground in Hartleys as above. Floors where delivery boys, maintenance men, and hundreds of other workers kept the store functioning.

Millie, her replacement, had finished serving Patsy and so Bea said, 'Please could you keep an eye on my customer in changing room three? I need to have a quick word with the delivery boys.'

Bea caught the door before it closed and slipped past them down the stairs. 'Just need to check what's in stock,' she said over her shoulder.

The men ignored her and continued their conversation about football. Bea didn't know how to start a conversation with the backroom boys. That's what Pippa had said on the night of Evans's Christmas reception. *She doesn't have a good word for the delivery boys or the despatch staff.*

'You are doing a very good job,' she said when they reached the basement. It caught their attention because they stopped talking and stared at her. They waited but Bea didn't know how to bring up Declan. Would they remember that she was the one who reported him to management? 'Stocking shelves and things,' she added.

One of the men nodded. 'Thanks.' They were going to walk away.

'Could you show me where the lingerie stock is held?'

'Same place it's always been.'

Of course, he knew that as a senior sales assistant Bea would know exactly where the stock was and what was being held in the basement and in the back of the department.

'What were you looking for? Maybe I can help you.'

Bea couldn't dither any longer, apart from anything else she had to get back to her customer. The basement was busy with supplies being unpacked and goods being wheeled across the floor on a trolley. One of the men went to assist a colleague, and the other looked over Bea's shoulder as if anxious to get on. 'I'm sorry to bother you, but I was wondering whether you knew, I mean *know* Declan Connor.'

There was complete silence as the thud of packages, whispers of crumpled paper, and the squeak of a trolley wheel came to an abrupt stop. The chatter of workers quietened as though a conductor had stilled their voices. All eyes were on Bea. *What had she done?*

A middle-aged woman with a bob and a snarly mouth separated herself from a group of workers. She looked Bea up and down as though she had no business being there. 'That's rich, asking after the poor bugger when it's your fault he became homeless.'

Bea felt light-headed. It was as though she were surrounded by a pack of wild animals. *Keep calm,* she willed herself. The old Bea would have said something to put the woman in her place. But the old Bea wouldn't have blundered into this situation. She was out of her depth. Ryan's words came back to her and gave her courage: *You're not afraid of going after what you want. Stop dwelling on the things that you're not and be proud of who you are.* She couldn't feel good about herself, knowing that she had walked past Declan every day and not seen him, or Ryan, or any of the other homeless people around King's Cross Station. She had to put things right by finding Declan, before Ryan found out that she had made his friend homeless.

Bea perched on a pile of boxes and thought carefully before she spoke. 'I was devastated to hear about Declan. Until he was reported missing, I had no idea that he was homeless. I realise now that if I hadn't opened my mouth things might have been different for him. If I could turn back the clock then believe me, I would.'

'Missing? I didn't know Dec was missing.' The man shook his head. 'How do you know this?'

Bea explained about the fliers Ryan was handing out to passers-by.

The woman with the bob tutted, 'Poor bugger,' but she looked a bit less scary and the rumble of the stockroom resumed.

'I'm trying to find him and thought if you or any of his friends could tell me something about him, it might help.'

Another of the boys in black joined them. 'I knew Dec. We were good mates when he worked here. You know he had a degree in economics and business? We had a pint in The King's Head once. He told me he grew up in a home for kids but it didn't stop him making something of himself. Don't blame yourself for reporting him. He was bound to have been caught sooner or later. Missing, you say?'

Bea nodded.

'He didn't keep in touch with any of us, so I can't really help you there. But if there's anything I can do, let me know. Yeah, a good guy – Declan.'

As Bea ascended from the basement, she felt as though she had left behind a great weight. It seemed that she had been forgiven by Declan's mates for ratting on him. How could someone just slip through the cracks like that? A man with a business degree and ambition? A person could lose their job and their home so easily. What stopped you from falling over the edge? Family? Friends?

'The staff room, please,' Jemima said the minute Bea stepped back into lingerie.

Bea followed Jemima's rigid back knowing that she was going to be reprimanded, but her mind was full of Declan and the unfairness of life.

'Where were you? Poor Millie. Her first day in lingerie.'

At first, Bea had no idea what Jemima was talking about, but then it came back to her – the rather large man who insisted he try on the leather and gold playsuit.

'Oh I'm sorry, Jemima. I only meant to pop out for two minutes. I got a bit caught up. Um, did it fit?'

'No, it bloody didn't. He got his equipment entangled and Millie had to set him free.' She sounded angry but a light danced in her eyes. 'He came hopping out of the changing room…' Jemima struggled to keep a straight face but then she caught Bea's eye and they laughed together.

It was a release to laugh. Bea could imagine the podgy man trussed up like a turkey, his face red. 'Ooh painful,' she said. And then as she caught her breath, 'I'm sorry, Jemima. Is Millie okay?'

'She'll survive. She'll have to get used to such things if she's to work in lingerie. But I am going to miss working with you.'

19

TWENTY-THREE SHOPPING DAYS TO CHRISTMAS

As soon as Bea got home from work, she prepared herself for business. She had declared an audacious plan to Alastair and was determined to deliver one. Suki Dee had requested her input, Evans believed she had more to offer given the opportunity, and Ryan thought her awesome. 'You've got this, Bea,' she said as she arranged notepad, highlighters, coloured pens, and stickers across her desk.

The clock ticked. She had never noticed how loud it was before. 'Something magnificent.' She twirled her hair around a finger. 'Think.' She tapped her pen on the edge of the desk. Maybe she was scaring herself by thinking too big. Start small and then build up. In the centre of her page Bea wrote, *Charity event.* Then, with a sharp pencil she drew an arrow and wrote, *A ball.* She shaded in the triangle of the arrow. Bea took more care drawing the next arrow. This time she used a blue pencil to colour in the triangle. *A raffle.*

Bea sighed. 'Okay, what is Suki Dee known for? What will

draw in the crowds?' She started a new page. 'Brainstorm.' *Big boobs.* Bea remembered them only too well. The thought made her uncomfortable and she drew a hard line through her first entry. There must be something else? 'I know. I'll define Suki Dee's current image.' Bea drew a stick figure on one side of the page and took her time drawing a thought bubble. With no idea what to write as Suki Dee's current image, Bea drew another stick figure on the other side of the page and wrote, *Humanitarian. See Angelina Jolie.* 'How to move from here –' Bea stabbed the page '– to here. Hmm.' It was no good. Her mind was blank.

Everyone wanted something magnificent from her – Alastair, Evans, Suki Dee. The thought of disappointing them filled her with shame. She had to make a success of this. The blank page was now filled with doodles, a high-heeled shoe, a sunflower, and random spirals. Bea screwed it up and tossed it in the bin. The clock's tick seemed to have got louder. Bea swiped it from the bedside table and marched out of the spare bedroom. In her own bedroom she looked for somewhere to bury it and alighted on the wardrobe. The top shelf.

As soon as Bea lifted the door, she knew what had led her there. How could she work when Declan's bag was waiting for her attention? 'Okay, Declan, I get it,' she said and hauled the bag out. 'I'll find you,' she whispered, as though offering up a prayer.

This time Bea was prepared for the odour of stale sweat and mildew that clung to the bundle of clothes stuffed inside. She closed her eyes and thought of Declan – young and full of life. It was as though he were in the room with her. Her notebook, coloured pens, and good intentions were now forgotten as Bea spread a towel over her bedspread and eased out a tangle of clothes: boxer shorts, T-shirts, a green rugby shirt with an Irish logo. There were a few odd socks and Bea lay them side by side. All five of them were completely worn at the heel and toes. They would offer no protection from the rubbing of shoes or the cold.

There was a faux leather wash bag and inside a toothbrush with flattened bristles – no toothpaste, a slither of soap, and a red flannel. This was what life was like for Ryan and Declan. The remnants of a life they once knew in these paltry possessions, as they struggled to maintain their dignity. To keep warm and clean. When she invited Ryan to use her bathroom she had been afraid of offending him. Why hadn't she realised that it was as important to Ryan to maintain his hygiene as it was to her, except this right had been taken away from him? How could she have been so self-righteous? Bea sighed. It was wrong that some people had so much and others nothing at all.

Her phone rang from inside her work bag, where it lay alongside her discarded heels at the bedroom door. Usually Bea disliked unexpected calls from her mum but this evening she was glad of the distraction. 'Hi, Mum.' She sat on the bed, one hand caressing a frayed sock.

'Bea darling. Is everything alright? You sound a bit distracted. If you're feeling a bit wobbly over the sale of the flat we can talk about it. I know that you hate change.'

Why did she do that? Mum's incessant worrying about her was undermining. Today she felt particularly fragile; the shell that protected her from the outside world was paper thin. It made Bea defensive and she snapped back, 'It's fine, Mum.'

There were a few seconds of silence and Bea knew that her mum was thinking through how to respond so that she wouldn't anger Bea more and she was ashamed.

'I'm sure it is, but you haven't told me where you plan to

live when the flat's been sold. Do you want to come back home, darling? It will be a bit of a commute but Dad could ferry you to and from the station.'

'No, Mum.' Bea hadn't meant to raise her voice. 'I mean, thank you but that won't be necessary. I can't tell you exactly where I'm going to be living but it's all in hand.'

Two heartbeats of silence. Bea could feel her mum's anxiety radiating across the radio waves.

'I hope you've been saving some money whilst living rent free. You'll need to pay a deposit. And have you checked out what you can afford? A shop assistant's salary can't be very much. You know it's expensive living in London. Do you want me to help you look, darling? Find somewhere suitable? Maybe live with a family who can check that you get safely back home of an evening?'

Bea's chest tightened and she held the phone away from her ear. Next door there was a blank sheet of paper when her future at Hartleys depended upon it being filled with wondrous plans. In one hand was a reminder of the life that Ryan, Declan, and hundreds of other people experienced in London, and in the other, her mum, telling her that she was incapable of looking after herself – that she would soon be losing the flat and had nowhere to go.

Bea took a deep breath as her mum had taught her as a child when she sensed one of Bea's meltdowns approaching. 'I told you that I had somewhere to live.' In the silence that followed, Bea felt her mum's reproach. They both knew that she was lying.

When she had disconnected, Bea felt overwhelmed with all that she had to achieve. Her priority ought to be work, but she had sat at her desk for over an hour without a single spark of inspiration. Now that Millie had replaced her on the shop floor, Bea was working full-time in the marketing department. There was no need to work all evening on the project as well. Tomorrow morning when she was fresh it would be easier; maybe an idea would come to her whilst she slept. Finding a flat, or a room in a house, couldn't be that hard. Leila said that there were apps and she had a flier somewhere. Feeling a little calmer, her equilibrium restored, Bea rolled the socks one by one and tucked them into a corner of the empty bag. As she folded each item of clothing, her heart reached out to Declan. *I will find you.*

Everything had been repacked, but there were no clues to help solve the mystery of his disappearance. Before stowing the bag away and getting ready for bed, Bea checked for hidden compartments. There was a zipped divider that she had missed. Bea opened it and found a large brown envelope labelled Confidential. It was wrong to open the envelope, but so was stealing the bag. Bea reminded herself that she was doing this to help Declan and Ryan.

'Here goes.' She slid a sheath of papers from the envelope. Mostly printouts from a computer. On first glance the information seemed random, a collection of websites, some printed on paper with an Islington library logo, others were photocopies. There was nothing to link them, although the pages were covered in arrows, circles, and heavy underscoring. The websites advertised everything from work opportunities to lucky charms that would guard against evil. Desperation to change his luck must have driven Declan to these unscrupulous sites. Then she saw Ryan's name printed on a deposit and took a closer look. It was confirmation of a deposit received from Ryan O'Marley on a flat in Islington dated March 2017. When she read the amount, Bea whistled – there was no way she could afford those prices and the landlord wanted two months' deposit plus a month in advance.

There was another interesting paper, a spreadsheet

presumably prepared by Declan or Ryan. Bea was inclined to think it was Declan, as Ryan seemed more of a practical person and Declan more bookish. The names of companies were listed in the first column, what they were selling in the next, then key information and wording from the websites and finally a column with personal email addresses and date of contact. Why had anyone taken the trouble to record this information? Were Declan and Ryan involved in some sort of dodgy business? They were both charmers, could they be con artists? It would explain why someone went after Declan. What if Declan and Ryan were the baddies? Poverty and despair could have led them into a life of crime.

Bea pored over the information, checking the websites on her computer looking for more clues, but nothing enlightened her. She had been staring at the spreadsheet for so long her eyes felt gritty. The email addresses could be people that Declan or Ryan had contacted. Bea didn't want to think that they had been trying to scam these people but she had to find out.

She set up an email account using the name Tabitha Twitchit – the name of a Beatrix Potter character, a cat who was a shopkeeper. Then, she sent an email to all of the addresses listed in the spreadsheet.

I hope that you will forgive me for contacting you but I have reason to believe that you have recently corresponded with either Declan Connor or Ryan O'Marley. I am carrying out a private investigation to find Declan Connor, who is missing. I would be grateful if you would be willing to talk to me – by phone or email. I will not ask you to pass on any confidential information.

She reread it several times before pressing send. Before going to bed she had one more thing to do – download the spare room apps. There were two apps and already Bea could see two or three promising adverts.

Tomorrow she would focus one hundred percent on the Suki Dee event. At least she had found some clues that might lead to Declan, and finding somewhere to live was looking more positive.

20

SEPTEMBER 2014

'Ryan. Where are you? What are you doing?' It was Caitlin. She hardly ever rang him and never in the daytime.

'On a roof.'

'Glad I asked. Can you climb down and phone me back?'

Ryan went to argue, to say no, he was working, but something in Caitlin's voice stopped him. She was twenty-one, studying agriculture in Cork. The last time he had seen her had been at Christmas.

His partner had gone off to find a slate ripper from a fellow roofer, and it was time Ryan took a short break to stretch his back. They were having an Indian summer and it always got hot up on a roof.

'Okay. What's up, sis?' Ryan sat in his truck, fiddling with his CDs. He would love to get a more up-to-date sound system but money was tight.

'It's Ma.' Caitlin caught her breath.

Ryan sighed. She hadn't looked good at Christmas, a bit breathless and lacking in energy. Da expected her to do too much on the farm. He knew that Ma covered the early milking shift several days a week because Da was too bloody mean to pay the farmhand.

'She died.' The words were a sledgehammer knocking Ryan senseless and he thought he must have misheard. 'It was a massive stroke. Da found her lying on the kitchen floor, he couldn't open the door because her body…' Caitlin broke off sobbing.

Blood rushed to Ryan's head, a roaring in his ears. *No.* Caitlin was wrong. Not Ma. She was only sixty-five. They spoke on the phone last week and she was fine.

'When?'

'A couple of days ago. Da had trouble getting hold of me, but I rang you as soon as I could.'

Ma had been dead a couple of days? When he was having a beer with his mates last night, Ma was already dead. Ryan went cold. He felt sick.

'He could have called me. Why didn't he tell me?' He was shouting at Caitlin. She was crying.

When was Da going to tell him? Not Ma. Not Ma. He tried to get it together, to understand how this had happened, as if knowing could change things.

'How? What? What was she doing? Why didn't Da call an ambulance? Did he even try and resuscitate her?' He slammed his fist on the dashboard.

'She was making bread. There was flour on her face and a lump of dough in her hand. She must have collapsed whilst kneading. The paramedics said she wouldn't have known anything. There was nothing anyone could have done to prevent it, Ryan.'

He never should have left her alone with Da, he expected too much of her – of everybody. His mouth was dry and his head ached as blood throbbed in his temple.

'Where is she now?' Why did he ask that? Because he wanted to see her to say goodbye, but not to a corpse, to his living, breathing ma. To hug her. To tell her how much he loved her. To say sorry for the grief he had caused.

'Da didn't want a wake at the house, so he arranged for her body to be taken to the funeral parlour. I'm sure you could see her if you want to.'

Typical of Da not wanting people to visit and pay their respects. It was all too quick. Why hadn't he spent more time with her this year? All of those wasted years after leaving home, he couldn't have them back. He wouldn't stand on the hill holding Ma's hand whilst she said, 'Will you look at that.'

'When's the funeral?' He was mentally checking his diary, thinking about what he would have to cancel, who he would have to contact.

'Next Tuesday. Ryan, come home. I need you. I can't bear this.'

The boys outside were laughing about something and gesturing at Ryan in his truck. If only he could return to the world as it was before he heard that Ma had died.

'I'll be home as soon as I can. Hold on in there, sis.' He didn't want to go back but Caitlin needed him and he was doing it for Ma.

21

TWENTY-TWO SHOPPING DAYS TO CHRISTMAS

Alastair was leaning so far back in his leather chair that Bea imagined it tipping over. He put his hands behind his head, expanding his chest. 'So, what have you got for me, Stevens?'

Blank sheets of paper, attempted brainstorms, and pretty diagrams with coloured arrows was all Bea had to offer. She looked thoughtful, and hopefully wise as she said, 'Um, well, I'm playing around with a few ideas. I haven't decided on one specific idea yet but...'

Alastair's hands came together on top of his head and he wriggled his fingers. The bizarreness of this cockerel impersonation took away any words Bea might have found to finish the sentence.

'Throw them all at me and I'll help you decide.' His fingers waggled furiously, dancing shadows across his bald head.

'Well, as I said before, a charity ball could be fun, but it would be difficult to set up at such short notice.'

Alastair's chair propelled him to a sitting position and he

brought his hands down on the desk with a thump. 'Unoriginal. You told me that you had a brilliant idea. Is that it?'

'No of course not, I hadn't finished.' Bea racked her brain for inspiration. She had to come up with something – anything. 'It could be like a garage sale.'

Alastair threw his head back and rolled his eyes.

'With celebrities and other regular customers donating things they no longer want. The proceeds could go to one of Suki Dee's charities.'

'Hmm. What else have you got?'

Bea was impressed with herself and encouraged she continued, 'A fashion show –'

'Boring.'

'Not if you had…' Bea looked to the ceiling hoping for a revelation. Nothing. 'Not if you had…homeless people as models. We could give them makeovers and donate to a homeless charity. Or –' she was on a roll now '– we could model clothes made from recycled materials. And donate to Friends of the Earth!'

Alastair's head was in his hands; when he looked up he seemed as surprised at Bea's resourcefulness as she was herself. 'Could work. Suki Dee's peeps are meeting with us on Monday morning. You'll need to prepare a short presentation.'

'No problem,' Bea said with authority. She could do this, even though it was the end of the working day and the meeting was first thing on Monday morning.

Before heading home, Bea had two rooms to view. She couldn't find the flier that the man thrust into her hand on the tow path but the rooms she had found on the apps were affordable. The first was a bedsit in a fashionable tree-lined road in Hampstead. It sounded promising.

Bea took the Tube changing to the Northern line at King's Cross. It would be a longer commute but in the summer months she could get off at King's Cross and walk along the canal. Maybe meet Leila for a coffee.

When Bea turned into Hampstead High Street, her heart soared. It was a wonderful place to live, with its boutiques and coffee shops. Tastefully decorated Christmas trees and statement minimalist decorations adorned the windows she passed on her way down the hill towards the address on her phone. After a fifteen-minute walk, Bea found herself outside a tall townhouse. The street was a combination of grand houses with security lights and alarms, family homes, some with wreaths on the door or twinkling lights in the foliage, and shabbier houses – many of these were divided into flats. Number 125 disappointingly fitted into the last category. Bea tried to remain positive as she waited for the landlord to join her.

'It's on the top floor.' The landlord huffed and puffed as he hauled himself up the stairs ahead of Bea.

She reluctantly followed, resisting the temptation to turn around and leave without seeing any more. The house was dirty, dingy, and smelt of twenty different meals being prepared, with wafts of garlic, onions, cauliflower, and mysterious spices overlaying the scent of previous meals absorbed now into the carpet and walls.

At the top of the stairs, the landlord stepped back so that Bea could view the room. It was barely bigger than Molly's storeroom. A rusty Baby Belling stood in one corner under the slope of an attic wall. Next to it, just two feet above ground, was a sink. A single bed with a naked lumpy mattress took up the rest of the room.

'The last tenant kept some boxes under the bed for his clothes and stuff.' The landlord said, following Bea into the tiny room. His bulk blocked the entrance and Bea felt claustrophobic. She had to get out.

Suddenly, they were plunged into darkness – a pitch black, the tiny window offering no glimmer of light. 'Metre,' the landlord muttered, as he squeezed past Bea, his sweaty flesh brushing her arm. 'Well?' he said, when the light came back on.

'No thank you.' Bea slipped past the landlord and raced down the stairs. She could still hear him panting and grunting as she stepped onto the street.

The next place had to be better than that one, Bea thought, as the Tube took her farther out of town to Golders Green. This room was a house share with six other people. The thought of communal living discomforted Bea. She needed her own space. It was hard enough being around people all day at work.

The girl who opened the door to Bea reminded her immediately of Davinia Grayson. It was the way that she appraised Bea, as though finding fault.

'We're interviewing potential housemates all weekend so we won't let you know until next week. My father owns this house and so as the landlady, I get the casting vote.'

Bea was still standing on the doorstep and she wondered whether this girl, Poppy, had already decided against her. 'So, how does this work?' Bea asked, imagining a formal interview process, with five more Davinias.

'You had better come in and take a look. Troy and Justine are out, but Gary's in the kitchen, and I think Tasmin's in her room.'

'The advert didn't say that it was a mixed sex household. When it said suitable for a female, I presumed –'

'Have you got something against men?' Poppy narrowed her eyes.

'No.' Bea gulped.

'Good, because you have to get on with all of the housemates. We're looking for someone who'll fit in.'

Bea guessed without having to wait for the call that she wouldn't be chosen to complete the set of *Friends*. That left one room to view. It was the type of accommodation her mum had suggested – a middle-aged woman letting her spare bedroom. The house was in Whetstone, a longer commute than she would have liked, but Bea was beginning to realise that with her current budget the options available to her were limited. This final viewing was scheduled for the next morning, and apart from that her weekend was free to concentrate on the Suki Dee event. Alastair had been intrigued by her outline ideas. Bea was confident that with some research and good preparation that she could deliver an impressive presentation on Monday morning.

22

TWENTY-ONE SHOPPING DAYS TO CHRISTMAS

Bea breathed in the aroma of freshly brewed coffee as she clasped two hands around a floral mug. A thick scarf had warmed Bea's breath as she hurried to the *Fandangle*, but sitting at the long table now, her skin zinged – flayed by the elements.

'What brings you here this Saturday morning?' Leila trilled in her sing-song voice. 'Not that I'm delighted to be seeing you, but you look like a woman on a mission.' Leila frowned, as though willing the thoughts from Bea's head.

Bea laughed, 'Well, you're partly right, because I can't think of a better start to the weekend than having a coffee in your cosy barge.'

Leila crossed her arms and tilted her head to one side. 'Of course. And the other reason?'

How lovely it was to be understood. Leila was right, ideas had been twirling around in Bea's head as she marched along the tow path, barely noticing the activity on the canal. 'Do you remember a girl at your party, dancing to the Potato Heads?

She wore a cute little dress made out of the ring pulls from soda cans. I was wondering if you knew where she bought it.'

Leila looked thoughtful. 'I think I know who you mean. She's a friend of Mouse. He'll be able to tell you more.'

It must have been the image of that dress, the metal links reflecting light as the girl danced on the *Fandangle*, that had given Bea the idea of a fashion show promoting recycled clothes. Fundraising for Friends of the Earth had also been inspired by Leila's party. Excited by the possibilities feeding her imagination, Bea shared her news with Leila.

'And the proceeds from this fashion show will go to Friends of the Earth?' Leila said clasping her hands together. 'That'll be fierce!'

Bea's face stretched in a smile that felt too big to contain. It seemed to come from her diaphragm, an energy that made her restless. Her palms tingled.

Roots joined them. 'I think it's going to snow again.' He rubbed his hands together and blew on them.

'Sit down and I'll fetch you a coffee,' Leila said.

Bea felt awkward left alone with Roots and she wandered over to the noticeboard. It was littered with fliers for community events – a school Christmas bazaar, a church carol concert, a heating engineer, and the very flier Bea had misplaced. *Rooms at competitive prices in central London.* Bea took a photo of it with her phone. Leila had not returned and so Bea returned to the bench to sit alongside Roots. It seemed rude to sit in silence and so she said, 'Have you heard anything from Ryan?'

'No. He'll be back soon. Business to attend to.'

Bea wasn't sure whether Roots was saying that *he* had business to attend to or Ryan. So, she nodded in agreement.

'Do you know Declan Connor?' Bea blurted out.

Roots clenched his jaw and narrowed his eyes. 'Leila says that you work at Hartleys?'

Bea nodded. Her face flushed.

'How do you know Declan?'

Roots was staring at her and Bea felt her skin scorch under his scrutiny. Did he know that she was responsible for making Declan homeless? If Ryan found out it could be the end of their friendship. It wasn't so bad admitting that she had reported Declan for sleeping in the store overnight – as the boys in black said, he would have been found out soon enough – it was her shame at walking past Declan every day on her way to and from work.

'I kept a brownie back for you,' Leila said, presenting it with Roots's coffee.

'Keep it for me. I'll come back later.' Roots glared at Bea, and then left.

'What's the matter with him?' Leila said, sliding back onto the bench. 'He can be a funny old bugger.'

Bea shrugged, but in her gut, she felt Roots's disapproval. Maybe it was because she worked at Hartleys and it represented a materialistic lifestyle. As Bea contemplated the gap between their worlds, she realised her stupidity. There was no way Hartleys could ask homeless people to model the recycled clothes. It would be insulting and insensitive. The very idea made her cringe with embarrassment. Perhaps Roots was right in his assessment of her; she was selfish and materialistic. If Ryan knew the real Bea he wouldn't say that she was awesome. The excitement that had been bubbling up in Bea now fizzled flat.

'Did you look up those accommodation apps?' Leila cut into her thoughts.

'Yes,' Bea said, suddenly weary.

'And?'

'Oh I looked at a couple last night. One was a disgusting bedsit that I wouldn't stay in if you paid me, and the other seemed to be looking for someone who would complete their cast of *Friends*.'

Leila screwed up her face. 'Not your cup of tea, then?'

'I don't think I was *their* cup of tea, and to be honest I wouldn't want to live with a group of strangers. Then, before meeting you this morning, I looked at a room in Whetstone. Apart from being too far out, it would be worse than living at home with my parents. The landlady told me I had to be home by ten every night or I would be locked out!'

Leila spluttered on her coffee. 'You're joking me?'

'I'm not. She wanted the income from letting her room but no inconvenience. I was to use her kitchen to prepare meals but only during specified hours – one hour in the evening and thirty minutes in the morning. All of my meals were to be eaten in my room – which was a bedroom with two single beds, flouncy bedspread, and those old-fashioned Roman blinds.'

'Okay. So that one's definitely out. What else have you got?'

'I took a photo of a flier on your noticeboard advertising affordable rooms. I'll give that a go. My options are limited on my current salary but if this event is a success I've been promised a promotion.' Leila nodded encouragingly, but Bea's spirits had been dampened. 'What if I don't pull this off, Leila? Sometimes I feel as though I'm pretending to be this efficient woman, but I'm not, and I'll get found out.' She had never admitted this to anyone before.

Leila touched Bea's arm. 'We're all of us frauds, darlin'. I live in fear of being discovered. You know I don't have any catering qualifications? I'm a hobby baker with a passion for cake. I don't even own this barge. Roots could kick me out any time he felt like it.'

'But you're always so cheerful and positive,' Bea said.

'And why wouldn't I be? I'm doing what I love in a place that I love.'

'You're lucky,' Bea said.

'We make our own luck. Trust yourself, Bea. I know you'll give it everything that you've got. And that, as my mam would say, is all you can do.

'Well, Roots didn't deserve that brownie.' Leila laughed as she removed a plate that was scattered with crumbs from between them. 'But we did.'

The taste of chocolate lingered in Bea's mouth, evidence that she was complicit in the crime. A couple of weeks ago, she wouldn't have contemplated eating something as fattening as a brownie. Being stick thin wasn't all it was cracked up to be. It didn't buy friendship or popularity – despite what she had imagined as a chubby teenager. People like the girl in the Golders Green house would always see through her. She couldn't fool anyone, and before long Ryan would find out too.

23

TWENTY SHOPPING DAYS TO CHRISTMAS

'She didn't bring us any brownies, Bear. Not even a sausage for you.' A chocolate Labrador lumbered in from a back room to join Bea and Mouse in the main living space of *No Worries*. It was clearly a bachelor pad as mechanical stuff and tools adorned surfaces rather than pot plants and silk throws.

Bea tickled Bear behind his silky ears. Next time, if she got another chance, Bea resolved to bring an offering of cake and sausage.

'You have a fan now. Poor old boy, he's got dodgy hips and can't get around much but he loves being made a fuss of.'

It was wonderful to be welcomed so warmly, as though she had been expected, and Bea's spirits lifted. 'I hope you don't mind me dropping in like this,' she said, and followed Mouse into his cabin. She had dropped by the day before on her way home from the *Fandangle*, but there was nobody home. Mouse leaned over an old table where an engine lay dismantled and set to work fixing it, as though Bea had merely popped out and returned minutes later. 'Only, Leila thought you might know a girl who was at the Potato Heads gig? She wore a dress made from ring pulls?'

Mouse didn't look up when he said, 'Sav. She's a fashion designer. Make yourself comfy. This won't take a minute. Just got to finish something.'

Bea settled herself amongst the cushions of a well-worn armchair. Bear licked her hand, before turning a couple of times and then with a low growl made himself comfortable across her feet. His solid presence a warm and comforting weight. Lulled by Bear's snores and the scratch and click of Mouse's work as he fiddled with the engine, Bea became drowsy. Minutes slipped by in a companionable silence interrupted only by the soft groans of Bear and the odd curse from Mouse. Bea was enjoying a daydream where she introduced a fashion show that was so extravagant it resembled an opening ceremony of the Olympics, when Mouse said, 'She has a shop in Brick Lane, Savvy Clothes.'

Bea sat up and Bear grumbled. 'Was the dress Sav was wearing one of her own designs?'

'I can't remember what she wore. Got it!' Mouse beamed and stepped back from the table. 'That should do it. I took some photos of the Potato Heads and I'm sure one of them included Sav. I'll just finish up here and then I'll see what I've got on the iPad. You'd do better to look up her website or visit the shop but you'd have to contact her first to check when it's open. Sav concentrates on sales through the internet and spends most of her time designing from home. The shop's a showcase for her work, but as I said, you'd have to ask her to open up for you.'

It was a start. If Sav was a recycled fashion designer, she could be very helpful. Working to a tight timescale, personal connections, and recommendations in the recycled fashion world would be invaluable and Sav would know the latest trends. She might even have a collection herself that was worthy of a Hartleys show. Reluctant as she was to leave the restful sanctuary of *No Worries,* Bea was anxious now to finish preparing her presentation for the next day.

'I've taken up enough of your time.' Bea stood up. Bear growled when she slipped her feet from beneath his soft belly. 'I don't want to leave you either.' She stroked Bear's huge floppy head.

'I'm almost done here.' Mouse frowned as he concentrated on something. 'Damn. I didn't see that.'

'It's okay. I'll look up Savvy Clothes on Google. If you find any photos of Sav in that dress, could you email me? Oh, and if you talk to her, perhaps you could say that I would like to meet with her to discuss her collection?' Bea scribbled down her email address and phone number.

Mouse was engrossed again in the mechanics of his engine. 'Sure. No worries.'

Bea smiled. The name of the houseboat suited him well – Mouse and Bear were so chilled. 'Have you known Ryan long?' Bea said.

Mouse looked up from his work. He narrowed his eyes and pulled on his beard. 'I don't really know him as such. We got talking in the summer when he was going for his run along the canal. I said he could use my shower any time he wanted. You know – there for the grace of God...'

That was typical of Ryan, drawing good people to him. 'Thanks for the coffee,' Bea said, wrapping her scarf around her mouth, and she left Mouse and Bear to tramp home in the freshly fallen snow.

There were lots of designers of recycled clothes on the internet. Bea was fascinated by the amazing designs using bubble wrap, shredded newspapers, magazines, and packaging. One ball gown had panels of contrasting colour crisp packets; a flapper-style dress was adorned with rows of sweet wrappers that shimmered in the light. The Savvy Clothes website was recycled fashion, but it looked a bit amateurish, compared to the leading fashion designers in that field. But, they were international designers from the USA, Italy, and France. Hartleys could attract top designers but not before Christmas. Bea created a board of images to show Suki Dee's people tomorrow. If only she could persuade them to wait until the new year, she could put together something sensational. Bea arched her back and rolled her head to ease the tension in her body after sitting at the computer for so long. Her presentation had a clear message: Suki Says, Save the Planet. The focus was on using what we already have. Finding value in things instead of discarding them. Bea had found a YouTube clip of an Italian recycled fashion show, the garments vibrant and original. There were still shots too; the many wonderful creations Bea had tracked down on the internet. She sighed with satisfaction. Her presentation would have impact and was bound to impress Suki Dee's people. Bea wondered whether it would be the assistant who had accompanied Suki Dee to her dress fitting and whether she would come alone or with another of Suki's staff.

It was a shame that it got dark so early, as Bea would have liked to return Declan's bag to the dilapidated barge. A walk would do her good, but it was very cold out there, and she didn't like the idea of venturing into the more desolate part of the canal beyond the graffitied bridge. It would have to wait until she could take some time out of the office, when it was still light. Before returning the bag, Bea decided to copy the table of information into an excel sheet. As she worked, she tried to find a pattern. There was one factor that all of the entries had in common. They were all too good to be true offers. What had Ryan got himself into? Her stomach knotted. Could Ryan's charm be part of his act? Had she already been taken in? Ryan had nothing to gain from a friendship with her, she reasoned. It wasn't as though he had been trying to sell her something. Maybe he was biding his time – grooming her. Bea cast aside the spreadsheet. She didn't know what to believe or who to trust. *Trust yourself,* Leila said. How could she trust herself when all of her life Mum had been telling her that she was a poor judge of character, that she was vulnerable – an easy target?

Ping. It was an email from Mouse. Bea ignored it at first. She had what she needed for tomorrow and wanted to focus her attention on why Ryan or Declan were interested in these websites. If she solved that mystery, she might come close to finding Declan, but her mind was a blank, and so she opened Mouse's email. He wrote as though they were friends and Bea felt comforted that at least through Ryan she had found Leila and Mouse.

The photographs had captured the chaotic exuberance of that day: the band with their outlandish instruments – a washboard and a ukulele, dogs and dancers vying for space on deck. Was that really her? Bea took a closer look; her hair whipped across her face and skirt flared as she spun around. How could she have been so uninhibited? And yet, nobody seemed shocked. A woman perched on a beer crate clapped her hands as she watched Bea dance. Where was Ryan? Bea scanned the photograph and then jolted when she saw the closely cropped hair and dark skin of the young man that she had followed to the old barge. He must have been looking for Ryan before he met him on the tow path. That's right, Ryan returned with the Armani bag. He must have been gone longer than she realised to have walked to the *Moby* and back.

To think that she had been dancing and having fun with strangers and Ryan wasn't even there. Like riding a bicycle for the first time, when her dad had let go of the seat.

Frustrated that she was no closer to solving the mystery, Bea opened her new email account. Seventeen emails were junk mail. A few obvious phishing ones. Bea worried that by exposing herself to these fraudulent websites she might get a computer virus. If the emails were to be believed, she was incredibly lucky as she had won not one but five prize draws and she hadn't even entered one. Delete. Delete. Delete.

Dear Tabitha. It was the pseudonym she had used in her email. *I have indeed had contact with Declan Connor and Ryan O'Marley. If you want information then it is best that we meet.*

It was as though someone had joined her in the room and was looking over her shoulder. Bea paced around her flat. Her palms pulsed with nervous energy. The email had been sent at 18.07 that day. Just ten minutes ago. She sat back down and typed.

Thank you for responding to my email. I am very interested to hear what you have to say. Perhaps we could talk on the phone?

Bea's heart calmed a little. She would telephone from work so that her own number would remain anonymous.

That's not possible. We must meet in person. This is highly confidential. I cannot risk anyone else listening in. I shouldn't even be writing to you. Maybe this wasn't such a good idea.

'Yes, it was,' Bea muttered as she started to type. *Okay. Let's meet.*

It has to be tonight. I'm going away for Christmas.

Maybe she could ask Mouse to accompany her. But what could she tell him without invading Ryan's privacy? She shouldn't even have this information, let alone share it with Mouse. *It would have to be in London. Somewhere public,* Bea wrote.

Waterloo Station?

What harm could she come to in a busy place like Waterloo Station?

Okay. What time?

How soon could you get there?

Bea checked her watch. *Seven-thirty?*

She would have preferred to meet earlier in the day, when it was light, but there should still be plenty of people around at that time. They told each other what they would be wearing. The informer, a man, would be wearing a Russian hat; they were apparently called Sherpas. Bea said that she would be carrying a copy of *Vogue*.

24

TWENTY SHOPPING DAYS TO CHRISTMAS

It was five past eight, thirty-five minutes after the time that Bea arranged to meet the informer. The station buzzed with anticipation as families prepared to be reunited for the Christmas holiday: a young woman sat by her case and spoke on a mobile, her face glowing and voice raised in exclamation, a young man scanned the departures board, a present wrapped in green foil strapped to his rucksack, and a family trailed past Bea wheeling cases. 'Will Grandpops meet us at the station?' a little boy chirped as he jigged to keep up.

But there was no sign of a Russian hat. Bea had looked up Sherpa hats on her phone, just to be sure. Maybe she was being too precise. There was a man in a fleece-lined hat – could it be? No, he had seen his mate and was walking away. She checked her phone to see if she had got the time wrong but he had clearly stated seven-thirty. Bea sent an email from her phone. *I'm under the clock. Where are you?* He hadn't wanted to exchange phone numbers and at the time Bea didn't mind, as she was reticent about sharing more information about herself than was absolutely necessary. Now, she thought it a mistake. He could be waiting under a different clock. If they missed each other, she might not get another chance to talk to him until after Christmas and by then he could have changed his mind.

Other people waited and left; a woman wearing a Santa hat with a jingling bell was greeted by a man holding a red rose. Just as well there was only one woman in a Santa hat. Bea wondered how many mistaken meetings there had been over the years; a red rose wasn't very original.

At a quarter to nine, Bea resigned herself to the fact that Mr Sherpa hat wasn't going to show. He hadn't answered her email. Maybe something unexpected had come up and he would contact her later to explain. She held up the front cover of *Vogue* as though it had his name printed on it but the only responses she got were curious glances, perhaps wondering if she was selling or promoting the magazine.

The meeting with Suki Dee's peeps, as Alastair irritatingly called them, was at nine-thirty the next morning. After working midday to eight shifts, it was going to be a struggle getting up at seven. She wanted to get in early to set things up and check that the YouTube clip worked. Ideally, she would have time to go through the presentation with Alastair and get his support on pushing for a delay until the new year to attract bigger names.

The Underground platform went from a straggle of people – a train having just left – to two people deep, as people lined the platform in wait. Conversations were about shows, meals enjoyed, plans for Christmas. Bea was still thinking about her meeting and honing in and out of other peoples' conversations when a train approached.

Out of nowhere, somebody barged into her. She toppled, her flailing hands grasping at air, as the rail line flashed beneath her. Then, a hand grabbed her upper arm and yanked her up, just as the train pulled in. It happened so quickly. She could have fallen beneath the train.

Bea looked for her rescuer. He – it had to be a man, his grip was strong, his hand span wide – did not make himself known. People milled around her and got on the train as if nothing had happened, and Bea wasn't entirely sure what had. Her knees were jelly and her hands shaking as she claimed an empty seat. It was just an accident – a clumsy drunk. She took deep breaths. It was the thought of what might have happened had she fallen. Bea shuddered. *She hadn't*. Thank God.

The journey home was a blur as Bea tried to make sense of the evening. Why hadn't the informer shown up? What if he had lured her to the meeting place to get sight of her so that he knew her identity and then followed her to the Tube where he tried to push her under a train? Bea shook her head; she was being ridiculous. It was just an accident. Those few seconds when she lost her balance, the sound of the train and then that grip on her arm, it felt like a dream. Bea shrugged off her coat and examined her arm; it was red and tender to touch. Had she been pushed or was it an accident, someone who had drunk too much jostling her? She ought to send a message of thanks to her rescuer through the free newspaper – she'd read them on her journeys to and from work – *Thank you to the kind woman who ran after me with my phone when I dropped it on the...* Bea stopped her musing to remind herself which line she was on and realised that it was her stop, Euston Station. She jumped up and exited just in time. Someone else must have done the same thing, as Bea heard the doors open and then close again behind her, as they did when something got trapped. For the rest of the short journey to Kings Cross, Bea was fully alert, jumping at her own shadow.

Her apartment was only a short walk from the station. It was well lit. Why was Kings Cross so quiet on a Sunday night?

Where had all the Christmas revellers gone? Someone was following her; she could feel their presence in the prickling of her skin. There was a movement in the periphery of her vision and she spun around, but whatever she glimpsed had been eaten by the shadows. The person who tried to push her under a train must have followed her home. The Tube door suddenly opening and reclosing behind her at Euston, it wasn't a coincidence.

The click-clacking of her heels echoed in the still night. Somewhere a cat cried. Granary Square was deserted, like a party when the last guest had gone home. A little breathless, she paused. A glug from the canal. The movement of a house-boat. Then, footsteps. Heavy, slow footsteps. They were getting closer. Nearly home. Bea jogged as much as her heels would allow.

At last, she was inside the apartment block. Safely behind the glass door. Bea peered into the darkness. Something moved in the light of a lamp, a shadow retreating. A couple passed by, their arms around each other. That could explain the footsteps. She couldn't see anyone else.

Bea let herself into her flat. Even then, she stayed very still before switching on the light. She checked all of the rooms, the walk-in cupboard, and under the beds. Satisfied that she was safe, Bea busied herself preparing for work the next day, but she was uneasy. Her email had rattled someone, and she was afraid that they might now know where she lived.

25

FEBRUARY 2017

It was a mystery where Da got his bottles of Scotch. Ryan didn't see him leave the farm – he would have to use the truck if he did – and Ryan would have noticed it gone. And yet, there were always empty bottles and a sour smell on Da's breath. It was one of the many things that they rowed about: How could they afford Scotch when they were struggling to pay wages? If Da could no longer work on the farm he could at least help keep the house clean; it was in a disgusting state. Then there was Ma. Ryan blamed his da for driving her too hard; he had no idea just how much Ma had done on the farm. Da blamed Ryan for breaking her heart and his betrayal in finding work as a carpenter behind their backs. Ryan didn't need Da to tell him that he had broken Ma's heart. He would never forgive himself for causing her pain, and if he hadn't left the farm, she wouldn't have had to work so hard. Her ashes wouldn't be scattered in St Agnes's churchyard, marked by her favourite flowers, primroses and cowslips.

'Caitlin and Sean should be here by five. I've put them in my room, so I'll take Caitlin's,' Ryan said.

Da was in his recliner chair surrounded by his paraphernalia: glasses, magnifying glass, newspaper and Sunday's colour supplement for the TV, a dirty hanky, nail clippers, medication, and Ryan was pretty sure if he dug around he would find a bottle of Scotch down the side of the chair. Da's eyes were half closed, but he wasn't asleep, just shutting Ryan out.

'So, you'll need to tidy yourself up. You don't want your new son-in-law seeing you with stains down your shirt and two days' growth.' *Or drunk,* Ryan thought.

He'd done his best to make the farmhouse welcoming for Caitlin and Sean but he couldn't work miracles. If they were going to live here and take over the running of the farm, they would have to find out sooner or later just how bad things were. Since Ma died over two years ago, Ryan had returned home and helped to keep things going. Caitlin had just finished college and had plans to work in New Zealand on a big dairy farm. Of course, she said that she wouldn't go and would move back to the farm, but Ryan persuaded her that Ma wouldn't have wanted that. So, Caitlin went to New Zealand and Ryan packed up his tools and returned to farming. Eighteen months later, Caitlin announced that she had married a farmer, Sean Fitzpatrick, a New Zealander whose family came from Ireland many generations ago. And now they were returning to the O'Marley farm to start their married life together. God help them.

'He's a proper farmer, not a dreamer like you. Knows his Jersey from a Hereford.' Da snorted as though remembering a joke. Ryan didn't ask, he knew it would be at his expense. 'When old Wallington's wife said they were after Jerseys in the market...' He broke off as he laughed.

'I was a kid. We'd never had Jerseys so how was I to know she didn't mean jumpers?'

'You weren't a nipper when you legged it across that field.

Thought our old bull was going to have you that time. He never did take to you.'

The same old stories; you'd think he would tire of them. They weren't funny the first time and yet Da retold them again and again. It made no difference that he had kept the farm going for the past two years whilst Da drank himself into a stupor. *Miserable git.*

'I was trying to catch a dog that had got in and was chasing the cows,' Ryan muttered. Da knew that a walker had strayed onto their land with a feisty terrier who had been let off the lead. If Ryan hadn't been fast, the bull might well have caught him. Da knew that he could have been seriously injured but to him it was a joke. It didn't help that Ma made too much fuss at the time. In Da's eyes, Ryan was a spoiled sissy – he had said so often enough throughout his childhood.

'That's what this farm needs – proper farmers, not a wuss.'

'Or a drunk.' Ryan thrust his hand down the side of Da's chair and retrieved an empty bottle of whiskey. He shook it in front of Da's face. 'Don't think I won't be glad to get away from you.' He couldn't say the words that formed in his head. It was as though Ma was there, her look of hurt and disapproval.

His hands shook as he tried to control his temper. 'Clean yourself up. I'm going for a run.'

'I'll be leaving the farm to them. Not you,' Da called after him as he went up the stairs.

Ryan sat on what was once Caitlin's bed and put his head in his hands. His breath came in shudders as he tried to stop the tears. He was a child again, humiliated and hurt. *He doesn't mean it.* His Ma's voice, but she was wrong. Ma always saw the best in everyone and for some reason loved the miserable shit. Downstairs the recliner grumbled as Da got up. He would have forgotten to take his medication – Ryan had counted the pills and put them in an egg cup but Da needed to be reminded. Ryan was no longer a child – he was Da's carer. Da may not deserve his care but until Caitlin arrived he was all Da had.

'Here.' Ryan held out the first of the pills in one palm and a glass of water in the other.

Da had tried to shave but given up midway, with two nicks on one cheek. He leaned against the kitchen table as he swallowed the pills. They continued with the morning routine as though they hadn't had a row. When Ryan had shaved Da and seen that he was dressed and ready to welcome Caitlin home, he left him in his recliner and went for a run.

Ryan paused at the top of the hill and got his breath back. Running was great for clearing his head, getting rid of the negative stuff. At the top of the hill, Ryan took a deep breath and surveyed the beauty of the land. With Caitlin coming home, it was time for him to move on. As his feet beat a rhythm across the fields his mind had been working – he would go to London. The guys on the building sites had stories about how they or their das had made a fortune working as casual labour in the golden city. He would earn enough to come back and build a log house. *Right here,* he thought. But that was just Ma's voice in his head. He would never come back to the farm whilst Da was alive and if he left the farm to Caitlin and Sean there would be no place for him. It hurt. Of course it hurt. He didn't want to be a dairy farmer but he loved this place. Saying goodbye to his home was like saying goodbye to Ma all over again. If he had a different relationship with the cows would Da have loved him? Was he really such a disappointment? What about all he had done these past two years: putting his life on hold, working for nothing to keep the farm going? Anger flared again and Ryan took off across the brow of the hill. Eventually, the steady rhythm of his breath and the beat of each footfall calmed him and the trance of running cleared his mind. This was an opportunity. Who knew what the future would hold? Da was doing him a favour. He could leave Ireland with a clear conscience and follow his dreams.

Ryan's pace slowed as he ran downhill towards the farm. Sweat trickled into his eyes and his limbs felt heavy and relaxed. His heart was as light as a helium balloon, full of hope and expectation for the future.

26

TWENTY SHOPPING DAYS TO CHRISTMAS

Her presentation was good. Bea knew this, and her outfit was stylish and professional. A green silk shirt dress with Brandon Maxwell heels, hair fashioned in a braided updo to keep it off her face. Bea was thankful that she had prepared her presentation before leaving for the meeting at Waterloo Station. The previous night's events had shaken her badly. Knowing what to wear had become second nature to Bea after years of studying fashion magazines. So, she should have felt confident as she made her way upstairs to the executive offices, her tablet and notes in a smart leather bag. It was a few minutes before nine, just enough time to go over the presentation with Alastair and check that the link to YouTube worked. Bea took a deep breath and pushed open the door.

Mr Evans's PA greeted Bea with a warm smile. 'Good morning, Miss Stevens. You are meeting in the Monet room. Would you like tea or coffee?'

Bea's heart fluttered. Her hands were sweaty. 'A glass of

water, please.' *Keep calm, Bea. You are a capable professional.* Bea steadied her breathing. 'Is Alastair here yet?'

'Yes. Go on through. I'm just making refreshments.'

That was a relief. They had time to set everything up. Maybe she shouldn't have made the YouTube clip a big feature of the presentation; technology wasn't always reliable. Alastair would surely agree with her that by postponing the event to after Christmas, they could stage something as grand as the Italian show in her presentation. Feeling more positive, Bea threw open the door.

Five heads turned to stare at her, two women and three men. She must have got the wrong room. 'Sorry.' Bea edged out and bumped into Alastair, who was coming in.

'Good, you're here. This is Bea Stevens.' He ushered Bea back into the room.

'I thought the meeting was nine-thirty,' she said a bit too sharply.

'We had some other things to discuss, but we're ready for you now,' Alastair said in a voice full of bonhomie, his eyes on the sharp and shiny people seated around an imposing conference table. The women favoured trendy thick-framed spectacles as though trying to conceal their beauty, despite glossy hair and expertly applied make-up. The men wore narrow jeans and colourful T-shirts with tailored jackets and waistcoats. And all of them were beautiful. Like models from the pages of *Vogue*. Bea almost felt sorry for Alastair in his grey suit and collarless shirt, a dull sparrow amongst the peacocks. 'As soon as the coffee has arrived, I'll make introductions and then the floor is yours, Bea.'

There was no time to do a run-through. The presentation wasn't good enough. She should have done more. Bea's legs wobbled. 'Alastair, can I have a quick word outside?' She would ask for assistance to set up the IT and get Alastair on side with a delay until after Christmas. They could do this, she just had to keep calm.

'Not now, Bea,' he said without even looking at her. If he had, she might have been able to convey non-verbally an urgent need to talk to him, but Alastair was in showman mode and Bea one of his performers.

Coffee was distributed and the beautiful people introduced. Bea focused on each face in turn avoiding eye contact as she had taught herself to do when her aversion to eye contact had previously given the impression of disinterest. Her heartbeat was steadier, and although she was aware of each breath it was at least a little deeper. Bea took a sip of water.

'This event is very important to Suki. It's key to the story we are telling this year – Suki Dee Licious, humanitarian. The celebrity with a heart.' A man in a silk paisley waistcoat looked earnest, as though he already doubted Bea.

A woman with glasses shaped like cat eyes spoke from across the table, 'It has to be big. Glamorous. Memorable. Something that will excite media attention. But of course, you know that, Alastair. That's why we've chosen Hartleys.'

If her future career and living in London didn't depend on the next thirty minutes, Bea would have skedaddled out of there faster than the discounted bargains on the last day of the sale. Alastair said her name and then there was silence.

This was it. Bea tried to imagine Ryan at her side. In her head she whispered his words: *You are awesome.* She took a deep breath and was deciding whether to remain seated or stand when Alastair prompted her.

'When you're ready, Bea.'

Bea stood up and then regretted it because her legs were shaking. She placed both hands flat on the table and tried to ground herself. If only this wasn't so important to her, she could do a perfect presentation. But it was. Her future depended upon the next few minutes.

'Good morning. I'm delighted to have the opportunity to meet with you to discuss my –' she sensed disapproval from Alastair '– *our* ideas. After considering a few options we have settled on one that I think will, um, deliver everything that Suki Dee is looking for.' Bea took a sip of water and hoped that nobody would notice her trembling hand. Alastair threw her a quizzical look. *If you wanted to know what I was going to say, you should have given me the opportunity to talk to you,* she growled in her head.

'If you could project onto the big screen, Alastair?' Could they hear the waver in her voice?

Alastair fumbled around with the technology but nothing happened. Alastair left the room to seek assistance and the beautiful people turned their attention to their phones, checking social media and messages. Bea was about to follow Alastair to brief him quickly on her presentation but he returned before she had the chance.

'We'll have it working in a minute. Why don't you start your pitch, Bea?'

The pitch was the presentation. Bea had intended to wow them with the amazing recycled fashion garments in the YouTube clip followed by a montage of stills, accompanied by the dramatic and eerie backing music of Costanzo Padovano as used in his own climate change film. Without it, she had nothing.

'I could just wait.' Bea wiped her damp palms on her thighs, leaving two greasy looking marks on the green silk.

Alastair shook his head. 'Just talk from your notes.'

Bea took a deep breath. 'Okay.' This time she remained seated. 'I was thinking, what are the important issues on the public conscience?' There were murmurs of approval. 'Climate change. Climate change. Climate change.' She had heard a politician repeat himself like that once in a speech and it had sounded good. 'When IT come to our rescue, I will show you what I have in mind.' Bea glared at Alastair.

At that moment the timpani drums echoed around the room, then a gong followed by a building of strings. The big screen flickered. Bea sighed with relief. It was going to be okay. Everyone was sitting up, waiting for the film. Bea knew that the outfits would impress them. She had worked hard to create a presentation with impact. The music was full throttle now. Bea had her back to the screen, she knew exactly how the images fitted with the music. The expressions of the beautiful people were not what she was expecting. She glanced at the screen behind her to see the Costanzo Padovano film playing, not the Italian fashion show or her montage of stills. She stood up. 'Sorry, that's not the presentation.'

'Turn it off, Bea, and speak from your notes.' Alastair didn't hide his impatience.

Bea was no longer nervous, she was furious. If Alastair had met with her before the presentation he would have known how important it was to get the IT right. They could have done a trial run. Now, it was too late and Bea knew that it wouldn't be Alastair who would be held responsible. She fumbled with her tablet, trying to find the images she had downloaded. The energy in the room had deflated. Bea was aware of looks being exchanged across the table. She held up her tablet. 'These amazing outfits have all been fashioned from recycled materials. This ball gown, for example, is made from crisp packets – and this dress from bubble wrap.' The tablet was passed around the room, but nobody looked very impressed. 'We are proposing a recycled fashion show to support climate change with the proceeds going to Friends of the Earth. It would be visual and topical.'

There was an uncomfortable silence and then a glossy-haired woman said, 'And how will this promote Suki Dee's humanitarian interests?'

Before Bea could reply, Alastair jumped in. 'Bea's going to use homeless people as models. The combination of saving the planet by using recycled fashion and saving people on the streets by giving them makeovers would give a clear message that Suki Dee has a heart of gold.'

No. No. What was Alastair thinking? Please don't let them think that's a good idea. Even Bea could see that a makeover wasn't going to be life-changing for someone living on the streets and there was no way that she was going to even suggest this to the likes of Sal.

'Maybe. We'll have to run it by Suki but if you can sex it up a bit.'

Bea's jaw dropped. *Sex it up?* Did they want a lingerie fashion show? She was about to ask, when Alastair put a cautioning hand on her wrist. 'He means something a bit more exciting – original.'

They hadn't said no and at one point Bea was convinced she had blown it – but homeless models? Alastair fluffed around Suki's peeps as they took their leave, promising to keep in touch with developments, and reassuring them that it would be everything and more that Suki Dee was hoping for. When they had gone Bea buried her head in her arms.

'They seemed okay with that,' Alastair said, returning to the room. 'Sorry about the IT. You should have said that you wanted to show a film.'

There was no point arguing, or complaining that Alastair didn't give her the chance to brief him. Maybe she should have sent him a message over the weekend, or arrived earlier. 'It was a good film,' Bea said.

They watched it together. 'Could you put something

together like that Italian show?' Alastair said, clearly impressed.

That was the response Bea had been hoping for from the beautiful people. 'If we could persuade Suki to wait until the new year, then yes, I think we could.'

'Not possible,' Alastair said, splaying his fingers like a mime artist. 'It has to be before Christmas or not at all.'

'Why did you say we would use homeless models?' Bea wailed.

'I was saving you. Didn't you see the way I turned things around?' He demonstrated with his hands. 'As I recall it was your idea.'

'Just an idea. A stupid idea as it happens.'

'Apparently not. Suki Dee's peeps love it.' Alastair rubbed his hands together. 'Looks like we're on! Good luck, Bea.' He shook Bea's hand and left her to gather her belongings and scattered emotions. How on earth was she going to pull this off, with just twenty shopping days until Christmas?

27

TWENTY SHOPPING DAYS TO CHRISTMAS

'How are you doing?' Alastair looked over Bea's shoulder, where she sat at a hot desk in the marketing department.

Since coming out of the meeting with Suki Dee's team, Bea had been trying to contact recycled fashion designers. The name Hartleys opened doors and Bea had at least managed to speak to a few PAs or other staff representing the great designers. There was definitely some interest; Suki Dee was an international celebrity and Hartleys had a world-wide reputation for glamour and glitz. It was when she said the event had to take place before Christmas that the conversation ended. Bea explained this to Alastair. 'If we could persuade Suki Dee to wait just a few more weeks –'

'It's not negotiable. The contractual agreement with Suki Dee is for the event to happen before Christmas or we don't get paid. In fact, there's a clause that penalises us if we pull out with short notice.'

It didn't matter what she thought. She had to make a success of this or risk losing her job at Hartleys, and with it the life she had dreamed of and worked towards for as long as she could remember. 'It's okay, I've got this. I just have to think.'

Alastair nodded, his brow furrowed.

'I have an idea, but I'll need to work outside of the office to hunt down some contacts,' Bea said.

'An idea that you would like to share with me?' The tone of Alastair's voice implied that Bea should do just that, but she wasn't ready. He hadn't been interested in hearing her thoughts before the presentation that morning.

'I don't think so. Not yet.'

'Fine. So long as you know what you're doing.'

'Does that mean I can work away from the office?'

'I don't care if you work in Piccadilly Circus, so long as you have a spectacular event ready for the week before Christmas. Could we at least agree a date, so that we can start to promote it?'

In counting down the days until Christmas, Bea hadn't even considered that it might take place sooner than 24 December. 'How about Christmas Eve?' she said. 'People will have finished their Christmas preparations and be ready to relax and perhaps more inclined to give generously.'

Alastair drummed his index and middle fingers on Bea's desk whilst biting his bottom lip in an embarrassing parody of a rock star. 'Gucci.'

Bea was confused. 'Do they design recycle?'

'*Gucci.* Cool. We can make a big deal of the homeless at Christmas. Suki's peeps will love it.'

'About that, Alastair. I don't think –'

One drumming hand raised like a baton, and Alastair gave Bea a steely look. 'Not up for debate.'

As Bea was leaving, Alastair told her to stay in contact at

all times and give minute-by-minute updates. 'With a deadline this tight we have to stay in close communication,' he said.

Pity he didn't think of that earlier, Bea seethed as she set off to find Mouse in the hope of getting an introduction to Sav. She had sent emails and left a message on the Brick Lane shop number but Bea couldn't wait for a response. If she could track down all of the fashion designers in person she would, but realistically, Sav was the only one she could appeal to face to face.

Bea popped home first to change and drop off her work bag. Just as she was about to leave there was a knock on the door. Through the spy hole Bea saw Stanley Larkin, the estate agent, with a thick-set Arabic-looking man. If she didn't answer the door, he would come in anyway; he must have used a key to get into the apartment block. It was irritating, but she was going out anyhow and they would be finished by the time she got back. Bea dived back into her bedroom and scooped up stray knickers and discarded shoes. Then she opened the door, pulling Larkin in with it, his key already in the lock.

Bear greeted Bea when she climbed on board *No Worries* by nudging his soppy head against her legs. She grabbed hold of his thick coat before he knocked her off her feet and made a great fuss of him.

'You'll be there all day if you're not careful. Come on, Bear. Let Bea get inside.'

Bea explained that she was working and meeting with Mouse was an important part of her mission. 'Please tell me that you have Sav's private phone number?'

'That's if she's in the UK. When I saw her at the Potato Heads gig, she said something about a trip to Venice.'

Bea's heart sunk. She had counted on finding at least a few local designers to pad out the show. So far, Sav was the only one, and if she was unavailable, Bea was screwed.

Mouse scrolled his phone. 'Shall I send you her contact details?'

'Yes please. Could you introduce us too? Say something nice about me? Ask her to help? People don't always take to me.' Bea blushed. She shouldn't have said that. Mouse would think her weird.

'Sure. But Sav will love you. I'll text her now. What do you want me to say?'

'Whatever I say will be wrong. Can I leave it to you?'

'There – done. I've told her that a top executive from Hartleys, who also happens to be a good friend, has seen her designs and would like to sponsor a fashion show. And I've given Sav your contact details.'

Mouse's phone pinged and he laughed. 'She's excited.'

Then Bea's. She read it out loud. '"I heard from a mutual friend that you are interested in discussing a fashion show to showcase my recyclable collection. I am busy up until Christmas but could meet with you in the new year." That's no good. I need to meet with her now!'

'Phone her,' Mouse said.

'What shall I say?'

Mouse rolled his eyes.

'Okay.' Bea took a deep breath and gave a silent prayer before phoning Sav.

Mouse watched as she spoke. 'I can't really wait until then.' Bea tried to keep her voice calm and professional. 'If you are unable to help –' Sav interrupted, anxious not to lose out on the opportunity to showcase her designs.

'Well?' Mouse said when Bea disconnected.

'I'm meeting her tomorrow at her showroom.'

'That calls for a drink, unless Hartleys's busy executive has other important business to attend to? A seasonal mead?'

Bear lifted his head and whined in protest of Bea's potential departure. She rubbed his ear. 'A drop of mead would be lovely. Sav agreeing to meet with me tomorrow is cause for celebration. Now if you could help me find a dozen or more homeless people to model the recycled fashion then I might just sleep tonight.'

The golden mead glugged into a tumbler and Mouse chuckled, 'You *are* joking?'

'I wish I was. It's such a stupid idea.'

Mouse poured a second glass. 'Whose idea was it?'

Bea swirled the honey liquor around the glass. 'Mine. I know – stupid. But I didn't expect anyone to take it seriously. I was just throwing around ideas – brainstorming. Then the moron in marketing told Suki Dee's team, and now they're expecting homeless models to be parading top designers' recycled fashion, and not only that they want *more.* They'll be lucky if they get a few students modelling the Savvy Clothes collection. I can't even get professional models at this short notice.'

'You'd better have another.' Mouse refilled Bea's empty glass. 'Talking of homeless – Ryan came by this morning.'

A warmth flooded Bea that was nothing to do with the mead. Her nerve endings tingled. He'd come back. But then she remembered the bag hidden in her wardrobe. She had to return it to the *Moby* before he found out it was missing.

'When did you see him? Did he tell you where he was going?'

'No, mate. I just happened to look up when he was walking by – around ten.'

Bea knocked back her drink. 'That was lovely but I have to get going.'

Could she sneak the bag back onto the *Moby* without meeting Ryan? First, she would have to make sure that he wasn't on the barge.

28

TWENTY SHOPPING DAYS TO CHRISTMAS

Bea flung a sunhat, pashmina, an old biscuit tin, and back copies of *Vogue* from the wardrobe shelf as she rummaged for the Armani bag. Tugging it free released a further cascade of magazines, flapping like birds to her feet. Why hadn't she returned it sooner? She had to get rid of it before Ryan noticed his bag was missing, if he hadn't done so already.

Buzz. Someone at the door. It wasn't the estate agent; he had a key to the apartment block. Bea froze. What if it was the person who followed her home last night? Should she pretend to be out, and if she did, what if they broke in and found her on her own? Bea's heart was racing. *You are being irrational,* she told herself. *Firstly, you don't know that someone followed you. Last night you were shaken up after slipping on the platform. It was probably because your heels were wet from the snow.* She took a deep breath. *Nobody followed you. Stop creating a drama out of nothing.*

Bea pressed the intercom and Ryan's face filled the screen.

She was so relieved to see him, she nearly buzzed him in. Ryan looked unkempt and it took all of Bea's resolve not to welcome him in so that he could bathe and share a meal. His eyes seemed to meet hers and Bea flicked off the screen. Thank goodness he had come back. It had occurred to Bea that she might not see him again and she was surprised at the depth of emotion that thought stirred.

Buzz. Buzz. And then a long, insistent *buzz.* Bea bit her lip and stepped away from the intercom, not trusting herself. He would leave in a minute or two and then she could return the bag, knowing that Ryan was away from the barge. When all was quiet, Bea checked the screen again and found that he had left.

Ten minutes later, Bea sneaked out of the flat, wearing a hat and a pashmina that between them covered her face and most of her hair. She passed Mike on the stairwell and he didn't acknowledge her so the disguise worked. Before Ryan had come into her life that was normal – Bea didn't notice her neighbours and they ignored her. Now, she couldn't come and go without at least one friendly hello, and Molly always asked after the lovely Irish boy. The Armani bag was inside a black sack, because the only carrier bags she owned had Hartleys emblazoned across them – a dead giveaway.

Ryan was on the steps in Granary Square. There were no visitors today on the astroturf and so he sat alone gazing at the canal. Bea wondered whether he was waiting for her to return home. She slipped past him unnoticed and strode on, with the canal to her left, towards the lock and beyond that the *Moby*. The horror of Ryan finding out she had stolen his bag was a smidgen scarier than stepping back on that rat-infested wreck.

With the bag safely stowed back under the floorboards,

Bea tidied herself up. She threw away the black sack, shook loose her hair which rippled from the braids she wore earlier, and prepared to greet Ryan.

He jumped up from the steps as soon as she approached.

'You may not want to get too close. I need a shower,' he said, keeping his distance.

'You can have a shower and I will prepare our lunch,' Bea said with a note of pride. She had been practicing how to make omelettes by watching YouTube.

Ryan's appreciation of the lunch she served made the effort worthwhile. 'Is this the same girl who tripped past me in her fancy clothes and choo choo shoes? The girl who didn't know how to boil an egg just a few days ago?'

'I may not have been able to boil an egg but everything else in my life was a lot better.' Ten days ago, she was in control of her life. She knew what each day would bring and the future was full of promise. How could things have gone so wrong, so quickly? 'Apart from meeting you, of course,' she added.

Ryan waved his fork. 'Are you sure about that?'

'Yes. I'm glad that I met you. I missed you when you went away. Why did you leave so suddenly? Where did you go?'

'To be sure, meeting me was the best thing that happened to you.' Ryan winked. 'I'm a tramp, Bea. A homeless vagrant.' His voice changed and Bea sensed his self-loathing. 'Where did I go? I'm a traveller. I go where I can find shelter, work, something to eat. I don't need a reason.'

'Oh.' Bea felt small. She had overestimated her importance to him. He was right; they were strangers who just happened to cross paths. This was what she did – misread things.

'I meant are you sure that everything in your life was better? For sure, you had choo choo shoes and a fierce look about you, but I didn't see much of your smile,' Ryan said.

Bea pursed her lips. 'Jimmy Choos. And I loved those shoes before the heel came off.'

'Jimmy Choos or Patrick's shoes, it makes no difference. What I'm saying is, you looked kind of smug, as though you had the world sewn up. But you didn't, Bea.'

Bea remembered that feeling. A self-created armour of protection, nothing threatened her daily pattern of life and she knew exactly where she was headed – straight to the top. Now, she wasn't even sure that she would have a job in the new year. 'Evidently not, look at me now.'

'I'm looking.' Ryan smiled, his eyes soft. 'You can't control the world, Bea, no more than you can still an ocean.'

'I know that. But I could at least prepare. Do everything possible to increase my chances of success. And I did. It's harder for me because it doesn't come naturally, fitting in.'

'Maybe that's because you're starting from the wrong place. Take those Jiminy shoes. You didn't go squeezing your foot into a pair that was too small or make do with ones that were too big? That would be daft. No, you found the right fit for your size and shape.'

It didn't make any sense at first but as Bea cleared away their plates she thought about how she came to be where she was today.

'I only got interested in fashion because I wanted to fit in at school. I thought that if I dressed and spoke like Davinia Grayson, the popular girl, then the other kids wouldn't pick on me.'

'Did it work?'

'Yes, it did. I'm good at pretending. I can be anybody if I try hard enough.'

'Except yourself?'

'Being myself isn't all that. Being myself is what got me into this mess.'

Ryan grinned. 'You're doing grand. Now, how about a stroll along the canal? There's something I want to be showing you.'

Bea was relieved that she had returned the bag in time.

29

MARCH 2017

Ryan reread the email confirming receipt of two months' deposit and one month's rent in advance for his flat in London. The down payment had taken nearly all of his savings, the one-way Sail and Rail fare from Dublin to London, the remainder.

'You don't have to leave, Ryan. There's room for us all on the farm.' Caitlin lingered in his doorway and Ryan was reminded of the many times he had gone to this room to comfort or tease his sister. 'I always wanted your room, but maybe getting married was a bit of a drastic move to get a room swap.'

'Sean's a good lad. I wouldn't have approved unless he was worthy of my little sis – but he seems okay.' Ryan grinned.

Caitlin stood behind Ryan at his desk and put her arms around his neck. 'England is such a long way away.'

'Not as far as New Zealand.' The printer whirred and Ryan reached across to catch the printed email when it emerged.

'I was only gone two years. When will you come back

home, Ryan?' There was a catch to her voice and she seemed to Ryan a little girl again, not the confident, experienced farmer who was pitching her plans for the farm to Da last night.

'I don't know,' Ryan said, and the uncertainty of his future hit him like a cannonball.

There was panic in Caitlin's eyes and Ryan felt a stab of guilt. No, Caitlin had Sean – it was time he thought about himself. He had worked on that bloody farm for two years with no pay as well as taking care of their da. But Caitlin was sitting on what had once been her bed, her face covered by a sheet of blonde hair, and Ryan was big brother again, trying to make everything right.

'It sounds to me like you and wonder boy have everything mapped out: business strategies and the like. Da wouldn't even agree to selling off one field of land when I suggested it, and yet he seemed perfectly okay with your grand plans.' Resentment crept into his voice but Caitlin didn't seem to notice.

She lit up. 'Sean has so much experience, he's worked on a transgenic cow research project – that's breeding genetically modified cows for therapeutic purposes.'

'You said.' Ryan's eyes had glazed over last night; he didn't want a rerun. But before he could change the topic, Caitlin continued.

'And the fully automated milking programme. That's where we met, when I was doing my internship.'

'We can't afford to pay wages, there's no way we can afford to go robotic.'

'You left before we set out our business plan,' Caitlin said. 'Sean thinks that organic, small dairy farms are what people want today – they have been turned off by the enormous dairy farms where cows are milked without any human contact. We want to keep the herd small – just eighty cows –

and develop an organic boutique dairy. I'm going to make artisan, luxury dairy products: yogurts, ice cream, and cheesecake. I've got an amazing recipe. Sean says that Cork has advantages over New Zealand.' She counted off on her fingers, 'We've a mild all-year round climate and really fertile soil so our grass is lush.'

Ryan slid the papers into the pocket of his rucksack. He wasn't leaving for another ten days but was already packed.

'Is that all you're taking?' Caitlin stopped her lecture, aware that Ryan was no longer listening.

'I'm travelling light. To be sure, I'll buy what I need in London, once I'm settled.'

'So, you really are going and I can't persuade you to stay?' Caitlin wheedled.

Ryan sighed. 'It's just that since Ma died… Well, Da and I…' He couldn't express the pain and hurt in his chest, couldn't find the words.

'I miss her too. It was harder being away from the farm. It felt as though I had turned my back on Ma, deserted her, even though she wasn't here. Does that sound mad?'

It had only been two years; maybe all three of them were still trying to find their way, to adjust to the crater-sized hole in their lives.

'Da fell apart when she died,' Caitlin lowered her voice.

Ryan bristled. 'You mean he took to drink. Became a drunk?'

'No. He worshipped Ma. She was the centre of his world.'

'And you would be knowing what Da went through these past two years? You were here to clean up after him, when he was too hammered to get himself to the toilet? To count out his pills and make sure he took them? To help him into the shower? To change the dressings on his leg?'

Caitlin gave him the same look that Ma did, a patient

warning in her eyes. 'I appreciate all that you've done, Ryan. If you hadn't come home to support Da and look after the farm, I couldn't have gone to New Zealand. But, I'm home now and I'll look after him. Just be kind to Da, he's an old man and whatever you say, he does miss Ma. That's why he's been drinking.'

Caitlin had been home for four weeks and in that time Da had transformed. He got himself up at seven every morning, washed, dressed, and shaved. When Caitlin teased him about his whiskey bottles, he had handed them over like a child caught scrumping apples. They didn't need him here. All of them were better off without him. Caitlin's words stung. *Be kind to Da*. What did she think he had been doing? He was too angry to reply and Caitlin looked as though she had settled in for a good heart-to-heart.

'What are you doing?' Caitlin said as Ryan tugged his shirt over his head.

'Going for a run.'

Caitlin took the hint and got up from the bed. At the door she turned and said what he guessed she had been working up to. 'I think that the reason you and Da don't get on is because he was a bit jealous of the relationship between you and Ma.'

Ryan put on his running T-shirt, ignoring Caitlin's psychobabble.

'Maybe you are too alike.'

Ryan glared at Caitlin as he started to unzip his fly.

'Okay, okay, I'm going. I'm just saying – you need to give each other some slack.'

As always, running helped. Caitlin was back and together with Sean they would take care of Da and the farm and he was free to get on with his life. *A flat in London.* Ryan had to keep pinching himself. It was in a fashionable part of central London and the rent was very reasonable. He'd done his research and signed up to a number of websites offering casual labour for builders and carpenters. He would earn three times what he could in Cork. His future glittered before him, as he descended the hill back to the farm. In two weeks' time he would be living in London.

30

TWENTY SHOPPING DAYS TO CHRISTMAS

Ryan was going to take her to the old barge, she was sure of it. Maybe it was because she knew what to expect, or perhaps Ryan had cleaned her up in preparation for this visit, but when she visited earlier, the *Moby* was cleaner than she remembered and Bea did not encounter any rats when she was stuffing the bag back under the rotten floorboards.

The tow path was peaceful with dusk beginning to draw in. A couple of ducks came in to land, skimming their feet on the water's surface. There was a gentle lap of the tide as it nudged the houseboats and muffled clatters from within the lit cabins.

'We usually walk in the other direction,' Bea said as they walked with the canal to their left.

'As I said, I have something to be showing you.'

Now was the time to confess to taking the bag. Ryan would be angry but if they were going to find Declan, they had to work together. Whatever Ryan and Declan had got themselves into, she needed to know. 'Ryan, when you were away –'

'Don't ask me, Bea.' Ryan stopped walking and turned Bea to face him. It felt intimate, his hands on her arms and the soft gaze of his caramel eyes. 'Okay, I'll be telling you what I can, but don't push me for more.'

Bea nodded, her mouth dry. Ryan let go of her arms and covered his face with both hands, as though trying to control his thoughts and tongue. Seeming more composed, he said, 'Okay. When I left you, I went into town. Tottenham Court Road. A friend told me that Declan was meeting someone the night he disappeared. I had an address. Some fancy offices.' He paused and shook his head.

'Go on,' Bea prompted.

Ryan sighed. 'They were empty. I asked around and it turns out they've been vacant for at least a year. It was false information.'

'This friend, how reliable is he?'

'He wants to find Declan as much as I do. Maybe we were grasping at straws. He could have imagined Declan said something, or just misheard. I don't know.' Ryan sounded defeated.

'Ryan, you have to tell me all that you know. If you're involved in something, it's okay. You can trust me. Let me help you. *Please.*'

Ryan turned back towards the *Moby* and strode ahead, his shoulders hunched up, his head bowed against the wind. Bea quickened her pace to match his. 'There's something I have to tell you, Ryan –'

Ryan stood still and held up a hand to Bea as if to silence her. Ahead of them lights danced on the wrecked barge. Torches. They seemed to flash on and off, but then Bea saw that it was the light going in and out of cover, like the sun flitting behind clouds.

'What's going on over there?' Bea said.

'River police.' Ryan turned around. 'Let's head back. I'll show you another time.'

'What? What were you going to show me?' Bea had to jog to keep up with Ryan, who stalked ahead, hands in pockets.

'Nothing. Nothing important.'

Before Bea could tell Ryan that she had borrowed Declan's bag, he said, 'I've told you too much already. I know that you want to help but you can't, Bea. If you get involved you will put yourself at risk.'

'At risk of what?'

'I can't tell you.' Ryan raised his voice and Bea felt as though she had been slapped. He sounded angry and exasperated as he continued. 'I shouldn't have come back. Look, forget everything. Forget me. Forget Declan. You and I live in different worlds. There's no use pretending otherwise.'

His words stung. She thought that they were friends and had become close, but obviously she had misread things again. There was a lump in her throat as she tried to catch up with Ryan. Now, she needed him more than ever. If what Ryan said was true then she was already in danger. Now she was certain that someone had followed her home from Waterloo Station. The same person who had given her a shove on the platform as the train came in. If they were trying to scare her, then they had succeeded. She had to tell him.

'This is where I say goodbye.' Ryan stopped when the astroturfed steps of Granary Square came into sight.

Tell him, Bea. She tried to think of the words but he was full of anger and she didn't know where to start.

Ryan took a bow, like a Shakespearian actor. 'It has been an honour knowing you, Bea Stevens. Have a grand Christmas. Have a grand life.'

Was he really saying goodbye for good? 'You can't go.' Bea

wanted to throw herself at Ryan and beat her fists against his chest. How could he do this to her? Didn't their friendship mean anything to him? Ryan was already walking away. 'Don't go, Ryan. There's something I have to tell you.'

He turned and blew a kiss. 'Happy Christmas, Queen Bea.'

There was nothing Bea could do but watch his retreating back. Where would he go? Not the *Moby*. Bea wondered what the river police had been doing on the old barge and then she realised – the bag! What if they found Declan's bag? If Ryan and Declan were up to no good then the contents of the bag could incriminate them. Was that why Ryan had taken off?

Bea was angry. He should have let her speak. First Alastair and then Ryan. Men and their self-importance. Did her voice matter so little? First, they don't give her the chance to speak and the next minute they say why didn't you tell me. Well, bloody Ryan could take care of himself. She had tried to help and he had walked out on her. And as for Alastair... Bea calmed herself as she approached her apartment block. As for Alastair, she had better check her phone for messages. It was eight in the evening and she hadn't communicated with him since leaving the office around lunchtime. At least she had made contact with Sav. That was something positive she could share.

Bea pulled out her phone with her keys and let herself in. She checked her phone as she climbed the stairs. Two voice messages from Mum. Nothing from Alastair. When she had shed her coat and kicked off her shoes Bea played the messages. The first said, 'Call me as soon as possible. I have some exciting news.' The possibilities flipped through Bea's mind: her sister, Lizzie, was pregnant again. Ollie, her nephew, had lost a baby tooth. Mum and Dad had won the lottery and so she didn't have to move. The second message threw water on any hope. 'We've sold the flat! Perfect timing.

You have to be out by Christmas and as you will be coming home then, you can stay here until you've found somewhere else.'

Bea's head ached. Her world was crumbling around her. To lose this flat would be to lose her independence. Brick by brick, everything solid in her life was being dismantled – her job, her home, and Ryan. How could he walk away like that? The anger had cooled and in its place was a profound sense of loss. Ryan. The flat. Her job. She was just tired. It had been a very long day: the presentation to Suki Dee's team in the morning, the visit to Mouse on *No Worries*, her subterfuge in returning the bag, and then Ryan's visit, and their walk, before he said goodbye. For good. There was no point in phoning Mum now, she would call her tomorrow. Bea sent Alastair a text message to say that she had a meeting with a recycled fashion designer the next day and so wouldn't be in the office until the afternoon. Then, she ran a hot bath.

As she sank beneath the geranium-scented bubbles, Bea's worries started to dissolve. A bubble caught the light and shimmered; an iridescent rainbow. She had relied too much on Ryan, read too much into his friendship. Bea caressed the rainbow and the bubble burst. She didn't need anyone. She coped better on her own. It was too difficult trying to understand people and Bea always got it wrong. Even Ryan. Bea had believed that Ryan understood her and she him, but once again she had misinterpreted. When would she learn? Ryan had gone. Perhaps it was just as well, if he was involved in something dark. Maybe they did belong to different worlds. Bea sighed and pulled out the plug. Bubbles sparkled on her skin, like an embellished ballgown. Tomorrow she was meeting Sav. That was definitely good news.

Bea's positivity continued as she got ready for bed. It was short notice to find somewhere to live, but not impossible.

There were options; she had viewed only three rooms so far. Then, Bea had an inspired thought. If she sold all of her designer clothes on eBay she would raise enough money for a deposit and a few months' rent.

'Sorted,' she said out loud. Then, relaxed and exhausted, she pulled back her duvet to climb into bed.

There, in the dip which cradled her shoulder, nestled a parcel wrapped in paper printed with holly. Bea clasped it to her breast. Ryan must have left it there when he visited that day. A warm glow softened any remaining tension that she had been holding within her core. That was so typical of Ryan. She hadn't been wrong about him. He did care. Bea tried to guess what was inside. Ryan had very little money and so whatever it was, she would treasure it. Something thin and slippery, kind of silky. She could save it to open on Christmas day or open it now. The need to feel a connection with Ryan persuaded Bea to unwrap the present. Her first Christmas gift that year.

It was white. A soft leather. So soft, it felt like a little white mouse. Then, Bea recognised her missing glove. That was odd, why would Ryan…? She turned it over and saw the crimson stain, like blood on snow. Her stomach churned. This wasn't a loving gift, it was some kind of sick joke but she didn't get it. There was a piece of paper tucked inside the glove. Bea tugged it out, afraid of what it might say.

She read and reread the typed message: *Be warned.* She threw the glove across the room as though it were a dead mouse and cowered against the bed's headboard. Whoever put it there might still be in the flat. Minutes earlier she had been naked in the bath. Bea knew it was unlikely, but until she had checked every room, under the beds, and inside the cupboards, she didn't feel safe. Even then, she was terrified. The only person who had a key was Stanley Larkin, the estate agent. He had been there earlier that day, when Bea was visiting Mouse.

Bea got dressed. It made her feel less vulnerable and there was no way she could go to sleep, knowing a stranger could get into her flat. The message was clear. *Blood on your hands.* Whose blood? Declan's? Ryan's? What did the sender think that Bea knew, or was about to uncover? Ryan was right, they inhabited different worlds. Maybe it was just as well he had disappeared from her life. Her priority now was to make sure that the flat was safe from intruders, to find somewhere to live, and above all to make the Suki Dee event a huge success.

31

NINETEEN SHOPPING DAYS TO CHRISTMAS

The smells, sights, and sounds of Brick Lane jarred Bea's senses as she ventured into a part of London that was new to her. Bright, bold murals postured on imposing buildings, Arabic music and the mingled scent of grilled meat, spices, the waft of musty clothes from vintage clothes shops and traffic fumes. Since leaving the flat that morning, Bea had felt as though she was being watched. She checked behind her every few steps and waited until the Tube door was about to close before jumping off. At least she was surrounded by people; until the door key was returned by Larkin, staying at home was more of a risk. Bea had tried to find out the identity of the last person to be shown around her flat by the estate agent but there was nobody in the office who could tell her. They did assure Bea that it wasn't possible for a client to take a copy of the door key because the estate agent wouldn't pass it to anyone else. This at least was some comfort, and Molly had instructions not to let anyone into her flat.

Bea tried to focus, to concentrate on preparing for her

meeting with Sav. She had been awake for twenty-six hours now and felt jet-lagged. The long hours of the night had been occupied by advertising her precious collection of designer clothes and accessories on eBay. Ashamed of having wasted so much money on frivolities when she should have been saving squashed any feelings of regret. The activity had helped to calm her as she waited for dawn. By the time it was getting light, everything had been photographed and catalogued. It was as though she had shed a past life. Each shoe, suit, and dress had a story.

Savvy Clothes was on a corner, the door and window frames painted teal. The side of the shop was in a residential street and the neighbouring brickwork covered in graffiti art, which included a lurid pink alien. Bea peered into the window but there wasn't much to see, just a suit jacket and waistcoat, fashioned from newspaper. Bea wondered whether the newspaper had been treated with something to make it waterproof; it looked stiff and starched. An oversized purple pocket watch was chained to the waistcoat giving a splash of colour. A girl with a bright pink pixie cut, who Bea immediately recognised as Sav, rearranged a silk scarf in the bottom of the window as she took a peek at her visitor. Instead of waving to identify herself, Bea crept away. Mouse had exaggerated her importance; Sav would be expecting a high-powered executive, not Bea, although she was dressed in a smart trouser suit and high-heeled ankle boots. One of two work outfits that she had not posted on eBay last night.

You can do this. You have to do this. Bea turned around and marched back, passing two young women in hijabs and she longed to be back in Hartleys doing what she knew – selling expensive lingerie. If only Ryan were at her side. Bea tried to conjure the image of Ryan, to hear his words of encouragement and Leila with her down-to-earth view of the world.

Then she remembered that Sav was a friend of Mouse. She was from the same world as her new friends and this gave Bea a little courage as a bell on the door announced her arrival into the silent shop. Sav didn't come out straight away and so Bea looked around her as she waited. There really wasn't anything else in the shop apart from the newspaper suit. It didn't fill Bea with hope.

'Can I help you?' Sav slipped into the shop from behind a panelled room divider.

Bea extended her hand. 'Bea Stevens from Hartleys, we spoke on the phone.'

Sav blushed. 'Oh, I'm sorry, I was expecting you but when you looked in the window and then walked away, I thought you were a customer looking for a clothes shop and that's not what this is…' She spoke quickly, breaking off to gasp for breath and wave her hands around. 'It's a showroom. I work in the back. Sorry, I should stop talking.'

Her anxiety relaxed Bea; she should have guessed that a friend of Leila and Mouse would have no pretences. 'Thank you for meeting me at such short notice,' Bea said. She had to sound professional if she was to entice Sav to commit to supplying a fashion show on Christmas Eve. 'Mouse thought you might have left for Venice.'

'You just caught me. Why don't you come through to my workroom and I'll make you a coffee?'

The Japanese-style panelled screen separated the sparse showroom from a magical cavern of chaos and creativity. In the centre of the room was a big square cutting table. Two sewing machines were on sewing tables at the sides of the room, and all around were rails of garments covered with sheets and materials: baskets of ring pulls and flattened tin cans, ruffles of crisp packets draped over a chair, swathes of newsprint and magazines pegged up to dry. Sav had transformed the things that people threw away into sumptuous trimmings and shiny trinkets – a magical haberdashery. Bea couldn't wait to see the clothes revealed.

When Sav returned with coffee, Bea told her about the fashion show and how it was to have good media coverage to promote Suki Dee's charitable work.

Sav was at first excited, but when Bea told her the date her face fell. 'I wish I had more time.'

'Perhaps you could show me your current collection,' Bea said, trying to sound like a fashion buyer.

Sav wheeled out two of the clothes rails. 'These are not all complete, more works in progress. If you'd met with me in the new year, I could have put something together for you.'

She made a face that Bea interpreted as regret and then folded back the sheet.

Bea drew closer, intrigued by the crackle and shine of the different textures.

'This rara skirt is made from crisp packets.' Sav held up a cute orange and red skirt that seemed to whisper as her hands stroked the ruffles and Bea imagined the delightful crackle it would make when swirling in a dance.

'You saw the jacket and waistcoat in the show room. I'm really pleased with them. I'm experimenting with the pocket watch.' Sav selected a waistcoat with a blue sardine hanging on a chain instead of a watch. 'I cut that from a catering can of sardines. I use tin cans a lot. Let me show you the bags I've made.'

Everything that Sav showed Bea was impressive, but very little was finished. There wasn't anywhere near enough for a show. 'I'll take everything that you have ready for Christmas Eve, but I'll need to know what you're providing and the sizes for my models.'

'Are you talking to anyone else?' Sav said.

'We haven't finalised the fashion designers that we are featuring yet.'

'When will you know?' She sounded anxious.

Bea shrugged. 'It will have to be soon.'

They agreed to talk again the following week, but Bea was realistic. Even if Sav completed all of the garments in her workshop it wouldn't be enough.

'How was your meeting?' Alastair rubbed his hands together, his eyes wide with expectation.

'Promising,' Bea said as she sought her desk, longing to be alone so that she could shut her eyes. Alastair nodded enthusiastically, he wasn't going anywhere. 'But…' There was no point in pretending. Nineteen days until Christmas and she had one local designer who may, if she was lucky, produce two or three garments in time for the show. They didn't have any models lined up, homeless or otherwise. It was impossible. 'Not promising enough.'

Alastair sat on the side of her desk. 'Okay. Give me a rundown of where we are: the designers who are interested, the models you are working with, that special *je ne sais quoi* that Suki Dee is expecting.'

Bea stared at Alastair in disbelief. 'It was yesterday morning that we discussed this plan for the first time. *Yesterday morning.*' It felt like weeks ago. So much had happened in that time: Ryan's leaving, the news that she had to leave her flat by Christmas, the blood-stained glove in her bed. The room tilted, and Bea took a deep breath. 'I've hounded all of the top recycled fashion designers. There is some interest but only if we postpone until after Christmas.' Alastair made a face, and Bea continued. 'The local designer

I'm working with is excellent. I viewed her collection this morning but we will need more.'

'Is that all you have achieved in one day? It's not as if yesterday was the first day of this challenge.' Alastair stood up to say this. Perching on her desk was for the friendly sharing of plans.

Suddenly Bea didn't care any more. All she wanted was a bed in a dark room. 'I can't do it, Alastair. I've tried, but it's impossible.'

Alastair sighed. He threw up his hands and cast his eyes to heaven. 'So now what? I have to go and tell Mr Evans and Suki Dee that Hartleys cannot deliver?'

Bea shrugged. 'If we just waited until the new year…'

Alastair shook his head. 'No. That is not an option. You do realise what this means for you, Bea?' His face was full of concern.

'Couldn't I just go back to lingerie?' Alastair's face was going in and out of focus as Bea tried hard to concentrate.

'You would have to backfill Alice's post, with protected pay.'

Bea had to find something to eat. She hadn't eaten anything since the omelette with Ryan – yesterday? Last week? She clutched the edge of her desk as the room swayed.

'Okay. Which department?'

'Children's toys. Don't decide now. Think it over. You do realise that that arrangement would only be until you serve your notice and then…Stevens?'

'Take a sip of water.' A glass was being pressed to Bea's lips. She opened her eyes to see Evans's PA bending over her. She was on the floor, propped up with pillows, her legs raised with a couple more.

'You fainted. I'm the designated first-aider.'

Bea looked around her. They were alone in the open office.

'Did Alastair speak to Mr Evans?' She remembered giving in her notice.

'No. Mr Evans is in Birmingham. There now, take another sip. You are still very pale. Are you getting morning sickness?'

'I'm not pregnant. I skipped breakfast.'

'If you're up to eating something, I'll get you a sandwich, and then I'll order you a cab. Is there someone at home who can take care of you?'

32

NINETEEN DAYS TO CHRISTMAS

Bea didn't want to return to her flat; she was afraid of what she might find. If only Ryan was there. He would probably have changed the lock by now. Bea smiled to herself. Even thinking about him made her feel better. Then, she remembered him raising his voice to her, telling her not to get involved. *Oh Ryan, what have you got yourself into?* She understood now, his need to protect her. But it was too late. Somebody knew where she lived and it was possible they had a key to her flat. What if they had paid Larkin to turn a blind eye whilst they took a copy of the key? She would have to change the lock as soon as she got home.

'You can drop me off here,' Bea said to the cab driver as they approached King's Cross Station.

The flat looked undisturbed. Her bed was littered with clothes and accessories where she had been sorting them out for the eBay sale. Just to make sure, Bea turned back her duvet and then inspected every room. Larkin hadn't returned the key and so she phoned his office.

'Hello? This is Bea Stevens. I phoned this morning and was promised that the key to my flat would be returned.'

A woman asked Bea to wait and a calming piano filled the silence. Bea's head was starting to drop when the woman returned to the phone. 'Mrs Stevens collected it herself this afternoon. I hope that's okay?'

'Yes, yes,' Bea said and hung up. Then she jolted – wide awake. That meant Mum was in London and on her way to the flat. Thank goodness she hadn't let herself in before Bea got home; her heart couldn't take any more surprises.

The doorbell buzzed and Bea's heart lurched. Mum was doing a little jig and blowing into her hands. She cast her eyes up at the camera and despite her misgivings, Bea felt a warmth spread through her. With all that she had experienced in the past twenty-four hours, it was a relief to see her stoic and loving mum – ready to fight anyone and anything that threatened her precious daughter. She suppressed a childlike urge to bolt down the stairs and throw herself into her mum's arms. Then, the reality of what she had done in resigning from her position at Hartleys struck her and she was filled with dread – a hollow pain, where dreams had once danced. Alastair couldn't have told Evans yet. If she phoned Alastair and said she had changed her mind, but it was impossible – no collections to show, no models, and Suki Dee wanted something *more.* Mum was waiting outside. One word from Bea and Mum would bundle her back home to the safety of suburbia and Mum's watchful protection.

If Bea was to keep her options open, she had to appear calm and happy. Mum would sense any weakness – a chink in her armour – and that would be it, she would be suffocated with love. Bea pressed open and awaited her mum at the top of the stairs.

'Mum, what a wonderful surprise. Are you in London to do some Christmas shopping?'

Her mum frowned. 'I came as quickly as I could. You sounded distraught last night.' Bea remembered with horror phoning Mum to find out who had a key to the flat. It must have been in the early hours of the morning. 'And when you said that you wanted the door key returned, well, I wondered whether a man had been *bothering* you.' Mum paused to give a meaningful look, as though she could extract the truth from Bea through her special powers.

Bea knew she had to think fast to achieve damage limitation, but her brain was scrambled through lack of sleep. She had summoned a genie and unless she was convincing there was no way it was going back in the bottle.

'Oh Mum. You shouldn't have driven all that way. I'm fine, I wouldn't have phoned you if I'd looked at my watch. You know me, once I get involved in something I lose all sense of time.'

Mum gave Bea a long look as if to say, *I'm not convinced.* 'No. You were right, darling. I should never have given the estate agent a key. It was careless of me. If I have put you at risk in any way…'

Bea was too tired to continue with her pretence. 'I'm really sorry I rang so late and woke you up. Here, sit down and I'll make you a cup of tea.'

Her mum settled in an armchair and allowed Bea to wait on her with tea and biscuits. A few weeks ago, Bea wouldn't have had anything to offer Mum except mini bottles of Prosecco awaiting successful sales day celebrations, but now she was fully prepared for visitors. Glimpsing the camomile tea, Bea felt a stab of pain and closed the cupboard door.

'I see that you've started packing,' Mum said as she passed Bea's bedroom door on her way back from the bathroom.

'Just having a sort-out.'

'You've got a lot to move. Why don't I stay the night and help you to pack things up? We could have a look at your new place together. See what else you might need and anything you want me to store I can take back in the car.'

'It's not definite, my new place. At least not yet.'

Her mum leant forward, as though about to pounce out of her chair. 'I thought as much. You haven't found anywhere, have you?'

Bea wanted to tell her mum everything. The weight of worry was too great to carry alone. The little burst of energy that had given her life when she prepared to greet her mum had now dissipated and Bea felt light-headed. 'I was sent home from work in a cab because I fainted.'

Before she got any further, her mum was at her side, feeling her forehead. 'I didn't think you looked right. You've been doing too much. Why don't you go and lie down?'

'You've only just arrived. I ought to –'

'I'm not a guest. I'm your mother. Let me look after you for once. I admire your independence but you need to learn when to accept help too, darling.'

'Thank you.' Bea's body felt heavy. 'Stay the night, Mum. It's too late to be driving back to Hampshire.'

Her mum yawned and then Bea. 'No wonder we're both tired. Are you sure that there was nothing more to your call? It's so unlike you to phone in the middle of the night. You must have had a good reason.'

It would have been so easy to unburden herself; she was exhausted and her defences were down. 'I was just spooked that a stranger had a key to my flat. I think that I had a nightmare and woke up. Yes, that's what happened. I'm really sorry that I woke you.' Bea yawned again.

'I hope you're not coming down with anything. Go on –

off to bed. I'll go myself in a few minutes. Tomorrow you can sort out what you want me to take back in the car. Dad and I will deliver it to your new place once you've settled in. It will make your move easier.'

In the one minute before she fell into a deep sleep, Bea was aware of her life unravelling. All that she had worked for and dreamed of. Her life in London. Her independence. The career she had aspired to. Ryan. An embroidered lace evening dress from the haute couture collection. Silk skeins rippling as they came undone. Glassy beads scattering with a clink as they hit the floor. Row by row. Until it had disappeared.

33

APRIL 2017

Oh, Ma, would you look at that? Ryan ached to have his ma next to him. The twinkling light of sun on water and the magnificence of the Wicklow Mountains as the ferry left Dublin Bay and the life Ryan had known and loved – the farm, Caitlin, his shabby old truck, and the carpentry tools he had been accumulating. Ryan took a deep breath of sea air and closed his eyes, enjoying the warmth of the sun and a breeze that ruffled his hair.

When Dublin was a distant blur of green and gold, Ryan went below deck. He wasn't a drinker and it was only eleven but the lure of St Patrick's bar – *a traditional Irish pub* – persuaded him to have a pint. He missed the camaraderie of the guys on the building site, after two years of living with Da and little company other than the cows. Caitlin and Sean were full of plans for the farm and Da had transformed since their arrival in February. He ought to feel pleased that Da and the farm were left in capable hands, but Da's ready dismissal of him hurt. Inside he was still the child who needed his father's approval and he hated himself for feeling like that. Da was a bastard. A bully. He ordered a pint of Guinness and resolved to put his past life behind him.

Apart from a splattering of shamrocks and piped Irish music, there was little to define the bar as typical Irish. The Guinness was from a can and didn't have the velvet and cream of a pint brewed in Dublin. An American couple were regaling the bartender with every detail of their Irish tour, and a fresh-faced lad sat at a table facing Ryan. In the corner five men were knocking back pints with shots lined up. They were loud and Ryan caught the young lad's eye as they exchanged a look of irritation.

'Where are you headed when you get to Holyhead?' the lad said.

'London. I'm doing the Sail and Rail,' Ryan said, but his voice was drowned out by a roar of laughter from the men.

The lad joined Ryan at his table. 'Do you mind? I couldn't hear you.'

Ryan was pleased to have his company and explained that he was taking an express train from Holyhead to London.

'Me too. Declan.' The boy shook Ryan's hand; an old-fashioned gesture for one so young, but it endeared him to Ryan.

'And where will you be staying?' Declan asked.

'In a place called Angel, isn't that a grand name?'

'To be sure. I'm staying in Issy something. Hold on, I'll have a look. I keep forgetting his address.' Declan checked his phone. 'Ah, here it is, Islington. This is my fella.' He flashed his mobile at Ryan and smiled indulgently at the image of a boy with black hair and olive skin. 'Ash. We met in Dublin when he was a student. Ash had to go back to London last year and he's been nagging me to join him. Thought I'd surprise him.'

There was a snigger from behind them; one of the louts was at the bar. Declan pocketed his phone.

'I think I might be living near Islington,' Ryan said. He

didn't have a smartphone, just an old-fashioned pay as you go; it didn't even have a camera. Ryan pulled some papers from his rucksack pocket. 'Here it is. The Angel Islington.'

Declan clinked his glass with Ryan's. 'Maybe we'll meet up and share a pint in good old London Town.'

'To be sure. You'll be the only person that I know in the big city.'

Declan left to get some air on deck and Ryan went through his papers, pinching himself that it really was happening – that he was going to live in London.

They would be docking in thirty minutes and so Ryan left the bar to greet Holyhead.

A woman passed by with two small children. 'There's an awful fight up there. They've been drinking.' She hurried the children away.

Ryan could hear the louts and strode up to the deck to see what was going on. Some poor kid was getting a kicking. 'Fuckin' Nancy,' someone shouted and aimed another blow at the boy on the floor.

Ryan knew it was Declan, and not caring that there were five of them, went to his rescue. He swung a punch and then another, surprising the thugs. It felt good. All of the anger that had been festering in him went into those blows and once he started he couldn't stop. When an officer in a white jacket pulled him away, Ryan's knuckles were raw and his head bloodied.

Ryan and Declan missed the shuttle service to Holyhead Station and the express train to Euston as they were escorted to the police station along with the thugs.

34

EIGHTEEN SHOPPING DAYS TO CHRISTMAS

Hearing her mum cluttering in the kitchen brought back childhood memories for Bea. She had slept for thirteen hours, and although refreshed, her heart was no lighter. Yesterday she had given in her notice by admitting defeat on the Suki Dee project. A temporary sales assistant in the toy department. Bea couldn't think of a job she would loathe more. There was no point staying in London. The friends that she had made were Ryan's friends and Ryan didn't want anything more to do with her. He was trying to protect her. The blood-stained glove was a warning, and if she had any sense she would go home with her mum to Hampshire. Forget Ryan. Forget Hartleys. Start afresh.

'Good morning, darling. I didn't like to wake you. There was nothing in your fridge and so I popped out and bought some bacon and eggs. Don't start telling me about calories. Nourishing meals and early nights are what you need.'

Bea didn't need any persuading. Since being introduced to Fandangle's bacon butties, she had let her calorie-controlled diet slide. 'Mum, about the flat,' she said.

Her mum put up a finger to stop her talking. 'Just a mo. Let me plate this up and then we can have a proper talk. You haven't told me anything about your new place or work. You said you thought you would get a promotion before Christmas.'

'There isn't –'

Her mum interrupted before Bea could say what she intended, that she hadn't found somewhere to live.

'Just as well you found somewhere.' Mum placed a fried breakfast before Bea and then sat opposite, her hands clasped as she prepared to deliver all of her news whilst Bea ate and listened. 'Poor, Lizzie. Such rotten timing. I don't know why Tristan has to have the house renovated just before Christmas. You know what he's like. Doesn't do anything by halves. Practically pulling everything down – walls –' she threw her hands up '– the bathroom and kitchen are coming out. How is Lizzie meant to cope with work and look after Ollie amidst all that chaos? Dad and I said, come and stay with us until it's all finished. It'll be a bit of a squeeze but we'll manage. It'll be nice to see more of Ollie and his school's closer to us really than them. More toast, darling?'

Bea's heart sank. Going back to Hampshire wasn't an option. She shook her head. 'No, thanks. When exactly do I need to move out?'

'I've said that you'll be out by Christmas but we need to get in house clearance and a cleaning company. I've had a word with Mr Larkin. They can arrange everything for us, but they will need the keys. Don't worry, so long as they have the keys when you move out.' Her mum took Bea's empty plate to the sink.

'Now tell me about your high-flying job. I'm so proud of you, darling. To be honest I was worried about you finding your way when you were at school. The psychologist warned us that you would always have your *problems* and with your funny ways I didn't think you would hold down a job.'

Mum meant well, but she was always trying to 'fix' her, instead of accepting Bea as she was – the way Ryan did. But Mum was right, she hadn't held down her job at Hartleys.

'You proved me wrong and I couldn't be prouder. Head of lingerie, you said on the phone? Knowing you have a good job and can afford to rent somewhere I don't feel so bad about selling Fiona's flat. My sister would be glad that she's helped you and now Lizzie. We're going to put some money in a trust fund for Ollie. Then, with your dad retiring…'

Bea tuned out. For years she had craved this approval and acceptance from her parents. Now that it had come, it was based on lies. She hadn't told Mum that she had the promotion, just raised expectation. Okay, she had lied about finding a flat, but at the time it was intended as a delaying tactic.

Her mum folded a tea towel and slipped it over the oven door to dry, just as she did at home on the Aga. 'Are you going in to work this afternoon or phoning in sick? I'm leaving for Hampshire about two, so let me have anything you want me to store.'

Sitting on the edge of her bed, head in hands, Bea tried to recalibrate following her mum's announcements. The first thing that she needed to do was find somewhere to live. Even a job selling kids' toys was better than nothing and her pay would be protected for a couple of months. Then what?

Ryan would tell her to get off her arse and show them all what she was capable of. She had known him only a few days and yet his voice was in her head, cheering her on when she felt like giving up. *I need to do this for Declan and Ryan too,* Bea thought. *Yesterday, I was exhausted but today is a new day. I will not be intimidated by these bullies. Whatever Ryan and Declan have got mixed up in we can sort this out. Ryan needs me to stand up for him.*

Bea checked her eBay account before phoning Alastair and was amazed to find that she had already raised over five thousand pounds. The only items remaining for sale were a pair of red suede ankle boots and a Michael Kors handbag. Bea discounted them, and then phoned Alastair.

'Hello, Alastair. Yes, I'm feeling much better, thank you. About yesterday –'

'I was disappointed, Stevens, but better you admit defeat now than disgrace Hartleys.'

'Have you told Mr Evans?'

'Not yet. He's away on business.'

'I've had time to reconsider. I *can* do this, Alastair. I was just tired.'

Bea could feel his disapproval in the weighty silence that followed. She filled in the pause by speaking first. 'After all, I have one collection and promises of others.'

'This local designer you told me about?' Alastair didn't sound convinced.

'Yes, Savvy Clothes. A fabulous collection. I know I can find more designers. Some of them may be local but the quality is good and if we can secure one or two big international names we should have enough for a show.'

'Can you do that?'

No, Bea thought, *but what was there to lose?* If she didn't try she would be out anyway. 'Yes.'

'And models?'

'I'm on to that today!' A thought had occurred to Bea as she spoke. She would make up some Christmas packages for the homeless and distribute them with an invitation to sign up for the fashion show. Nothing was impossible.

'If you're sure?' Alastair still sounded cautious.

'Absolutely! I won't let you down, Alastair. Trust me.'

One minute after disconnecting her call, Bea's phone pinged. She had sold the handbag and shoes. Now, she had to find somewhere to live.

Bea left her mum cleaning the inside of kitchen cupboards, whilst she posted her parcels – all of the garments wrapped in tissue paper and polythene mailing sacks. When her mum had been vacuuming the lounge that morning, Bea had requested a viewing of a flat near the Holloway Road Tube station, just two stops further along the line from King's Cross. It was through the agency advertised on the flier that Bea had found on the *Fandangle* notice board. The rent was within Bea's budget, which was a surprise, because it was a self-contained flat that she wouldn't have to share. It was also immediately available, subject to two months' deposit a month in advance and references. *Miracles do happen*, Bea said to herself as she strode along the Holloway Road in search of Tufnell Terrace.

It couldn't have been more perfect, the proximity to the Tube station and the setting – a little row of terraced houses. The flat was on the ground floor with a secluded courtyard garden. In the summer she could plant pots with geraniums, like the displays on the houseboats. Aunt Fiona's flat had never stirred such feelings in Bea, it had just been a place to sleep, but this little flat called to her. It promised a new life – one of domesticity and belonging.

'I want it!' Bea exclaimed when the landlord, a thickset man with swarthy skin, had finished showing her around. He narrowed his eyes and gave her a curious look as though he doubted her intention. 'Really. I want to rent this flat.' *More than anything*, Bea finished in her mind.

He kept his gaze on her and for a fleeting moment Bea had a sense of recognition, as though their paths had crossed not so long ago. Maybe he shopped in Hartleys. If she had sold him women's lingerie, it would explain his apparent discomfort in her presence. *Or*, it could just be because that's how people reacted to her for a reason that Bea no longer tried to understand.

'I'll need the deposit and two months in advance,' he said. 'Places like this are snatched up but I'd like to secure a tenant as soon as possible. I'm going abroad in a couple of weeks and I don't want to leave it empty.'

Bea was torn. Her instincts told her not to be rushed into handing over so much money but she had fallen in love with the place and didn't want to risk losing it. 'I would need a signed contract first,' she said.

'No problem. You do realise that you won't find anything else of this quality at the price I'm asking?' He gave her a long look as though trying to weigh her up.

'Why is that?' Bea said, still wary. Her sister, Lizzie, always warned her that if something seemed too good to be true, it probably was.

'I'll be honest with you,' the man said, rubbing his bristly chin, 'I have a cash flow problem and need the money now. A couple of other people viewed it but were put off by the main road. I've only just reduced the rent for a quick let, because I need to secure another property abroad. If you're not interested I'll easily find another tenant.'

'I am interested. I'll send the deposit today. If you could send me a contract.'

'Okay. You'll need to send the money by bank transfer. Here are my details.'

Bea photographed the information scribbled on a piece of paper, as well as stowing it away in her handbag. She wasn't leaving anything to chance.

'If we can settle everything by tomorrow, you can move in next week. If that suits you.'

'Thank you. Thank you,' Bea enthused. Her luck had changed and she had a feeling that all would be well. She couldn't wait to tell Mum that she had a moving date.

The next job on Bea's list was to buy pairs of thick socks, toiletries, hats, and scarfs for her Christmas parcels. She would include an invitation to participate in a fashion show. Maybe she should offer a fee as an extra incentive. A few weeks ago, she wouldn't have dared to approach homeless people and engage them in conversation. At least Ryan had taught her not to make assumptions about people – good or bad. People were people. Bea found it hard talking to anybody and homeless people were no different. But, she was on a mission and nothing was going to stop her from achieving her goal.

'I'm home, Mum,' Bea called as she dumped her bags in the hallway. As well as buying gifts for the homeless, she had bought Christmas presents for Mum, Lizzie, and Oliver. For the first time that season, Bea felt a little Christmas magic.

Her mum had left, leaving behind the scent of J'Adore and a scrumptiously clean flat. As promised, she had taken away heavy items such as spare bedding and books. Next Thursday Bea would order a cab to take her remaining belongings, a suitcase, and duvet to the new flat. Her own garden flat, in the heart of London. She was an independent woman. Bea whooped with joy and did a little dance.

It would have been fun sharing this news with her mum but Bea was glad to have back her solitude. Any fears about intruders had been swept away with the dust that had gathered in the corners of rooms. The fridge had been filled with healthy food: salads, cold meats and cheese, yogurts, and a few ready meals. Bea smiled; at least Mum knew that she wasn't up to preparing a meal from scratch. Omelettes were her limit. However, no harm in changing the lock. While, she waited for the locksmith Bea contacted her new landlord. The contract was a simple one. She checked it and then she paid the deposit and rent. One thing at least had gone to plan.

35

EIGHTEEN SHOPPING DAYS TO CHRISTMAS

Twenty parcels, fourteen for women and six for men. Bea had included sanitary towels and tampons for women and disposable razors for the men. Alastair had insisted that the homeless charities were consulted on how best to engage the models and already they had restricted Bea's endeavours: they were not to offer financial reward as it would encourage substance misuse. On how to recruit volunteers, they remained silent, probably thinking, as Bea did, that it was a stupid idea. So, no help really. If they knew Bea had included razors in the packs then they would probably have vetoed those too. Weighed down with two carrier bags, Bea crept around St Pancras Station peering at the prone and huddled figures, trying to find suitable models. It was impossible, beneath the layers of clothing and dirty world-weary faces Bea had trouble guessing age, build, and sometimes gender. With only twenty parcels to distribute, it was like laying a bet on those most likely to volunteer. A meal in Hartleys's restaurant and a twenty-pound Hartleys gift voucher were being offered as payment for modelling the recycled clothes. The third time Bea circled the station she made her move. A young woman, possibly a size eight, she was so thin and drawn, hunched against a wall, her knees pulled in to her chest. Bea crouched down next to her and the woman tilted her head like a curious robin.

'Can I get you a hot drink or something to eat?' Bea said.

The woman slouched back, as though disappointed. 'Nah. Have you got any money?' She flashed her eyes at Bea, defiant and accusing.

Bea hesitated, unsure whether to give the woman some money or offer the parcel and invitation. The light in the woman's eyes extinguished as quickly as it had fired and was replaced with a blank dead gaze devoid of all hope.

Bea handed her a parcel. 'A Christmas gift. It's nothing much but you may find something useful in there.'

The woman didn't respond; she had retreated back into her own world and so Bea placed the parcel by her side and scrambled up, the speech that she had rehearsed about the fashion show unsaid.

Bea scribbled in her notepad the number on the parcel and a brief description of the girl but Bea had not asked her name, age, or dress size. This was going to be even harder than she had thought.

Rather than make a fool of herself by staying around the station where her clumsy attempts might be witnessed by rail travellers or CCTV cameras, Bea headed for the Euston Road. There was no reason to be spooked, no reason for the prickling sensation on the back of her neck, a heightened awareness of being watched, of being followed. Bea spun around and a parcel toppled from her bag. Her instincts were wrong; the people who milled around her were intent on their own purpose, none of them interested in Bea.

It was a little after ten and so a number of people were still curled up in sleeping bags in the shelter of nooks and alcoves afforded by the buildings. The pavement sparkled with frost and Bea reflected on what it must have felt like, trying to sleep when you were freezing cold and afraid to close your eyes. The body burrowed in a thin sleeping bag, that Bea was standing over now, had very little protection from the elements. Unsure who was hidden within, she crouched down and whispered, 'Can I get you a warm drink?'

A groan came from inside and some movement, then the scent of stale breath and tobacco, as an old and weathered face emerged. His long beard reminded Bea of Gandalf the Wizard. Definitely not model material. But this poor old boy would benefit from warm socks and a hat. Bea bought him a cup of tea and sat with him as he opened the parcel, marvelling over each gift. It was as though they were a normal family, opening Christmas presents from under the tree. He tried on the hat and socks. His poor feet were blue with cold, his toenails in desperate need of cutting as they curled in on themselves and bit cruelly into his skin.

'Have you got any baccy?' he said.

Of course, Bea bought him a packet of tobacco and some cigarette papers. She wished that she could do more for him, but his reaction to her kind deed made her feel that she had given him the world.

'God bless you. God bless you,' he repeated again and again. He kissed her hands and then held them between his. 'An angel. That's what you are. An angel sent by God.'

It was hard getting away, as the old man wouldn't stop telling Bea how wonderful she was and it was embarrassing with passers-by staring at them. He stuffed the wrapping paper into his sleeping bag to keep himself warm, and Bea guessed that the flier with information about the fashion show had gone the same way. Another parcel wasted if you thought of it that way, but Bea couldn't – not when it had brought him so much joy. But, she wasn't Mother Teresa; she was on a mission and had to distribute the remaining eighteen parcels wisely.

With so many homeless people in the area, it should have been easy for Bea to find eighteen possible models but as she approached people of all ages, male and female, the responses did not improve. An old woman, a similar age to Sal, told Bea that she was a model and an actress. She could have been once – who knew? But now, she had most of her teeth missing and hair sprouting from a large mole on her chin.

There were ten parcels left but Bea didn't know how much longer she could do this – it was so depressing. As she talked to people living on the streets, she was exposed to their world and their hopelessness and desperation crept over her like fingers of damp fog. Warm socks were always well received and one boy had been overjoyed with the toothpaste and toothbrush but Bea felt inadequate and foolish. They needed so much more and her offering felt like an insult, as though she thought herself Lady Bountiful. The purpose of her venture was to find potential models but Bea had stopped bringing attention to the flier when one man shouted obscenities at her believing she was making fun of him.

As she trudged along St Pancras Road with the intention of scouring Camden Town for recruits, Bea could not shrug off the feeling of being followed. She paused to admire a church with a tree-lined churchyard set back from the road. A bawdy shout followed by raucous laughter, then some jeering, came from within the grounds. Bea climbed a few stone steps and entered the churchyard through a gate. Mature trees provided a screen for whoever was gathered there; when they were in leaf they would provide welcome shade and a burst of vibrant green. Bea's shoe scuffed the ground and the scent of leaf mould and peaty earth filled her nostrils. She breathed in the crisp air and as it filled her lungs she felt its cleansing power. Meandering between the trees, enjoying a respite from the city, Bea almost forget what had drawn her there, then she saw four men and a woman sprawled across some gravestones as they passed around a bottle. They hadn't seen Bea and she contemplated returning to the busy road. If someone was following her, she was making herself vulnerable by venturing into a secluded area.

One of the men was holding court, telling a tale. The woman shrieked with laughter and there followed some banter between them.

If she handed out five parcels, there would be only another five to distribute. They were unlikely models but so were the other eight people who had received parcels that morning. A blackbird surveyed Bea from the head of a gravestone and sung a few notes of encouragement. Yesterday, she had made a vow to be more careful and here she was taking a risk. *Now you're being as paranoid as Mum,* Bea thought. What was the point of avoiding her mum's overprotectiveness if she was going to place the same restrictions on herself? A magpie cawed. And Bea ventured forth.

'Hi,' she said.

Nobody responded at first; it was as though a veil separated their two worlds and the group neither saw nor heard her. When Bea squatted down on a gravestone next to the woman, they all stopped what they were doing and stared.

'We're not doing any harm,' the woman said, her face pinched in self-righteous anger.

'I didn't mean to disturb you,' Bea said. 'I just wanted to say hello.'

They continued to stare.

'Um, I thought you might like –' Bea fished in her bag for a parcel which she held up like a trophy '– one of these.' They continued to stare.

Bea handed a parcel to the man sitting closest to her. He looked as though he was in his forties, tattoos across his fingers.

'What's this then? A box of handkerchiefs with my name embroidered on them?' He addressed the group, not Bea, and was rewarded with guffaws, but some of the tension was defused.

'Nothing much, just some things that might be useful. Have a look.' Bea watched as he tore off the wrapping paper. The others were more interested in a bottle of vodka that the woman was hanging on to amidst shouts of protest to pass it on.

The man picked through the contents of the parcel but seemed unimpressed. ''Ere, Joe, you could use this.' He threw a tube of toothpaste across the gravestone at an old man. There was more laughter but Joe pocketed the prize.

'I've got one for each of you,' Bea said, as she passed them around.

The woman grabbed her parcel and felt it as though trying to guess what was inside. 'I'll save it for Christmas Day,' she whispered to Bea and Bea felt like crying. If only she could give her more.

'What the fuck!' The man who had received the first parcel was reading the flier.

Bea's face went hot.

'Fucking models? You taking the piss or somethin'? Hartleys? Like we shop there?' He screwed up the flier and tossed it away.

'Go buy us some booze,' a man with a thick beard said.

'Yeah. Get more vodka,' the woman said.

They were all looking at Bea. Laughter had turned to aggression as it often did when people were drunk.

Bea clambered up. 'Okay.' She had no intention of buying them alcohol but it was an excuse to make her escape. Three unopened parcels lay abandoned between the gravestones but she couldn't take them back. This wasn't going very well at all.

'Bloody do-gooders,' a voice shouted after Bea.

In her hurry to get away, Bea took the wrong turn and found herself deep within a copse. A twig snapped behind her. Convinced that she was being followed, Bea blundered on, afraid to turn around and meet her pursuer. She prayed that she would come across an exit to the street. Bea couldn't face walking back past the winos. Then she came to a brick wall, too high to climb. If she followed the wall it should lead to an opening. A rustling of leaves and a thump from behind. Bea ran. She stumbled as her feet found hollows and slid across the damp, slippery leaves. Footsteps were close behind. *Thump. Thump.*

'Wait,' a man shouted.

Bea crashed through the trees, no longer looking where she was going. *Whack.* She fell hard onto her back. Everything hurt. The footsteps were running towards her. Bea tried to get up but she couldn't move; the pain in her back, her foot, and her head rendered her helpless.

36

EIGHTEEN SHOPPING DAYS TO CHRISTMAS

'Why didn't you stop when I shouted?' An Asian man was standing over her. His face came in and out of focus.

'What happened?' She had been running away from someone or something.

'You hit your head on a low-hanging branch.'

Bea wriggled her legs experimentally and cried out as a sharp pain burned in her ankle.

'Don't move. Just lie still for a few minutes, that was quite a blow to your head.'

Bea tried to look at him but the light was too bright and so she closed her eyes.

'Do you mind if I take a look at that ankle?'

Bea shook her head. She wanted to ask him who he was and why he had shouted for her to wait. Had she dropped something? That's right, she was delivering parcels to homeless people.

He eased off her ankle boot.

'Ouch.'

'Sorry. It's a bit swollen but you may have just sprained it. How's your head?'

Bea opened her eyes again; the light was less harsh but she had an almighty headache. 'I should be okay now but thanks for stopping.'

The man was still nursing her foot. 'I think that you'd better come back with me until we're sure that you don't need to see a doctor.'

Bea yanked her foot from his grasp and cried out in pain. Then, with lots of *ow, ow, ows,* she struggled to her feet. 'Ooh, a bit dizzy.' She put a hand to her head as the forest swayed. What was she doing in a forest?

'Please, let me look after you until you're feeling a bit better. We can jump in a cab and be back at my place in ten minutes.'

No. No. No. She didn't know this man. His face was familiar but it triggered feelings of panic and distrust. 'I don't know you.'

The man smiled. 'My name's Ash. I'm a friend of Ryan O'Marley.'

Bea felt woozy and lost her balance. Ash caught her. 'Steady.'

She took a closer look. 'I saw you talking to Ryan outside the *Fandangle* and my flat. How did you know where I lived?' Could he have been responsible for putting the glove in her bed?

'Ryan told me to meet him there. Are you okay?'

Bea struggled to her feet. A raucous laugh came from the graveyard and Bea remembered her embarrassing encounter with the winos. Then she spotted her carrier bags where they had tumbled, the remaining red and green parcels strewn across the glade like Christmas decorations. Ash followed her gaze.

'Don't worry, I'll pick them up.'

'Were you following me?'

Ash had his back to her as he gathered the parcels. Now was her chance to escape but even if she did try to run away, it would be more of a hobble and Ash would have to support her, which would defeat the purpose.

'I was. Ryan asked me to keep an eye on you.'

On hearing his name Bea was filled with warmth and a longing to see him.

'Do you know where he is?'

'I do.' He tucked the parcels into Bea's bag. 'I can take you to him.'

Bea wasn't sure whether she could trust this man. What if it was a ruse to entice her to go with him? If he had tried to push her on the platform and then put the glove in her bed, what else was he capable of? Despite these thoughts, Bea instinctively felt that she could trust this man. He had gentle eyes and a soft voice. If Ryan had asked him to keep an eye on her, then he did care. It wasn't her imagination. To see Ryan now would make everything okay. She had to see him. 'Where is Ryan?'

'At my place. It's not far but we'll have to take a cab. You can't walk anywhere. In fact, we should really take you to the hospital.'

'I'm okay. Can we go to Ryan straight away?' Bea hated hospitals and now that she knew Ryan was within reach, she didn't want to waste another minute in finding him.

The cab took them to a street of terraced houses in Islington. Some of the houses were smart with newly painted front doors, shiny door knockers, and black glossy railings. Others were tired and neglected. Ash led Bea up the steps to the front door of a particularly grubby-looking house. Yellowed labels identified the occupants of the flats with an assortment of buzzers and bells. Ash supported Bea with one arm as he opened the door. Although her head still throbbed, Bea's vision and balance had improved. Her ankle however was extremely painful and without Ash's support she would have had trouble walking.

'We'll get some ice on that once you're sitting down,' Ash said.

The house smelt of stale and pungent spices from meals once cooked behind the many closed doors. The carpet, an indistinguishable colour, had absorbed the odours of cat wee and cigarette smoke.

'How many people live in this house?' Bea asked, giving a silent prayer for her good fortune in securing her beautiful garden flat.

'Twenty-four, I think. Six bedsits on each floor and there are four floors. Oh, and a basement, so at least a couple down there, I should think. The landlord crams in as many people as he can. One more step. Are you alright there?'

Bea nodded as she supported herself on the stair bannister and Ash unlocked the door to his bedsit. 'Hold on a minute.' He disappeared inside.

Ryan was behind that door. Ash would be telling him that he had found Bea. What if Ash was wrong and Ryan didn't want to see her? It felt as though a bat was hurtling around in her belly trying to break free.

The door opened and Bea's heart stopped. It was Ryan. He was clean shaven and his hair once again a startling blonde.

'Sure enough, it's Bea Stevens. I didn't believe what I was hearing. And will you look at that gash on your head. Oh Bea, what have you been doing to yourself?'

His voice full of warmth and camaraderie warmed Bea's heart.

Ash peered over Ryan's shoulder. 'Help her in. We need to get some ice on that ankle.'

Bea allowed them to settle her in a threadbare armchair and arrange the furniture so that she could raise her wounded ankle on a coffee table. Ash found a bag of frozen peas to place on her foot. Bea squirmed; she hated the feeling of ice against her skin.

'Can't you find a towel to wrap those in?' Ryan said, catching the expression on Bea's face. How did he know her so well?

'I should go and buy some ibuprofen,' Ash said when he returned with a dirty grey hand towel.

'No. Don't go anywhere.' Bea closed her eyes. 'We need to talk about Declan.'

37

APRIL 2017

Handcuffed in the back of the police car, Ryan was escorted from the ferry to the police station in Holyhead. His jaw may have been broken. His knuckles bled. Battered, bruised, and bloody, but Ryan felt at peace, the rage within exorcised. The beating he had given the thug was deserved but it was something else that had fired his fury: an anger that had been brewing the past two years.

A police officer took Ryan's statement. The other lads must have been interviewed in different rooms as he hadn't seen them since the police boarded the ferry. His intention had been to break up the fight but then he just lost it. Forgetting his tender jaw, Ryan covered his face with his hands and then yelped in pain. He had been the last man fighting. Voices were calling him off but he had lost control, and then an officer was pulling him away from the man who lay on the deck, curled up like a hedgehog.

'What happens next?' Ryan asked. Surely, they would let them all off with a warning. How could the police determine who was to blame? It was just a brawl.

The police officer did not reply. She left Ryan alone in the room. He should have caught the express train to Euston Station. By now, he would be in London ready to start a new life. The adrenaline had left him and Ryan felt ashamed. He was an eejit. It wasn't even his fight. At thirty years old you'd have thought he would have learnt when to walk away.

'We need to take photographs of your injuries.' Ryan was escorted to another room for this procedure and the taking of fingerprints.

Eventually, a more purposeful confident policeman met with Ryan and he surmised that this was a senior officer. 'Where are you staying in the UK?' he said.

'London. I have an address in my rucksack. I'm renting a flat.'

'I'll need the address and confirmation from your landlord before you leave.'

Ryan sighed with relief. He wasn't going to be sent directly to prison or kept in a cell overnight. They would sort this out and he would be settled in Peacock Court before the end of the day.

'We'll need to be able to contact you when we have a date for your hearing.'

All the nerves in Ryan's body stood to attention. 'What hearing? What are you charging me with?' He took a deep breath to cool his temper.

'Mr Fenton, the man who you attacked, is pressing charges for GBH. We think the lesser charge of ABH more appropriate, given your statement and the nature of Mr Fenton's injuries. However, it's yet to be decided.'

'What about *my* injuries? Can't I press charges too?'

The police officer smiled. 'I wouldn't advise that, Mr O'Marley. Hopefully, your case will be heard in a magistrates' court and the sentence will be minimal. That's if you're sensible and don't contest the charge or make a counterclaim. I shouldn't be saying this but Mr Fenton has connections. If he didn't, we would probably have let you all off with a warning.'

At last Ryan arrived at Euston Station. His excitement at starting a new life in the big city had been squashed; all he could think of was the trial and whether he would get a prison sentence. Everyone around him seemed to know where they were going as they dragged cases or marched with intention, talking business on mobile phones. Nobody seemed aware of anyone else, as though they were the only people on the planet. Maybe he was just a country lad.

A teenage boy sat huddled by a wall outside the station and Ryan found five euros for him. He had instructions to telephone his landlord as soon as he arrived so that he could collect the key and with renewed optimism he made that call. He would miss the beauty of his homeland, the lush green fields of Ireland, but there was something vibrant about London. His new life was about to begin.

'I've arrived. A bit later than expected but I'm ready to collect the key.' Ryan smiled at a mum who was wiping chocolate from the face of her toddler.

'I'm sorry, Mr O'Marley, but we can't release the key to you.'

The mum wheeled the pushchair past Ryan, but he was no longer smiling.

'Why? I need it tonight, I've nowhere else to stay. You said it would be ready for me today – this afternoon.'

'Hold on a moment, you need to speak to my boss.'

A man came on the line, someone Ryan hadn't spoken to

before. 'I understand that you were detained by the police earlier today.'

He didn't think that the police would have made immediate contact. Eejit, he should have guessed and given them the wrong number, said he couldn't remember and would let them know later – after getting the key.

'I haven't been charged with anything. It was all a misunderstanding.'

'I'm sorry but we have to decline your application as your right to rent and references don't meet with our scrupulous standards.'

'But you can't do that. I've handed over six thousand euros as a deposit and rent.'

'It's in the contract that you signed.'

'Well, you've got to be giving me my money back.'

'No, we don't. It's all in the contract.' And then, after muttering some nonsense about legal processes, the man hung up.

Ryan stared at his phone in disbelief and then flung it across the square. *Eejit. Eeejit. Eejit.* Now he had busted his phone. A middle-aged woman glared at him as though he had shouted the profanities that crowded his head. They couldn't do that. He had handed over all of his savings. All he had left was – Ryan checked his wallet – a hundred and twenty euros. Enough to go straight back to Ireland but what would he say? Da would mock him and he would lose all self-respect. He could afford one night in a hotel, but then what? The police wouldn't be able to find him. Should he tell them that he had no address? No, they would deport him.

It was dark now and Ryan was exhausted after his journey and the fight and trauma that followed. He would use what little money he had to buy a sleeping bag and find somewhere to bed down for the night. Maybe talk to the kid he'd seen earlier; he would know the best places. Tomorrow, he would search for some work – casual labour as a carpenter. Life in the city hadn't started out as he had hoped, but it could only get better.

38

EIGHTEEN SHOPPING DAYS TO CHRISTMAS

Ryan and Ash exchanged a glance, as if trying to signal to one another how much they could tell Bea. She had to come clean and tell them that she was already involved. It felt too hard and so she started with another confession.

'I knew Declan before he was homeless. If it wasn't for me he might still be carefree and safe, the way I remember him.'

Bea stole a look at Ryan, but could not read his face.

'You can't take all the credit. It was my fault he became homeless,' Ash said.

'And mine that he's missing and possibly even...' Ryan didn't finish the sentence but they knew what he meant. Finding Declan alive was becoming less certain with the passing of each day. He wouldn't have abandoned his friends. Everyone who knew Declan described him as good-natured, generous, and loyal. She felt a deep shame at how she had wronged him – not the reporting of his staying overnight in the store, she was just doing her job – the fact that she had walked past him every day on her way in and out of work without even seeing him. Bea couldn't forgive herself for that. How could she have been so selfish, so self-obsessed?

Ash closed his eyes as though in silent prayer. Ryan looked as though Declan had died and that he was responsible. His sadness pierced Bea's heart. She wanted to hug him and tell him that everything would be okay. Maybe it would if they worked together. If Declan was alive, they had to find him.

'If you both tell me everything you know about Declan's disappearance. His last movements on the night he went missing. *Everything*.'

Ryan sighed. 'Oh, Bea. You don't know what you're asking.'

It wasn't going to be easy getting Ryan to share his troubles. Whatever he was mixed up in he didn't want to involve Bea. She was going to have to tell him that she already knew too much.

Ash took a deep breath. 'I loved Dec. We fell in love when I was a student in Dublin. I'd never had a boyfriend before, but there was something special about Dec.' His voice faltered and he turned his head, wiping away a tear. 'I miss him every day.'

Ryan put a hand on Ash's shoulder and Ash continued. 'When I moved back to London, I didn't expect to see him again. Like a holiday romance – but a uni one.' He gave a laugh full of sorrow.

'Nobody here knew that I was gay. My family are strict Muslims. I couldn't tell them about Dec, it would bring shame on my family. I know I was a coward. I should have been proud to be Dec's boyfriend – I was, but it had to be kept a secret. Dec surprised me when he turned up on my doorstep. It was an awesome surprise. I was ecstatic to see him. But when he said that he was going to live in London and expected to stay in my bedsit, I didn't know what to do. Do you mind?' Ash picked up a box of cigarettes.

Bea shook her head. As he lit one, she noticed that his hand was shaking.

'If I had more courage I would have invited him to live with me. I loved him. I love him. It's my fault he's gone missing. If anything has happened to him, I'll never forgive myself.'

'You're not responsible and neither is Bea. Maybe if you'd kept your mouth shut instead of blathering, Declan wouldn't have lost his job. Maybe he would have found somewhere to live and not ended up on the street.'

It took a couple of seconds before Bea realised Ryan was talking about her, and then she went cold. 'Who told you?'

'Roots.'

Bea tried to remember exactly what she had said to Roots, the day he walked out of the *Fandangle* in a strop. It had been enough for him to put two and two together.

'It doesn't matter, Bea. I'm not blaming you. You're no more responsible for what happened to Declan than Ash.'

'You must have hated me when you found out.'

'No. It made sense when Roots told me. If I hadn't got to know you then I might have hated you, but no – I could never hate you, Bea. And you weren't responsible for what happened to Declan, not really. I was.'

'I'll make some coffee and a camomile tea,' Ash said, getting up. His movement broke some of the tension in the room. 'How's your foot, Bea?'

She didn't want to make a fuss when her injury was nothing compared to what might have happened to Declan, but her head ached and she still felt woozy. 'I'm not great, but I'll survive.'

'We shouldn't be throwing all this at you. I'm not convinced that you shouldn't see a doctor. How about Ryan makes the drinks and I pop out for some ibuprofen?' Ash said.

Bea was grateful for some quiet time. Whilst Ryan cluttered away at the tiny counter that was an excuse for a kitchenette, Bea closed her eyes. Cold water trickled down her ankle and she adjusted the towel to absorb the condensation. The burning shame that Ryan knew her indifference to Declan as she passed him on the street was uncomfortable. 'You don't have to wait on me, Ryan. I'm fine now, really.' Bea sat up in her chair; she didn't deserve his kindness.

'Ah, be sitting still, you're doing grand. Here.' He handed her a mug of coffee. Bea dried her foot with the towel. It was a little swollen but she could rotate her ankle without crying out in pain.

Ash returned with a paper bag. 'How are you feeling?'

'Better, thanks. Just a headache and a sore ankle.'

'Do you feel sick or dizzy?'

'Not really.'

Ash gave Bea a couple of tablets to swallow with water but refused to take any money from her. They drank their coffee mostly in silence, knowing that there was still much to tell. Ryan took up from where Ash had left off.

'Declan was a good mate. We met on the ferry from Holyhead a couple of years back. It seems much longer.' He paused, maybe reflecting on all that had happened since. 'Some stuck-up louts had it in for him. Gave him a beating.'

'Bastards.' Ash spat out the word, his face tight with anguish.

'So, I did what anyone would do. I went for them.'

'You had a fight?' Bea asked.

'Ooh yes. Quite a fight. I just lost it. Police pulled me off. Threatened to charge me because the guy I knocked out had connections high up.'

'That's not fair, when the other men started it,' Bea said.

'There's a lot in this world that's not fair,' Ryan said. 'I should have reported back to a police station in London but I never did. When I became homeless they had no way of finding me and so I never found out if I had been charged.'

'I was jealous of your friendship with Dec,' Ash said. 'I shouldn't have been. And then when he went missing, I blamed you for getting him into trouble.'

'It was my fault. Declan wanted to see justice done. He didn't blame Bea or you for making him homeless, but by Jaysus he wouldn't let the villains who stitched me up get away with it.'

'That's what I don't understand. Who 'stitched you up'? How was Declan defending you? Does it have anything to do with the spreadsheet in Declan's bag?'

Ryan's shoulders tensed and he turned to stare at Bea. 'How do you know what's in that bag?'

The confession had not come out the way that she had planned.

'Never mind. It makes sense now. That's how you attracted attention to yourself. Ash told me that he was following one of the villains and saw him jostle you on a train platform.'

'It was you who grabbed my arm?'

'Yep, me again,' Ash said.

Bea tried to recall if she had seen him and then gave up. Thank goodness he had saved her. She daren't think what might have happened if he hadn't been there. 'You said that Declan was going to meet someone in an office near Trafalgar Square, the night he went missing?' Now was her opportunity to find out exactly what was going on.

'We must have got it wrong,' Ash said.

'I told you. There was nobody there. Just empty office space.'

'But why? What are you involved in, Ryan? You have to tell me so that I can help you.'

'That's exactly why I can't tell you, Bea. I stopped seeing

you so that you didn't get more involved. When Ash told me that someone tried to push you under a train, I knew I had done the right thing. Jaysus! First Declan and now you. I couldn't bear it. *Please* promise me you will forget everything. Where's the bag now?'

'I put it back where I found it,' Bea said.

'Okay.' Ryan took a deep breath. 'Have you told me everything?'

She couldn't tell Ryan about the glove. He would definitely keep his distance then, or put himself at more risk by confronting her intruder. The thought of the glove made her retch. Ash grabbed a used cereal bowl from the sink. 'Use this.'

The nausea passed with no need for the bowl but Bea was shaken.

'That's enough for today,' Ash said.

'No. You have to tell me more. What do the spreadsheets mean? Are you and Declan involved in some dodgy business, Ryan?'

Ryan's face darkened and Bea recognised the same anger she had experienced briefly the day he left her. If only she didn't blurt things out. It was hard thinking of the right things to say and the right tone. With a thumping headache and a throbbing ankle, she didn't stand a chance at subtlety.

'It doesn't matter what you've done. I just want to help you, Ryan.'

'And that is exactly what I don't want you to do. I told you to forget about it.'

'I think it's time I took you to A & E,' Ash said.

'Declan must have been onto something,' Bea persisted.

'*That*.' Ryan stabbed a finger at Bea. '*That* is what I'm afraid of. You're relentless when you want something. I thought Declan was tenacious but you are savage. I should have just stayed away from you.'

Please don't, Bea wanted to beg. Nothing mattered so long as she had Ryan in her life. Blood on her hands. The warning was clear. Lives were at stake if she meddled in this business. Her involvement was risky for all of them, but to walk away as Ryan wanted her to would be to give in to these bullies. She couldn't do that. It wasn't right.

'Let's cool it.' Ash put up his hands. 'I'm going to drop Bea off at A & E. Don't shake your head, Bea, you've got to be checked over.'

Ryan's face had relaxed a little but his body was still tense. 'If you don't go I might have to phone your mum.'

Bea was about to protest when she realised he was teasing. They shared a look, one that made Bea feel as though she had been forgiven, but she couldn't promise Ryan that she would forget about the spreadsheet. Whatever mystery Declan had been trying to solve, she was going to finish what he had started.

Reluctantly Bea allowed Ash to phone for a cab. 'Before I go, take my new address. Mum sold the flat and I've got to leave before Christmas. Oh, and here's a Christmas present for you.' She tossed a parcel to Ryan. 'And you, Ash. It's nothing much, just a few odds and ends. Ignore the flier inside – it was a moment of madness. Ryan knows that I'm prone to those.'

Bea suspected that she wouldn't see Ryan for some time. She was going to miss him. 'You will come and find me, Ryan? As soon as you can?'

Ryan nodded. 'Of course. You need someone to remind you not to wear Jimmy's shoes when you're walking on ice. And I see that you're still wearing heels. Haven't you got a pair of snow boots?' He was trying to lighten the mood and she loved him for it.

'Only *little* heels. I don't even know what snow boots are.'

39

EIGHTEEN SHOPPING DAYS TO CHRISTMAS

If she hadn't vomited spectacularly missing a cardboard bedpan and spraying the toes of a pretty Polish nurse, Bea might have been sent home from Accident and Emergency with a dressing on her forehead and instructions to take it easy. However, vomiting was one of the indicators on a list that a male nurse was checking against Bea's symptoms.

'I can't be admitted,' Bea snapped. Suki Dee's event was in eighteen days and so far, she had just one designer and Sav didn't even have a collection ready. Her day spent as Santa Claus had not brought her any closer to recruiting models. No models. No recycled designer collections. She shouldn't even be wasting her time waiting to see a doctor. 'I've got to go.'

'Irritability.' The nurse clicked his tongue and put a hand on Bea's shoulder, pinning her to the chair.

'I'm not irritable. It's the noise in here and the lights.' She felt disorientated and giddy, hating too much stimulation at the best of times, being in A & E was a nightmare, not helped by her sensitivity to the light.

The nurse pursed his lips and then rolled his eyes at Ash.

'I can't do this. I've got to get out!' Bea felt panicked. It was the air, hot and thick with the coppery smell of blood and antiseptic.

'Let's move her into a cubicle so that she can lie down,' the nurse said to Ash as if Bea wasn't there, and they each took one of her arms.

When Bea had been settled on a trolley behind some curtains, a sick bowl tucked by her side, the nurse said, 'I don't like the look of her.'

That was a bit personal, Bea didn't much like the look of him either. 'I don't always dress like this, it was because I was being Mother Christmas.'

'Hmm, change in behaviour,' the nurse said. 'Leave her with us, I'll get her admitted to the assessment ward for twenty-four hours. You say that she lives on her own? Is there a next of kin we can contact?'

Forty-eight hours. She wouldn't be discharged until Saturday night. Two days when she should be working.

'What's your parents' number?' Ash said.

'You mustn't tell my mum. *Please* don't contact her. Okay, if I'm dying and you *really* have to –'

'Take my number,' Ash interrupted Bea. The nurse gave him a sideways look and they grinned at each other. As Ash passed him his phone number their hands met and lingered for a few seconds. *Don't mind me,* Bea thought. *I'm only the patient.*

And so, Bea was admitted to a busy, noisy ward, dressed in a hospital gown. The forty-eight hours passed in a confusion of waking and sleeping, of doctors shining torches into her eyes, nurses inflating an armband and prodding her with a cold thermometer. Fortunately, she wasn't sick again and painkillers relieved her headache. By nine on Saturday evening, Bea was discharged home in a cab. Her phone had been stored in a bedside locker and so Bea had missed the two voice messages from Alastair and a couple of emails.

The first voicemail said to call Alastair as soon as she got the message. The next the same, but more impatient. Then, 'Where are you, Stevens? Blast you. I told you to keep in touch at all times.' He muttered to himself as he disconnected. Oh dear, Alastair was really pissed. Bea switched to email. The first was sent early in the day and simply said that Alastair had been unable to contact her by phone and could she telephone him.

The next email started *Dear Miss Stevens.* That wasn't a good sign. Mr Evans had been copied in; this was going to be bad. The words blurred and a sharp pain stabbed at her temple. Bea couldn't look at the screen; it was making her nauseas. She would wait until she got home and then minimise any damage. Why hadn't she just phoned Alastair on Friday morning to let him know she was in hospital? Now he thought she had gone AWOL. It didn't help that she had admitted the task was impossible and offered her resignation from the role. Not contacting Alastair since Thursday morning when she had tried to persuade him that she had just been overreacting, it was no wonder he was spooked. If the Suki Dee event was a disaster or cancelled at short notice, Alastair would take some of the flak. Bea couldn't blame him for trying to protect himself, but couldn't he have given her time to explain before involving Evans?

The unread email taunted Bea. She couldn't ignore it any longer and once she was sitting at her kitchen table with a mug of camomile tea – because she thought it might calm her – she opened it and prepared for the worst. It read like a formal warning – *you've got to get your act together or you'll be out.* Not in those words. The email said that Suki Dee was visiting the store on Monday for a dress fitting and would like an update on arrangements for her charity event. Alastair wanted a written progress report from Bea by midday yesterday. The email went on to say that he was disappointed in her failure to communicate, despite clear instructions from him to do so, and that if he wasn't satisfied that adequate arrangements had been made, he would be recommending that Bea step down from leading the project.

Bea didn't blame Alastair; he was covering his back. She still had a chance to turn things around. Suki Dee wanted an update on Monday. Bea had made some progress; she just had to come over as confident and in control. After sending a conciliatory email to Alastair explaining that she had been admitted to hospital but would be back at work on Monday, Bea crawled into bed.

40

FOURTEEN SHOPPING DAYS TO CHRISTMAS

By Sunday, Bea was feeling stronger. She could go a couple of hours without a headache and only felt dizzy or sick when looking at a computer screen. No closer to finding a leading recycled fashion designer, she tweeted an invitation for recycle designers to contact her if they would like to show their collection at a high-profile event in December. There may be fashion school graduates like Sav who would jump at the chance for the exposure that Hartleys could offer. That was all she could do, for now.

Apart from seeing Ryan again, the best thing that had happened in the past few days was securing her wonderful flat. Bea hugged this gift to her and felt a warm light of optimism. As affirmation that all would be well, and because she needed to get out of the flat, Bea took the Tube to Holloway Road. It was unlikely that she would be able to take another peek at her new home, but she could explore the area – find the best coffee shop and discover any hidden treasures. In the three years that she lived in Kings Cross, Bea had only just discovered the wonders of the canal and she wasn't going to make that mistake again.

This new home signified a new start. *I'll join in more, maybe go to an evening class for advanced Russian. I'll invite Leila to supper – first I'll have to learn how to cook.* In Bea's imagined world she was a different person, transformed into a domestic goddess with a diary full of social engagements. As she had already ventured into a land of fantasy she went further and imagined Ryan at her side, teasing her playfully at her shortcomings whilst beaming with pride. And then she saw Peacock Court. That was the address on Ryan's deposit confirmation. Lost in thought, she had wandered far from the Holloway Road. It was a wonder that her feet had taken her here, to the very address where Ryan had lived when he first came to London.

Peacock Court was impressive. Once three very grand houses, they had been converted into flats. Each had a porticoed entrance, with stone steps and glossy black railings. Bea had marvelled at her good fortune in finding the wonderful garden flat in Holloway, but this surpassed expectation. When Ryan mentioned that he was leaving his family farm when he met Declan on the ferry to Holyhead, she had assumed that he was from a poor farming community. To afford to live here, he must have been reasonably well off. Bea tried to make sense of the spreadsheet again. If only Ryan would tell her more about his life, it might shed some light on what had happened to Declan. For example, how had he come to be homeless?

Thinking made her head swim and Bea had to steady herself by clutching the railing to Peacock Court. It was foolish of her to have walked so far when she was meant to be resting and she still had the journey back unless there was a bus because she couldn't afford a taxi. A middle-aged man came out of the front door of number two.

Bea gave her best smile. 'Hold on.' She hurried up the steps as though she knew where she was going and he held the door open. 'Thanks.'

Ryan's flat was on the second floor, Flat D, 2 Peacock Court. Bea had tricked her way into the building, caught up in an imaginary world, where Ryan lived happily behind one of these doors. Now that she was standing in the carpeted hallway, two flats on either side and a staircase to the second and third floor, Bea felt foolish.

A girl leant over the bannister, her blonde hair falling in skeins like Rapunzel. 'Can I help you?'

Caught unawares, Bea astounded herself by tripping out a plausible lie. 'My friend rented flat D, a couple of years back. We kind of lost contact and I was wondering if he left a forwarding address or something.'

'Oh. I see,' the girl said, as though she understood too well Bea's true motive.

It took a few seconds for Bea to catch on. 'Oh no. It's not like that. He wasn't a boyfriend or anything,' she stuttered.

A flash of gold as sun from a skylight danced on the girl's hair. She lifted her head and the light was gone. 'You must have the wrong address, these are all owner occupied.' It was said with an air of contempt as if renting a property was a sign of social status. Bea thought of Ryan now; the only place he could call home was the rat-infested *Moby*.

'Although, the owners of flat D did try to let it on Airbnb when they went on a round-the-world trip a couple of years ago. The residents' committee put a stop to that, after a few undesirables got in. Look, have you got an appointment with someone in this house? If not, you'll have to leave. Jeff should never have let you in. I've told him about that before.'

The girl had to be mistaken; Bea had seen the deposit confirmation, although it was ridiculously low for a property this opulent. 'Maybe I could have a quick word with the owners of flat D' she said.

The girl sighed. 'I'd better introduce you so that Marlene doesn't blame Jeff for letting you in. The residents' committee are coming down hard on that sort of behaviour. I wish he would listen.'

Bea felt sorry for getting Jeff into trouble. He was going to get an earful from Rapunzel.

Marlene was much more accommodating than the girl and invited Bea into her home. A slinky grey cat wound itself around Bea's legs as she sat in an armchair waiting for Marlene to return with coffee. It was good to rest. Bea closed her eyes, bright lights played behind her eyelids, and a sharp pain bored into her temple.

'You've gone very pale.' Marlene stood over Bea holding a tray of coffee and biscuits.

'I'm sorry, I shouldn't have bothered you. It's just that I was passing and I knew this address.' She was rambling, her tongue felt thick and clumsy in her mouth. 'I…I…should be at home resting. The hospital said…'

'Oh dear.' Marlene sounded a little afraid. 'Is there someone you'd like me to call?'

'No. No thank you.' The words that Bea should say wouldn't come to mind. Even if she wasn't suffering from a mild concussion, Bea would have found this social situation challenging. A few weeks ago, she wouldn't have dreamed of walking into a stranger's home.

Marlene perched on the edge of a sofa, as though ready to run. 'You said that your friend rented our flat a couple of years ago?'

'Yes. Yes.' Bea tried to focus on why she was there. 'He paid a deposit and everything,' she stumbled on.

'Oh dear,' Marlene said again. 'We didn't know anything

about it. I'm so sorry. Of course, once we found out, we stopped letting the flat. What's your friend's name?'

Marlene wasn't making any sense in Bea's muddled brain. She took a sip of coffee and the luxurious grey cat jumped up and made itself a nest in her lap.

'If he's bothering you tip him out.' Marlene relaxed back against a cushion, for some reason she now seemed reassured that Bea wasn't mentally unstable. 'I've kept some of the tenants' post. It was the least that I could do.'

'Ryan O'Marley,' Bea said as she stroked the cat's bony spine.

'Help yourself to a biscuit. I'll have a look in the drawer. O'Marley. It rings a bell.'

It was a beautiful flat. Three tall sash windows looked onto the street, where a watery winter sun reflected off the roofs of cars. Bea hoped that Ryan had been happy here for at least a few months before he became homeless. He knew so much about her, but shared so little about his life. It was as though he were ashamed of what had become of him.

'Here, I thought I had a letter for Ryan O'Marley. It's a bit old, I'm afraid. I do hope it wasn't urgent.' Marlene passed Bea a white envelope with a handwritten address. Before she released her grip, Marlene said, 'Will you be sure to give it to Mr O'Marley?'

'Yes. I promise.'

Bea tucked the letter in her handbag. She'd seen what she came for – the flat where Ryan once lived. And she had a letter to send on to him at Ash's address.

Soon Bea would be living in her new garden flat. It wasn't quite as grand as the flat Ryan rented but not far off. Leila was wrong, there were some beautiful flats to be rented in central London for a fraction of the cost she had suggested. Bea had a surge of elation. Tomorrow Suki Dee was visiting the store.

She would be calm and confident, restoring Alastair's faith in her. The last few days had been a blip: the shock of finding her glove, a sleepless night, and then the concussion. Now, she was back on track. As she waited for the 73 bus to take her home, Bea glowed with positivity.

41

NOVEMBER 2017

The white van was parked a couple of streets away from the soup kitchen, but Ryan knew the number plate and so he was prepared. He'd been living on the streets for seven months and although he would never get used to the dehumanisation and barbarity that he experienced each and every day, he had at least learnt how to keep himself safe. The first night he slept rough; he was woken in the early hours by a drunk pissing on the pavement, the spray of his urine spotting Ryan's cheek. Disgusted and furious, Ryan packed up and walked the streets until dawn trying to keep warm. He soon learnt that being pissed on was the least of his worries. The homeless – that faceless pack of sub humans, were fair game for thugs, unscrupulous police officers, and other rough sleepers. There were no-sleep zones and that included many of the hostels. Soup kitchens, food banks, church shelters, and drop-ins provided some structure to Ryan's week; he got to know other rough sleepers and volunteers and had even found some casual work from time to time which had supplemented his jobseeker's allowance, until it stopped last month. He tried to look out for newbies; their bewildered expressions and the way that they clung on tightly to their possessions marked them out. Like the kid who was hanging outside the soup kitchen as if unsure whether or not to go in. Ryan passed him without speaking. He would go inside in his own time, when hunger had won out over humiliation.

The scum from the white van were already inside, loitering close to the queue pretending to be homeless. Ryan caught Jenny's eye as she ladled lentil and vegetable stew into a young woman's bowl. The woman turned and passed the bowl to a child; he couldn't have been more than five years old. Stew slopped over the sides of the bowl, making orange splashes on the grey tiled floor. Ryan saw that the woman had a baby strapped to her front and went to help.

'Shall I carry that, mate?' he said to the child. The boy shrunk back hugging his bowl.

'You'll be alright with Ryan,' Jenny said to the woman.

The woman nodded to her son and he let Ryan take his bowl.

'Let's find you a table,' Ryan said.

'Don't worry, I've got my eye on them,' Jenny said in answer to Ryan's questioning look. The men in the white van had been making frequent appearances and during that time at least two regulars had disappeared.

Ryan sat alone eating his stew. Jenny had slipped him a couple of extra rolls, which he had stowed away for later. The weather was still mild but autumn would soon turn to winter and Ryan was glad that he had friends like Jenny, people who he would have to rely upon if he was to survive his first winter on the streets. He watched the newbie join the queue. Someone else had their eye on him – one of the scum from the white van.

Seeing the young woman with her kids reminded Ryan of Caitlin. He hadn't communicated with her since leaving Ireland and he knew that she would be worried and sad. He was sad too. He missed his little sis, even when she was in New Zealand they had kept in contact with emails, texts, and the occasional phone call. He had given her his Peacock Court address but her letters would have been returned unanswered – 'not known at this address'. What was she to think? That he had given her a false address so that he could break all ties with his past life? He would never hurt her like that, and yet he had. When he tried to imagine Caitlin's pain, and he did frequently as a kind of punishment, it hurt him like a hand squeezing tight around his heart. Once, when he was left waiting in a job centre office beside a phone he lifted the receiver hoping to make a quick call but he was disturbed before he had finished dialling. The woman was kind and invited him to make his call – she didn't know it was to Ireland – but Ryan declined, apologising profusely. It was his charm and good manners that had kept him afloat; he could not afford to get on the wrong side of people who had the power to smash his fragile world.

It was time to get back on the road. The volunteers were clearing away the pans of stew and old ladies from a local church were arriving with their leaflets about God's love, piety and compassion creasing their brows as they tilted their heads to tend to the poor.

'Want to earn a few bob – cash in hand?' One of the men from the white van was talking to the new kid. 'A guy I know has some work going. It's hard graft – bit of labouring if you're up for it.'

The kid's eyes sparked with light and Ryan's heart sunk. He didn't want to get involved but someone had to tell him.

'Sure. It's good of you to give me the nod.'

And he was Irish. Ryan couldn't turn away. 'Leave the kid alone.' He stood tall and threw back his shoulders. If he had to knock the guy out he would – for the two hopefuls who had jumped into the white van last month and never been seen since.

The man's mate joined him and they boxed Ryan in. 'What business is it of yours?'

Ryan was about to let his fists fly when Jenny pushed her way between them. 'You two are banned from this soup kitchen. Get away from here if you don't want to be questioned by the police.' Her voice was fierce but Ryan could see her hands shaking and he was sorry that he had put her in that position.

The men shouted a few obscenities. One of them spat at the ground by Jenny's feet but she continued to glare at them until they were out of sight. 'I've reported them, given the police the registration number of the van,' she said.

'Ryan? Ryan O'Marley?' the kid said when they were alone.

On hearing his name, Ryan felt as though he had been handed a gift; it was so rare to hear his name spoken and yet it was almost all that he had. But he couldn't place the kid. Maybe he was from Cork, a kid brother of one of his schoolmates.

'This is the second time that you've saved me. I didn't get to thank you the first time. You've no idea how pleased I am to find you. Declan. Remember?'

Ryan hadn't forgotten the incident; he might have been living in his fancy London flat if not for the brawl, but he didn't expect to see Declan again, certainly not in a soup kitchen.

'I went looking for you,' Declan said and Ryan felt as though someone at last cared about *him*, Ryan. Not just as a homeless man who needed their charity.

'You gave me your address – Peacock Court, Angel. It's a poetic address to be sure.'

'Yes, I said we'd have ourselves a pint of Guinness together. Can't offer you anything like that now.'

'If I had the money I would be buying you a bottle of whiskey, never mind a pint. You got arrested for defending me and I never got to thank you.'

They fell into step together and without discussing where they were headed they walked and talked until they found themselves on the canal tow path by the Islington tunnel. Declan told Ryan about his surprise visit to Ash and the disappointment that came a day or two later when, after a blissful reunion, Ash explained that Declan couldn't live with him. He told him about the temporary job in a department store, where the security guards turned a blind eye to him bedding down at night, and how that all ended. Ash took him back but things didn't work out and so he had been sleeping rough for the past three weeks. There was no bitterness in Declan's voice; he sounded as optimistic and full of life as he had seven months ago when he talked of his plans on the ferry.

'So, you were duped,' Declan said when they were resting on a bench watching the flow of water as it gently butted against the barges.

This was Ryan's favourite place. He had stayed close to the Angel, liking the image that the name conjured, and because it was where he was headed when he arrived in this foreign city. The canal and some of the green spaces along its bank were a find. He was even on nodding terms with a few of the people who lived in the houseboats.

He offered Declan his water bottle. 'Duped? How so?'

'The scam. I went to Peacock Court and heard how a fraudster had conned people by getting them to pay the deposit on a flat that wasn't available for rent. The owners were overseas at the time. I heard it all from the caretaker. The residents' committee were up in arms but the owners tried to play it down because they were afraid that they would be implicated. Fortunately, only a few people were duped, but that's no help to you, mate.'

'You mean I would have lost the flat anyway? Even if I hadn't been arrested?'

'You never had it, friend.'

For seven months Ryan had believed it was his temper that had lost him his home and savings. Hearing that it was his stupidity did not make him feel any better. But he was so mad. So angry. He wanted to get hold of the shithead who had done this to him and squeeze the living breath out of him.

Declan touched his arm and the warmth of his friendship eased some of the tautness in his muscles. 'You saved me twice. I'll help you get even. We'll find the people responsible and make them pay.'

Ryan had no idea how they would do this but Declan's solidarity and friendship made him strong. They would find a way.

42

FOURTEEN SHOPPING DAYS TO CHRISTMAS

'A goodwill ambassador. Or a medal, like.' Suki fluttered her manicured hands, the golden talons mesmerising Bea, who was sitting on the opposite couch, as though it was every day she had an audience with the star. 'What do you call it?' She clicked her fingers.

'A Victoria Cross?' Bea said, feeling that some response was required from her. Alastair shot her a warning look. He had told Bea to say as little as possible.

'Shakira got a medal from the United Nations Labour Agency for her work to help children. I thought *Suki*, it's time you used your power and influence to make a difference in the world.' She dipped her head for two beats and then shone her beautiful face at them – camera-ready.

'That's very commendable. Hartleys would be honoured to play a small part in your humanitarian journey,' Alastair said.

Suki beamed and sat back in her chair. 'I can't wait to hear what you have planned for me.'

Alastair and Bea exchanged a look. They had met beforehand, for what Alastair called a frank and meaningful discussion about Bea's position at Hartleys, and the event. He was, he said, trying to risk assess the situation. Somehow, Bea had managed to convince him that she was on the edge of creating something marvellous. It was an exaggeration, but Bea had nothing to lose. If the event was a disaster she would lose her job, but if she backed out now then she would have a couple of months grace working as a junior in the toy department before being kicked out anyway. Bea believed that against all of the odds she could pull it off. It was too important not to. Everything depended upon her success. Her amazing flat. A life in London. The career she had always dreamed of. It was within her grasp. She just had to spin straw into gold.

'Your PR team would have reported back on our initial plans,' Alastair started.

'Yes, yes.' Suki waved her hands like an overexcited child. 'But I want to know *everything.* Can I see the designs? Have you told the poor unfortunates what Suki Dee Licious is doing for them? I want beautiful, gorgeous clothes on the waifs from the streets and a narrative...' She paused to think and Bea felt uncomfortably hot.

'A narrative about *love.* Love and compassion. How we need to save this planet.' She raised her voice as though already addressing the United Nations.

Bea couldn't keep quiet any longer. This woman may look like Aurora – Sleeping Beauty from her favourite Disney film – but she had no idea what she was talking about.

'We can't get homeless people to model unless we can give them something that they want or need.' Ignoring the barrage of piercing looks that rained upon her back and Alastair's noisy cough, she continued, 'What good's a Hartleys gift voucher to someone who lives on the street? They need warm clothes, bedding, toiletries, food, healthcare, jobs –' Bea ticked these off on her fingers as she gained steam.

'With respect, Miss Stevens,' Alastair hissed. Bea could hear the tightness in his jaw. 'Hartleys are being very generous. We sell everything that a person could want. Hartleys have been known to sell an elephant and even a helicopter in our long and illustrious history.' He laughed as though he had said something original, not the same old line that Evans recited at public gatherings.

'I don't think a homeless person would want anything like that,' Suki said and her perfect eyebrows came together as she considered this possibility. Then her face opened – maybe she was afraid that a frown would cause premature wrinkles – and she smiled at Bea. 'What do you think we should give them?'

Bea had given this some thought. 'Couldn't we give them vouchers to use in charity shops? They could buy a lot more for their money. And it would support the charities too.'

'I like it!' Suki clapped her hands together and held them as though in prayer. 'It would be *wonderful* publicity. But is that enough? I want this event to launch my new image. We'll give them all makeovers, of course. And have some wonderful stories that will make people weep: How the opportunity to be a model for a day turned their lives around. Ooh I love it! Now, who are your designers? I want the clothes to be fabulous.'

Alastair was looking a little pale, and so Bea replied, 'Have you thought, Suki…' She paused to build the suspense, so much hung on Suki's reaction, she had to give this her all. 'About working with local designers? Supporting fashion students and graduates? You would be helping young people to launch their careers.' Suki widened her eyes and encouraged, Bea went a bit further. 'Without your support, who knows those young designers could become homeless themselves.'

Alastair clicked his tongue. Maybe she had gone a bit too far.

'Hmm. I'm not sure. I don't want this to be an amateur event, like something from the local community centre. We may be working with homeless models but this has to be top-class. And I need something more. The press will be there. If this is a disaster you could ruin my reputation. You could completely destroy my image.' She was red in the face now and Bea remembered, too late, the demon who terrorised her dresser when she couldn't fit the cleavage enhancer.

'I don't think Miss Stevens was suggesting a Christmas bazaar at the church hall.' Alastair chortled. 'Good heavens no. This is Hartleys. Rest assured that your event will be worthy of our reputation as the world's number one luxury store. Miss Stevens's ideas may seem a little...progressive, but I am confident that you will be impressed when it all comes together.'

Suki Dee nodded and then turned her attention to her mobile. 'I have an engagement at eleven. Can you call my dresser? She should have finished with your wardrobe people by now. And my driver?'

Bea stood up to leave. 'If that's all, I'd better get back to the important job of organising the most talked about celebrity event of the year. Well, December. There were bound to have been other celebrity things this year, in fact, other Suki Dee special events. This will be –'

'Goodbye, Miss Stevens,' Alastair cut her off before she could do any more damage.

Bea scuttled out of the store before Alastair had the chance to discuss their meeting. She needed medication for her head and a few miracles. Bea had attracted some fashion designers as followers on Twitter. One of them was Sav, and she had local contacts. Maybe the incentives for models had been wrong but the charity idea was genius. Ryan was right, when she wanted something nothing could stand in her way. But with just two weeks until Christmas, she was running out of time.

43

THIRTEEN SHOPPING DAYS TO CHRISTMAS

'All systems go!' Bea announced as her laptop fired up.

She absolutely *had* to concentrate, to focus every bit of her attention on the project and not get distracted by the mystery of Declan's disappearance. She had posted Ryan's letter, care of Ash, that morning. Marlene, the owner of his Peacock Court flat, would no doubt have preferred Bea hand it to him in person. It had been sent eleven months ago and so it could have waited until Bea saw him but she didn't know how long Ryan would be staying at Ash's address.

She hated being away from Ryan, which was crazy as she had managed perfectly well without him for twenty-three years, but when he was with her she felt kind of anchored – the currents of everyday life stilled. She felt as though something inside unfurled and basked in the warmth of his smile, his unquestioning acceptance of who she was. At least he would have somewhere to stay over Christmas, if he and Ash didn't drive each other mad living in such close proximity. They both had quick tempers.

Bea shook herself; she had to concentrate on the fashion show. 'Designers,' she said as she clicked on to Instagram. Her plan was to spend a couple of hours on social media following up any leads on prospective designers, and contacting charities to discuss the voucher idea. Then, she was going to have another go at approaching homeless people, this time with a more attractive offer.

It was a good plan, but within thirty minutes Bea had switched from looking at #recyclefashion to Declan's spreadsheet which she had copied into an excel sheet. Declan had put his life at risk life in seeking justice for Ryan. Sitting in Ash's bedsit, none of them had given voice to what they all feared. That Declan had been murdered. The thought was unbearable and Bea forced it from her mind, in case thinking the unthinkable made it happen.

Despite looking up the websites listed in the spreadsheet repeatedly, there was no clue. The businesses were all different and apart from a few key phrases such as, *once in a lifetime* and *unbelievable results*, there was nothing to link them. Tabitha Twitchit's email account was now flooded with scam offers and whilst Bea was thinking her fingers automatically clicked and deleted them. On autopilot, she nearly missed the personal email addressed to Tabitha.

Dear Tabitha,

I know that this is not your real name, as I am a big Beatrix Potter fan. I am really sorry to hear that Declan is missing and I pray for his safe return. Declan was very kind to me and my boys. You see, we were the victims of a scam. I am so ashamed of myself for being conned like that, I should have known better. In short, I lost my life savings. We have been living in bed and breakfast for the past eight months. This will be the worst Christmas of my life. My kids don't understand why we can't have a Christmas dinner and it will break my heart when they find out that Santa has only left them one present each and not even new. I don't know what Declan was planning to do, but he said that he was gathering information about similar frauds, so that he could see justice was done. I never expected to get my money back, but it would have given me some satisfaction to see the villains pay for their crime. There must be others like me. I hope that he did not endanger his life in his pursuit for justice. It is a cruel world. I hope that your Christmas is better than mine. Do let me know when you find Declan. I will keep him in my thoughts and prayers.

Regards,

Chloe Winters (Mrs).

Bea's mind raced. Declan was seeking justice for Ryan. So, Ryan must have been the victim of a scam too. A sense of foreboding pushed its way up from her diaphragm and lodged like a stone in her throat. The spreadsheet must have helped Decan to find links between the scams. Why hadn't she seen this herself? Then, Bea did what she should have done days ago – she looked up each of the businesses on Companies House, where all limited companies are registered with details of their trading history. Every single one of them was a subsidiary of Kassab Enterprises. Bea swallowed hard.

When something seems too good to be true, it probably is. Bea could hear her sister Lizzie's warning in her head. Was her flat too good to be true? It felt like a miracle, to find this jewel of a place – with the little courtyard garden. No, the landlord had explained why he had reduced the rent and wanted a tenant who could move in quickly. She was just being paranoid. Her breath steadied and she tried to refocus on the fashion show.

Bea clicked her screen back to Instagram. An Italian designer had mentioned spending Christmas in the Scottish Highlands. It was worth following this up. She made a call to the designer's booking manager. But as the phone rang, Bea felt her nerves tingle. The landlord's face came to mind and again she tried to pin down where she had seen him before.

'Paco Pauletto. Posso aiutarla?'

'Puoi parlare in inglese per favour?' Bea replied. She had to concentrate.

'Of course. Can I help you?'

The booking manager was unavailable but Bea explained to his assistant that she was organising a spectacular event to be hosted at Hartleys by Suki Dee Licious. She did not mention the timescale. The assistant assured Bea that the booking manager would phone her as soon as he was available and that he would be excited by the proposal.

For at least three seconds Bea was filled with optimism but then an ugly thought nudged away her happiness. The morning that she let Stanley Larkin, the estate agent, into her flat, he had a man with him. A swarthy-looking thickset man. That was where she had seen her landlord before. It was the same day that the glove had been placed in her bed.

Bea rummaged through her desk drawer, looking for her contract. Her heart was racing now. The contract had slipped inside one of her notebooks and Bea shook it free. Now, she smoothed it out and tried to view it dispassionately. The wording was what she would expect, nothing suspicious there. It wasn't on headed paper, so no company name to check. She was just jumping to conclusions. Imagining things. Maybe her landlord just reminded her of the man who visited her flat. It all made sense though. Ryan's flat in Peacock Court. Marlene said that she 'knew nothing about it'. Bea didn't know at the time what she was talking about. Rapunzel had said something about apartments being let on Airbnb. If Ryan had been conned by Kassab Enterprises then Declan was close to exposing them as con men. That was why he had gone missing. It also explained why Ryan was homeless.

44

TWELVE SHOPPING DAYS UNTIL CHRISTMAS

At Tufnell Terrace, a middle-aged woman opened the door and greeted Bea with a warm smile. 'Hello, I've just warmed some mince pies.' Then she frowned. 'Sorry, I don't remember your name. You are here for the fundraising coffee morning? Come in.'

A couple of women joined her on the doorstep, one of them clutching a plastic container. They too were waved in. Bea hesitated outside, wondering whether to just leave or follow them. She didn't know if she could bear to see her dream flat occupied, but until she had absolute confirmation that the flat was not for rent, then wishful thinking might lead her to delude herself.

Matronly bottoms jostled for space around a long table as home bakers lovingly arranged their cakes. Bea spied a lemon drizzle cake, an impressive Victoria sponge oozing scarlet jam, and flapjacks which the baker, a woman wearing a long skirt and multicoloured jumper, repeatedly told anyone within earshot were vegan and gluten free. None of the offerings came close to Leila's chocolate brownies, and Bea felt a surge of pride for her new friend.

'Would you like a Rocky Road?' A woman about the same age as her mum waved an open tin under Bea's nose. They looked good, but that wasn't why she was there.

'No thank you.'

'Has Jennifer offered you a tea or coffee?'

Bea nodded and wandered over to the French windows. The little courtyard garden where she had planned to plant geraniums was sparse. She shouldn't really be there – gate-crashing the party. Now that she knew the flat was occupied, she ought to just leave.

The owner joined her. 'I planted some spring bulbs before going away in October but didn't bother with winter flowering plants this year. Are you a keen gardener?'

Bea sighed. Maybe she could be a gardener, if she had a garden. 'Not really. Have you lived here long?'

'About three years. It's a wonderful neighbourhood. Really friendly as you can see from the number of neighbours supporting this children's hospital coffee morning. I'm a Friend of the Hospital. Which is your flat?'

This one, Bea's heart cried. It was everything that she had imagined it to be, but it would never be hers. 'Oh, I heard about the coffee morning from a friend. Are you spending Christmas here in this flat?' she said, just to be certain.

The woman gave a quizzical look, and Bea worried that she had somehow given herself away. 'Most of Christmas, you know how it is, family members to visit. Who's your friend?'

'She's over there,' Bea said, and when the woman turned her back she slipped out of the front door.

All of the money that Bea had raised by selling her clothes had gone. Tomorrow, she had to leave Aunt Fiona's flat and hand the keys to the estate agent. Kassab had stolen more than her money, he had stolen her dream – a future that she had been so sure of she had already started to live it in her head. Her journey to work, the little deli on the corner where she would buy brie and ham off the bone for impromptu lunches with Ryan. Bea travelled in to the office, going through the motions as though she was a normal person. Her body functioned, as though unaware that inside she was a wreck. Humiliation. Shame. Disappointment. And grief. A grief that made her want to howl and hammer her fists. It wasn't fair. How could she have been so stupid?

'Press releases.' Alastair pounced on Bea the moment she arrived at her desk. 'What have you got for me?'

Bea took a deep breath. She had to focus on the Suki Dee event or she would lose her job as well as her home. The knowledge that she had got it so wrong shook Bea's confidence and so when she responded to Alastair it was in a tremulous voice.

'The charities. I phoned the charities and they agreed to sell us gift vouchers.'

Alastair fixed his stare on Bea and she used this to steady herself. 'Mind, Shelter, and Crisis have all agreed.' Her voice grew stronger, more authoritative.

'Gucci.' Alastair clapped his hands together. Bea was about to correct him when she remembered this was Alastair's new word for 'cool'. 'Designers?'

'Savvy Clothes. Paco Pauletto–'

'You got Paco P?'

Bea nodded. She hadn't exactly, but his booking manager's pa seemed keen. 'And Lucille Vine. Possibly.' This was a bit of a stretch as she only had an email response asking for more information.

'More. More.' Alastair waved his hands as though directing traffic towards him.

There wasn't any more. In fact, there was a lot less. 'Hmm. I'll have to get back to you when things are a bit more definite. But, looking good.'

'Models?'

'Now that we have the gift vouchers to offer instead of Hartleys vouchers we might attract a few models from the street. Perhaps we could book a few professional models as well, just to boost numbers?'

'Maybe.' Alastair cupped his chin. 'Okay. But only as a last resort.'

Satisfied that Bea was making progress, Alastair returned to his inner sanctum and Bea slumped over her desk. For twenty seconds she sat with her anguish and then anger kicked in. How dare he rob her of her savings. Not just Bea, Chloe Winters, Ryan, and all the other people Kassab Enterprises had conned.

Alastair stalked out of his office with a pile of papers under his arm. He would be gone for some time. When she was sure that nobody would overhear her call, Bea phoned the police to report the crime. A woman took her details and made sympathetic noises, but Bea got the impression that her story would just be entered on a computer for future reference. There must be something she could do. Bea trawled the internet to find out about other peoples' experience and read about a man who had taken his case to the Royal Courts of Justice. As a result, the fraudster's bank account was frozen and the stolen money reimbursed. Bea seized upon this and phoned her sister, Lizzie, who was a solicitor.

'What's wrong, Bea?'

'Nothing's wrong. Why should anything be wrong?' Bea felt her hackles rise. Why did her family always assume that Bea would get into some kind of trouble? That she couldn't look after herself? 'I just phoned for some advice. For a friend of mine.'

'Oh okay.' Lizzie sounded distracted and Bea imagined her turning her attention to her computer screen. 'Can you take this through to Jeff?' Lizzie was speaking to someone else. 'Go on,' she prompted Bea.

'I'm asking for my friend, Ryan.' Bea told Lizzie about the scam and asked whether it was worth approaching the Royal Courts of Justice.

'It has been done in the past, but it can be a very slow process. There are so many of these scams. Has your friend reported it to the police?'

'Yes, but they weren't very helpful. Mum said something about you staying with her while your house is renovated.'

'We've already moved in. It was a nightmare at home. Not much better at Mum and Dad's, because we're all a bit cramped. Dad has had to give up his office for Ollie and I know Mum has cleared her own clothes out of the wardrobe in the spare room to make space for me. They've only got one bathroom and no separate toilet, so it's not ideal, but very kind of them. Mum told me you've found a garden flat. Way to go, Bea! I told Mum that you're a sharp cookie and that she has nothing to worry about as far as you're concerned. Hold on.' Lizzie must have covered the mouthpiece as her voice was muffled. 'It was the sixteenth. No – eighteenth.'

'It's okay, Lizzie. I'll see you at Christmas. Give Ollie a hug from me.' She hung up. Staying with Mum and Dad definitely wasn't an option. Tomorrow she would be homeless.

45

ELEVEN SHOPPING DAYS TO CHRISTMAS

'I've arranged a meeting with the media team for Monday at 2 pm. We will need *everything* – the models' names, back stories, designers and links to their collections, media contacts for the charities. Catering? Have you spoken to Delaney? Prosecco or champagne? Canapes. Ask for Christmassy ones.' Alastair fired off these instructions as he prepared to leave the office.

Bea's head swam with the enormity of what was required. Maybe she had misled him a little bit in pretending that all was in hand. The time to admit that it couldn't be done had passed. Evans and Alastair would be furious. Hartleys's reputation was at stake. Bea didn't want to be anywhere near Suki Dee when she found out. If she had admitted defeat she would have lost her job anyway, and so there was nothing to lose by giving it her all and hoping for the best. She gave Alastair a weak smile. 'Don't worry. I'll have everything ready for our meeting next week.'

'Monday. Two pm,' Alastair said firmly in case Bea had any doubt.

'Yes. Monday at 2 pm. I'll be there – with everything you need.'

'Good. Then I'll be getting off. Don't stay too late.'

Bea didn't have a home to go back to. She had given the keys to the flat to Stanley Larkin on her way into work. Her suitcase was in the staff room – just the clothes she hadn't sold, and some toiletries. Mum had taken her books, and she had left her bedding in a black sack with Molly, so that she could collect it when she had somewhere to stay. It was a problem that she would have to resolve soon as it was already dark outside.

'I won't. I'm expecting a call from Lucille Vine's office at nine. It will be 4 pm in New York. It's just easier to take it here as I have all of the information at hand.'

'Okay. Let security know if you're still here after ten, because that's when they like to make sure everything is locked up. Don't want you locked in!' Alastair chuckled as he left Bea to get on with organising the big event.

She hadn't given catering a thought, but it was only five-thirty. Mr Delaney, head of catering, would still be in his office. Arranging the catering was the least of her problems, and the catering staff were always very accommodating as they were used to providing refreshment for big functions, often at short notice.

The food hall was still busy as late-night shoppers filled their baskets with festive delights. Glacé fruits in wide trays sparkled red, orange, and green beneath the Christmas lights. Customers queued to select treats from a glass-fronted counter with mouth-watering chocolates and truffles. Shopping baskets were filled with luxury Christmas puddings, elaborate gingerbread houses, and tins of biscuits. If Christmas was all about toys for children, for adults it was the feasting on fine foods. Bea thought about Ryan, Sal, and

Declan. Sal stuffing the bag of croissants inside her coat as though it was the only meal she would receive. Ryan nibbling the ham sandwich to make it last. Christmas would be like any other day for them, and others living on the street. Maybe a church or soup kitchen would provide a festive meal for a few, but it would be no different to any other day when they queued up in the hope of some nourishment. Where was Declan? Would they find him before Christmas or was it too late? Bea knew that the chances of him still being alive grew less every day.

'Mr Delaney's office is out the back. Go down Refrigerator Row and turn left at Salami Street. It's on the corner of Baker Avenue.'

Bea followed the girl's directions, along the underground corridors that were used to transport goods to the Food Hall. She passed a man wheeling a trolley filled with hams and then she smelt freshly baked bread, and saw a door marked Head of Catering.

Mr Delaney was very accommodating and for the first time in several days Bea was filled with confidence. If only the other tasks were as easily achieved. Above ground, the store looked magical and Bea took her time returning to the office. She missed working on the shop floor in the days before Christmas. As there was some time to spare she dropped in to say hello to Jemima and the team.

'Oh Bea, thank God. Could you be an absolute darling and help out? I've been on my feet for seven hours without a break. The buyer's just been in marking everything down and shoppers are trailing her like seagulls following a plough.' Jemima was pale and looked tired.

'Of course. Take a break and I'll cover until you get back.'

When Jemima returned with a little more colour in her face Bea extracted herself from the crush. The store closed at nine and it looked as though they would continue to be busy until then.

'I'm going to have to get back to the office,' Bea said reluctantly. Selling lingerie was a walk in the park compared to what she was expected to achieve by Monday.

'Could you get one of the boys to collect these garments for dispatch?' Pippa called after her. 'Most of them are for your friend Suki Dee.'

When Bea let herself back into the office, there was a scribbled note on her desk from Alastair's PA. Paco Pauletto wanted her to send information about the event. The bookings manager hadn't said no when Bea confessed the date, but he wanted to know the names of the other designers who would be showing recycle collections, media coverage, VIPs attending, how the garments would be stored and other details. Encouraged by this communication, Bea put together a professional response. She told Paco Pauletto that Lucille Vine of New York, Anastasia Delov, and a new UK designer, Savannah, were being considered, amongst others. All of which was true. Anastasia Delov was based in Paris and Bea was trying to persuade her team that this event was one she couldn't afford to miss. However, none of Bea's emails or calls had been returned.

The office phone rang at nine-fifteen, startling Bea, who had lost track of time. It was the New York call. She had high hopes for this one. If Lucille Vine agreed, and Paco Pauletto, she could pull this off. *Please let them say yes*, she willed God, or any kindly spirit who might grant her wish.

The conversation started well and Bea's palms tingled with anticipation.

'When were you thinking of holding this event?' The question Bea dreaded.

'Well, that's the exciting news.' Bea spoke in her most

upbeat voice. 'We thought Christmas Eve. Perfect for fundraising as people wind down for Christmas and great for media coverage highlighting what Christmas will be like for the homeless.' She hated saying 'the homeless'. It was as though Ryan and Sal weren't people just – the homeless.

'Eleven days' time?' The voice sounded incredulous, as though Bea's suggestion was absurd, and they were right. It was.

'That's right,' Bea said.

A security man poked his head around the door. Bea held up a hand to stop him interrupting, and then nodded her head in reply to his unspoken question — yes, she knew they wanted to lock up.

The telephone conversation did not get much beyond the date. Lucille Vine's office tried to negotiate a date in early January and Bea left it open, just in case Alastair had a change of heart.

Bea gazed out of the window where all seemed quiet. The sea of shoppers had at last subsided, and only a few store staff could be seen in the street lights as they made their way home. That was where Bea should be headed, but where was home? She hadn't made any arrangements, as her head had been full of the Suki Dee event. It was ten at night, too late to arrive uninvited at the *Fandangle* or to ask Mouse if she could crash out on *No Worries*. It didn't feel right asking these new friends to give her a bed for the night. Ryan hadn't imposed on them, and they were more his friends than hers. She couldn't go back to Hampshire. It would be so humiliating. And where would she sleep? On the sofa? It wasn't fair to Mum and Dad.

The store was plunged into darkness. Security must have thought she had left. Bea crept out of the office, using the torch on her phone. The staff restroom where she had left her case was quiet. At this time of night, the cleaners and maintenance staff would have left the building, and so it was just her and the security staff. Nobody would notice if she slept in the staff room just for one night. It was too late to find anywhere else and she couldn't afford a hotel room.

Bea made herself comfortable in an armchair and surprised herself by nodding off. She awoke just after midnight freezing cold. People who were sleeping on the street would be much colder; at least she had shelter. Bea's teeth chattered and so eventually she decided to risk creeping to the linens department on the third floor to borrow a throw.

There was no sign of security. Everywhere was so quiet and still it was hard to believe that just a few hours ago it had been heaving with customers. Bea sat on the edge of a bed and listened to the silence. Nothing. No distant sound of traffic. No music. Not even the scratching of a mouse, the hum of a fridge, or the rattle of a radiator. Absolute silence. Her limbs were heavy and her head ached. Bea pulled back the plump duvet. It was as light as a cloud. The pillows smooth and crisp. She slipped off her shoes. It wouldn't hurt to have a little nap in the luxury of this bed. Just a few minutes' rest and then she would borrow a blanket and sleep upstairs in the staff restroom.

Bea snuggled into the downy nest and fell fast asleep.

46

TEN SHOPPING DAYS TO CHRISTMAS

10 February 2019

Dear Ryan,

I don't know why I am still writing to you at this address as you haven't answered any of my letters. Millie, my old school friend, tried to look you up when she was in London but she didn't think that you lived at the address you gave us. Was it always your plan to disappear or did you make that decision when you arrived in London? If I had known that I might never see you again, there are things I would have said. One of them being – don't go. I miss you so much. You have always been there for me – my big brother. I know that I'm married now and you probably think that I don't need you any more but I do. I need you to tell me that everything's going to be alright, that Sean and I can make a success of the farm, that Da's not going to suffer, and that I have big enough shoulders to carry all of this. But I don't!

Yesterday, Sean was seeing to the herd and so I tried to help Da shave. I nicked his chin and you should have heard him yell. 'Where's Ryan? Get Ryan to shave me.' It was all he would say. It's always Ryan. I've tried to explain to Da that you're in England but he doesn't remember. His memory is so poor, he wouldn't know the time of day if I wasn't there to tell him when to eat and go to bed. Sometimes he thinks that I'm Ma and he's so sweet and tender, I almost want to be her so that I don't disappoint him.

Maybe I am writing this letter as a kind of therapy because I can't talk to you. Please don't be dead, Ryan. It hurts like hell to know that you don't want us in your life. What did I do to make you hate me? Was life really so bad that you had to run away and start again? If that is what you have done then I will try and wish you well, but it's hard because I'm so angry with you for walking out on us. You left me, Ryan. But please, please don't be dead.

If this letter does by some miracle reach you then I'm begging you to come home. Da has lung cancer. He's dying, Ryan. I'm doing my best to care for him but he keeps on asking for you.

What I'm trying to say is that we all miss you. You have left a hole in our lives. It was hard losing Ma but for you to walk out like that – it was cruel. I am angry, Ryan. Angry and sad. This letter will probably never reach you. But if it does – do the right thing. Come home.

Love Caitlin.

Folded inside the letter were three twenty-pound notes. Enough for a one-way ticket to Dublin. The torrent of emotions that swept through Ryan knocked him like a breaker wave and dazed, he lowered himself into a chair. Fury at the fiends who had conned him and fury with himself because he was the cause of Caitlin's pain. *Eejit. Eejit. Eejit.* Ryan held his head in his hands. Stupid eejit, he hadn't thought about the effect his homelessness would have on his sister. He had been too caught up in self-pity and the need for revenge.

His throat tightened. Da was dying. And he was asking for Ryan. What if he was too late? Caitlin sent this more than ten months ago. He had let them down badly. Two Christmases had passed since he left home. Did Caitlin hope each year that he would be home to celebrate the season with his family?

Ryan leapt to his feet. It wasn't too late. He could get the next flight and be back before New Year's Eve. What a fool he had been. Ryan swiped away angry tears.

He wrote a note for Ash. *I am going back to Ireland on the next available flight.* Ryan tapped his pen, trying to decide what to do, then he continued. *If you get any news about Declan, please let me know.* He added the farm address. *I'll let Bea know I've gone. Don't give her my address. Watch out for her. Thanks for letting me stay. Ryan.* Short and sweet. There was no need to say any more.

Ryan gathered his things, and then pulling the woollen hat, thoughtfully provided by Bea, over his ears he began his journey home. Back to the farm. To Da and Caitlin. His eyes were just weeping because of the cold wind. He was leaving London. Leaving Bea. Forever. The pain in his heart was to be expected. It was hearing about Da, and Caitlin's distress; it wasn't the thought of never seeing Bea again. How could it be? He had known her only a few weeks. Those silly high-heeled Jiminy shoes. The way that thoughts flitted across her face, and her nose twitched, when she was deciding what to say. Ryan smiled to himself. It was when she forgot to censor herself that she really came alive. He had watched the layers of pretence melt like snow until the woman she truly was shone bright and clear.

Although Ryan thought he was heading for City Airport, he found himself outside Bea's apartment block at Granary Square. The lump in his throat had refused to shift and he knew that he had to see Bea just one more time. To explain why they must say goodbye, and to thank her for letting him into her flat and her life on that snowy night. Two men were carrying Bea's sofa out through the entrance hall. Ryan stood aside to let them out of the door and then slipped in before it closed.

'You're too late. She's gone,' Molly said, coming out of her storeroom.

Ryan knew that Bea was moving, she had given him her new address, but he thought it was in a few days' time. It was probably just as well. They needed a clean break. So long as he was still in her life, she would not give up in her pursuit of justice. Bea was more relentless than Declan, and although he tried to keep positive, Ryan was afraid that Declan may have paid with his life. He couldn't risk the same thing happening to Bea.

Molly held the door open as the men returned. 'Look at the mess on my floor,' she said, tutting at the footprints made by wet boots. 'No point mopping until they've finished. Is there much more?' she called up the stairs after them.

'Thanks, Molly,' Ryan said. He might as well go straight to the airport. There was no point leaving a note. Bea had gone.

'Not so hasty. Come into my office and I'll make us a brew. It's time I had a break and the warmth will thaw you out.'

Her kindness brought a fresh wave of sorrow, and so Ryan hid his face by turning away to pull off his hat. He fumbled with an inner pocket of his jacket, and when the hat and his emotions were carefully packed away, he followed Molly into her little den.

'Just hot water with a splash of milk, please,' Ryan said.

Molly removed a teabag from his mug and poured the hot water. 'She left yesterday. I have a phone number but no forwarding address, although I can give you Mrs Stevens's if that's any help.'

'I wanted to let her know that I'm going back to Ireland.'

Molly asked him what arrangements he had made for his flight. When he told her that he was just going to turn up at the airport and see what was available, she insisted on helping him to make enquiries. There was a City Jet flight to Dublin at two-thirty which had available seats.

'Now, how about you phone Bea? I won't listen. Go on. Use my phone.' Molly gave a gentle smile which reminded Ryan of his ma. What was the matter with him today? All of this blubbing. He nodded, unable to speak, and Molly left him alone in her storeroom.

The phone went straight to voicemail and so Ryan left a message. 'Bea. This is Ryan. I'm sorry I couldn't say goodbye in person. I'm going back to Ireland because my da is ill and my sister needs me.' Ryan paused, unsure how to continue. 'Okay. Well, I probably won't see you again.' His voice wavered and he swallowed hard. 'I know you will wow Suki Dee. You are incredible, Bea Stevens. Don't let anyone tell you otherwise. Okay. Have a good Christmas and new year. And everything.' He hung up before he said too much.

Molly insisted on kissing him goodbye. 'You're a good lad. If ever you need anything you just come and find me.'

His flight was in three hours. There was time to visit the *Moby*. He would collect Declan's personal effects, his driving license, and a lucky charm shamrock, and destroy that wretched spreadsheet. Then he would go straight to the airport. As he walked along the canal Ryan mentally said goodbye to the place. He had met some amazing people – Mouse, Leila, Roots, Molly, and Bea. That evening he would be back on the farm with Caitlin and Da. He prayed that he wasn't too late.

As Ryan stooped to enter the cabin, he was aware of a presence and felt uneasy. A man dressed in black was at the far end, his face in shadow. The *Moby* didn't belong to Ryan, although he had come to think of it as a kind of home. Who was the intruder? Ryan or the man who was watching him, like a cat about to pounce? The cabin was crowded with the two of them. He just needed to collect his things and then he didn't care who moved in.

'Ryan O'Marley?' the man said, and Ryan froze. He didn't need this now. Just as he was about to leave for Dublin. 'Do you know this man?' The man in black was showing Ryan something cupped in his palm.

'Can we talk up on the deck?' Ryan said. He needed some air and the light was better. It was also easier to run.

On deck, Ryan took Declan's driving licence from the man. 'Who are you and why are you interested in Declan?' His body tightened.

'It's you I'm interested in,' the man said.

47

TEN SHOPPING DAYS TO CHRISTMAS

T*hud. Thud, thud.* Bea thought at first that she was in Hampshire. It sounded as though Mum was sorting out the airing cupboard, dropping piles of sheets to the floor. *Thud.* No, she was still in London. Not her flat, she had handed the keys to Larkins before going to work, and she was still in … Hartleys! Bea flattened herself and wriggled further under the duvet. She was fully clothed, her suitcase tucked out of sight in the staff restroom. It had gone quiet. Bea peeked out the side of the duvet. A trail of sensor lights followed a delivery man as he strolled across the floor and then disappeared through a door. He hadn't spotted her. Bea slipped out of bed, fumbled for her shoes, and then strolled out of the department as though she had arrived at work early and had every right to be there.

When Alastair arrived at ten, Bea had been hard at work for three hours. Her attention had darted between finding fashion designers and researching how to get some resolution for the people who had been scammed.

'You're in early, Stevens. Anyone would think you spent the night here.'

Bea snapped to attention. 'Who told you that?'

Alastair chuckled. 'Pleased to see you working hard. Shall we meet at –' he checked his watch '– three? Have a catch up? We're meeting comms at 2 pm on Monday, so best to be prepared.'

He didn't wait for an answer as he strode across the open plan office to his glass cubicle. Bea realised with some relief that he had been making a joke about her staying in the store overnight. She had to sort out some accommodation today. Another wave of anger at bloody Kassab and the misery he had caused had Bea reaching for her phone again.

'I can't wait until the new year.' It was the fourth time that she had spoken to Sonia Sparrow, a senior clerk at the Royal Courts of Justice that morning. 'I've sent you all of the paperwork, my application to the court, and evidence of fraud. Why can't you just freeze Kassab's accounts? You've got his bank details. Do you want more? I can send you more statements from other people they've conned.'

'No. No. You've sent enough,' the clerk said, a note of panic in her voice. Bea had fired off email after email. 'I'll ask the judge to prioritise it next week.'

Alastair returned to the office humming a Suki Dee song. He waggled his eyebrows at Bea.

'Why not today?' Bea smiled into the phone.

At the other end Sonia Sparrow tried to explain that there was a backlog of cases. Bea wasn't having any of that.

'I'll come in and see him myself. Okay. No, I can't wait until then. You're open on Saturday so I'll pop in then. Why not? Okay, I'll phone you. In case you need more…um…' Alastair was watching her, a questioning look on his face. 'Information,' Bea said.

'One of the fashion design team?' Alastair grinned. 'Well done, Stevens. You've yet to tell me the *wow* factor. Detail is important: catering, stylists for the models, invitations. I could get my PA to sort them out to take off some of the pressure. But don't let's forget the wow factor. I know you wanted to surprise me but now is the time to reveal all.' He sat on the edge of her desk.

The bloody *wow factor*. This was where she needed Rumpelstiltskin's help to spin those bales of straw into gold. 'I'll update you on everything this afternoon when we meet,' Bea said, feigning an air of confidence.

Fuelled by coffee Bea went into overdrive. She would have to trawl the streets again at the weekend in the hope that her new offer might attract a few models but she wasn't optimistic. It sounded so trivial. An insult. Bea wasn't sure that she could follow it through. Fortunately, the model agencies that she contacted that morning were more accommodating than the fashion designers. Portfolio photos were sent from two agencies and Bea was confident that she could find suitable models. It was a contingency plan.

By midday, Bea had a definite no from Anastasia's office in Paris. Paco Pauletto declined soon after when Bea was forced to admit that Lucille Vine and Anastasia would not be participating. Again, there was an offer of reconsidering if the event was postponed until the new year. That left Savvy Clothes. Her one and only recycled fashion designer.

Sav picked up on the first ring. 'Bea. I was just about to call you.'

Alastair was hovering by Bea's desk waiting for her to finish her call when a huge man swaggered into the office. Alastair stood up and asked if he could be of assistance.

The man held out his hand to Alastair; it reminded Bea of a tinned Christmas ham. 'Adams. Security.'

Bea froze. He had come to report her. Of course, they would have seen her on the CCTV cameras; they were everywhere. Sweat prickled her brow.

'I've been busy.' Sav was talking and Bea tried to concentrate, but she was trying to listen into Alastair's conversation at the same time.

'I'll tell my staff to be vigilant,' Alastair said and the security man nodded.

He winked at Bea as he left and she felt a chill down her spine.

'Can I have a look this afternoon?' Bea said, tuning back into Sav. 'At your showroom? Okay, I'll be there in under an hour. I can't wait.'

Alastair smiled when she hung up. The security man couldn't have reported her.

'Can you confirm timings for the invitation? Jen is going to get some printed.'

Bea nodded. 'I have to pop out to view a collection. The UK designer I told you about. I may get back after three. Could we push the meeting back a bit?'

'Okay. Four-thirty?' Alastair said. Now that he was confident Bea had everything in hand, he was all smiles and congeniality. The only hope Bea had now was for a Christmas miracle. Even if she managed to string Alastair along this afternoon, she would have to come clean on Monday when they met with comms.

Bea's heels clicked as she hurried down the staff stairs. It was quicker than taking the lift when the store was crowded. She made a mental note of what she had to do before meeting with Alastair. At the bottom of the stairs, she checked her phone to see if Delanie had confirmed catering. There was a voice message but Bea didn't recognise the number. She hoped it wasn't Sav cancelling, although she knew Sav's number.

'Okay. Well, I probably won't see you again.' Bea gasped. Her wave of delight at hearing Ryan's lilting voice was replaced with panic. This time it sounded as though he meant it. 'I know you will wow Suki Dee. You are incredible, Bea Stevens. Don't let anyone tell you otherwise. Okay. Have a good Christmas and new year. And everything.' He couldn't disappear out of her life like that. Didn't he know what he meant to her? Bea could cope with losing her flat and her job, but she couldn't imagine a life without Ryan. He had phoned from a mobile. Bea's hand shook as she returned the call.

'Hello?'

'Who is that?' Bea said.

'You rang me. Who are you?' an irritated voice replied. Then Bea recognised the voice.

'Hi, Molly. This is Bea Stevens. Is my friend Ryan with you?' Bea sighed and her body relaxed. She cradled the phone as if it were Ryan. A smile warmed her. Everything was going to be alright.

'No, love. Didn't he tell you? He was catching a plane at two-thirty this afternoon to Dublin.'

No. No. It was already 12.30. 'Thanks, Molly. I'll see you soon to collect my bedding. Thank you for letting Ryan use your phone.'

There was just enough time, if she was very lucky. Bea withdrew some money on her overdraft and hailed a cab. 'I have to get to City Airport in less than an hour,' she begged the driver. She had to catch Ryan before he went through security.

48

TEN SHOPPING DAYS TO CHRISTMAS

'You can't go through security without a boarding pass,' the assistant said to Bea with a fixed smile on her beautifully made-up face.

'You don't understand. My friend is going back to Ireland and I may never see him again. I have to tell him something important.'

Behind her, a man in a suit sighed.

'Sorry,' the girl said, and turned her attention to the next in line.

Bea was not going to be dismissed so quickly. This was important. 'There must be some way that I can get past security to see if my friend is in the shopping and restaurant area. His flight isn't until two-thirty and I rushed to get here in time.'

The girl's smile faltered and she looked weary. 'No. It is not possible. Now, can you please move away so that I can check in the people who are flying with us today?'

The man behind Bea stepped forward, but Bea wasn't going to leave. 'How much is a ticket? I'll buy one.'

The man tutted and stepped back. Behind Bea, passengers murmured. She didn't care; they would just have to wait.

'You can't buy a ticket here. This is just for check-in. You'll have to go to enquiries.'

It was nearly two when Bea finally got the attention of someone who could help her. 'There is a seat on the two-thirty flight to Dublin but it's £68. If you had booked online you could have got it at a third of the price.'

'But I'm not even getting on the plane,' Bea wailed. 'There must be something you can do to help me get through security. I have to tell Ryan, that I – well, I've got something important to say and I'm afraid that if I don't speak to him before he flies I might never see him again.' Bea felt tears welling. She had to tell Ryan what he meant to her. The thought of never seeing him again was unbearable.

A call went out for Ryan O'Marley to report to one of the City Jet staff, and then Bea sat down to wait.

It was five when Bea eventually got back to the office, feeling miserable and defeated. Ryan had not answered the call. He was so suspicious after what he had been though, she might have guessed that wouldn't work. If only she had answered the phone when he called. Bea tried to imagine a different scenario with her persuading Ryan to stay in touch. What could she have said to change his mind? Not the truth. Bea wasn't sure that she could even admit it to herself – that she had feelings for Ryan. Ones that were new to her. That she couldn't imagine her life without Ryan. This revelation made Bea's head reel. Everything else seemed insignificant in comparison. But this time Ryan wasn't coming back.

Alastair had left the office for the weekend, despite Bea's message that she was running late. She had dropped in at Sav's workshop to apologise for missing their meeting, but the workshop was closed.

There was a note on Bea's desk. *Email a full report to me at the weekend. Everything. We have to be fully prepared before meeting comms on Monday. That includes the wow factor.*

If Bea sat up all night, she wouldn't be able to achieve the impossible and there was no Rumpelstiltskin to help her. But she had to make one last concerted effort. Unless there was a Christmas miracle, Bea would have to confess on Monday that she had misled Alastair and the event would be cancelled. She would lose her job.

The hours slipped by as Bea revisited all of the fashion designer sites and fired off emails offering the moon, if only someone would agree to show their collection. The security man did not visit the office to remind Bea to go home and so she was surprised when the lights went out at ten-twenty. If security didn't know that she was there then she might as well risk one more night in the store. Bea was emotionally and mentally drained. Where could she go at this time of night anyway?

The sofa in the staff restroom was not as comfortable as the divan bed but she was less likely to be discovered. A click and then a whirr. The refrigerators in the staff restaurant or maybe the heating. It was three in the morning and Bea couldn't fall off to sleep. All she could think about was Ryan. He would be in Ireland now. Would he even think of her once he was with his family? She was glad that he was going to be reunited with them before Christmas. It was selfish to be sad when this was the best outcome for Ryan. Maybe he would have second thoughts and contact her once he was settled. There again, she might remind him of a time he wanted to forget. Ash might pass on a message from her.

A light reflected off the window; it looked as though it

came from inside the building. Bea rolled onto her side and hugged her coat around her. She should have borrowed a blanket, it was too cold to sleep. A door creaked. Eerie. It was as though someone else was walking around the fifth floor.

A pool of light marked the edge of the door and then extinguished. A torch. Someone was prowling around. Footsteps. Then torchlight.

The door opened. The same security guard she had seen talking to Alastair swung his torch in an arc, illuminating fragments of still life – an armchair with a discarded magazine, a dirty mug on a coffee table. The light dazzled Bea as it settled on her and she shielded her eyes.

'Sorry. I can explain,' she said.

Then it was dark. He didn't say anything but she could hear his laboured breath as he crossed the room.

Bea hugged her handbag to her. 'I got locked in,' she spoke into the dark. Why didn't he use his torch?

A shape shifted; she could feel his presence filling the room.

'Turn on your torch so I can see you,' she demanded, afraid now.

'Why didn't you wait for me in the bed? We would have been more comfortable there.' His voice came from behind her.

Bea stood up. Where was the door? She was disorientated. Did she have her back to the door? Could she find her mobile and use her torch? No, she had to get out now.

Like a trapped fly, she flew at the corners of the room, groping for a door handle.

'Don't be like that. I'll keep your secret. You can stay here as long as you like. Use the facilities. I won't say a word.'

He was everywhere, his bulk blocking her exit. She could smell his body odour. Then a hand snaked out of the darkness and grasped her arm. 'You've done it before. It's not as though you're a virgin.' He laughed.

Bea kicked and screamed. She tore at his face and then she ran.

'You'll be sorry,' he shouted after her. 'Bitch.'

Her legs wobbled as she took the stairs two at a time. *Slow down. You can't afford to fall over. Not now. Not here.*

Out through a fire exit into the night. Maybe a fire alarm would sound; she didn't know and didn't care. Bea ran from Hartleys without looking back until she found herself on the edge of Hyde Park. It was bitterly cold. The park was closed but the darkness beyond the gates threatened her. He had crept into her room, a menacing shadow, and Bea couldn't shake off the fear. She imagined that she saw shapes moving, as though predators lay in wait. All around, eyes were watching her.

Bea pulled her coat tightly around her. In two hours the Tube would open and she could go back to Hampshire. A hearty breakfast, a log fire, and an outpouring of love from Mum and Dad. Love and concern. Followed by their affirmation that Bea needed protection and should never have been encouraged to go it alone in London. That she was a very bright girl, but not a good judge of character – too trusting and naïve. That people took advantage of her. That somehow Bea always got it wrong. And they were right. Why else would she be walking the street, having narrowly escaped being raped, and almost penniless having been conned out of her savings?

Bea had enough money for a train ticket to Hampshire. She could stay for Christmas, sleep on the sofa, and then look for another job in the new year. She thrust her hands deep into her pockets and trudged on through the night, past Buckingham Palace towards the river. Bright lights and sparkle adorned the buildings but at this hour it was quiet.

At London Bridge, Bea looked out across the river. Tower Bridge was illuminated, as though decked out for Christmas in strings of fairy lights. She peeked out from her scarf and watched the vapour trail as her breath warmed the air. A man and his dog sat midway along the bridge. 'Mind if I join you?' Bea said.

The man stroked his dog's head, a Jack Russell, and the dog whimpered in its sleep. Bea made herself comfortable on the pavement alongside them. She had been walking for nearly two hours and was glad to rest her feet.

'You from the church? Or the Sally?' he said.

Bea felt inadequate. She had nothing to offer this man – no light of hope or love of God. 'No. I'm Bea. Just Bea.'

He nodded. They sat in silence. Bea didn't feel any need to talk. The dog twitched his legs as though running in his dream. Eventually the man said, 'It's warmer under the bridge, but safer up here.'

'When the café's open I'll buy us a coffee,' Bea said.

He didn't reply. Bea's mind drifted. Tomorrow she would visit the High Court and again on Monday. Kassab was not going to get away with stealing her money. She would expose him as a fraudster who had brought misery to heaven knows how many people.

The wind whipped up a newspaper from under the dog's paw, and Bea caught it before it blew away. 'Mind if I sit on this?' Bea said.

The man shrugged and Bea opened out the paper to provide a wider mat. A news story caught her eye. Homeless man found dead in a disused railway station near Kings Cross. Just – *a homeless man.* No name. It was as though his life was unimportant. His dead body an inconvenience.

'Have you read this?' Bea stabbed at the story. It was unjust.

The man nodded. 'It happens.'

'What do you mean, it happens?' Bea was angry at his acceptance.

'Look around you. It's a dangerous place. Me and Skoot can take care of ourselves, but some of them – the kids, girls – it's tough. Some of them just give up.'

A man in a big overcoat walked close to the road giving them a wide berth.

'How did you come to be here?' Bea's voice softened. She understood now that everyone had a story. Nobody was born homeless or destined for it. If not for her family, Bea could have become homeless herself.

The man didn't answer at first, and then he said, 'I worked in the city. Lost everything on a bad investment – not just me, there were my clients too. Thought I had golden balls but turns out I'm just a sad old geezer like everyone else. I used to walk past people like me. Never thought I'd end up here.' He laughed but it was hollow and self-mocking.

Was it really so easy to slip through the cracks? To be packed away like Christmas decorations when you lost your dazzle? Ignored and forgotten.

'We should make more noise. Make people see us and listen,' Bea said, unable to keep the anger from her voice.

The man grunted and looked away. Bea felt him disengage, the same way that people did at parties, pretending to go in search of a drink when they just wanted to find someone more interesting to talk to. She didn't care. An idea was kindling, spreading its warmth like energy within her breast.

'Have breakfast on me,' she said and slipped a fiver under Skoot's collar before scrambling to her feet.

Never mind her failure in finding designers and models. She had been given a platform. A stage. Suki Dee wanted the media to cover her event. This was a gift. An opportunity to be heard. To give a voice to people like this man, to Ryan and Declan, and the anonymous homeless man who had died in a disused railway station.

Suki Dee wanted something 'sexy' that would put her on the map. Bea was going to make a noise that nobody could ignore. Being polite, trying to fit in didn't work. It was time to use her difference to make a difference. *Maybe,* Bea thought as she started to run towards the Tube, *I've found the shape of my foot.* This random thought stopped her in her tracks and she reflected on what Ryan had said. *Know the size and shape of you and then find what fits.* Maybe she didn't know how to make small talk, or charm customers, was a bit impulsive and too trusting. But, she was tenacious – Ryan and Evans had remarked on this – and compassionate – the injured cat, and Ryan, being examples of this. Bea started to run again. And smart. Mum was always telling her that she was clever.

'Who cares about being head of department?' Bea shouted into the early morning air. A passing cyclist twisted his head and his bike swerved. 'I'm going to make a noise that nobody can ignore. Expose the fraudsters and give homeless people a voice!'

49

NINE SHOPPING DAYS TO CHRISTMAS

Ash leaned out of a window, his hair standing on end, his chest bare. 'What do you want?' He didn't add, *waking me up at six in the morning.*

For the first time, since running to Monument Station, Bea questioned whether Ash would be as excited as she was about her plan.

'Oh, it's you. Hold on. I'll put on some clothes.'

The window slid shut and others opened. 'Sling yer hook.' 'Bugger off.' 'D'you know what time it is?' Between them, they made more noise than Bea.

'Ten past six,' Bea shouted back.

A few minutes later Ash met her at the front door. He glanced up and down the road before letting her in. Bea felt foolish as she traipsed up the stairs behind him. Ash hadn't looked pleased to see her. 'I'm sorry if it's a bad time,' Bea said, pausing on the stairs.

'I thought you were someone else,' Ash said. His voice was sad and defeated.

Bea thought of Ryan and her heart contracted. She knew

what it was like to miss someone. To hope against hope that you would see them again. 'Sorry,' she whispered.

Ash cleared some clothes off the sofa so that Bea could sit down.

'Who did you think I was?' Bea asked. She didn't like to pry, but neither did she feel like coming out with her plan. It seemed a bit egotistical and overblown in the reality of the new day.

'It doesn't matter.' Ash shook his head. There was no mistaking the sorrow in his voice.

'Were you expecting Ryan?' Bea said.

Ash reached for a folded newspaper and passed it to Bea. It was the story of the homeless man who was found by a couple of developers in York Station, a disused railway near Kings Cross. Bea scanned the story for the second time that morning. 'Do they know who it is?' she asked.

'They think…Ryan…'

No. Not Ryan. Bea was screaming inside. It couldn't be. He left a message on her phone yesterday. No. Ryan was in Dublin. Bea's breath steadied. Ash's head was in his hands. She ought to offer him a drink or comfort, but Bea was immobile. She could not shift her fear that Ryan was dead.

The buzzer startled both of them. Ash left Bea to look out of the window.

'Who was it?' she said, when he returned.

Ash didn't answer. He seemed to be having difficulty controlling his emotions. A key turned in the lock.

'Well?' Ash said.

'Sorry, mate.' Ryan handed Ash his key, which had been thrown from the window in a sock.

Bea wanted to fling herself at him. To feel the reassurance of his broad chest. His heart beat. Holding her steady. Keeping her still.

Ryan caught Bea staring, as though he had only just noticed she was in the room. As their eyes met, Bea felt a charged energy between them. Discomforted by the intensity of emotion, she looked away.

'Did you get my message?' Ryan said in his singsong voice.

Bea collected herself. 'Yes. You should be in Dublin.'

'To be sure I would, if the guards hadn't stopped me catching my flight.'

Bea was confused.

'The police,' Ash explained.

'River police. They found Declan's bag on the *Moby* a few days back.'

'The day we saw them checking her out?'

Ryan nodded. 'The bag was taken along with other ID to help them find the owner. They were trying to get him to pay his fines and arrange for the old girl to be towed. It was only when the death of a homeless guy was being investigated that a potential match was made with Declan's ID.'

'So it was him?' Ash's voice was croaky.

'Sorry.' Ryan nodded his head. 'But it's gobshite that Declan took an overdose.'

'Dec never touched drugs. It was those bastards.' Ash swung his arm across the kitchen counter, sending a tin caddy bouncing across the floor.

They sat in silence as emotional energy ricocheted off the walls.

'Why don't I buy us all some breakfast?' Bea said. She needed fresh air and time to think.

In the café, Bea cupped her hands around a large Americano; the steam warmed her face and she imagined herself thawing into a pool of water. Her feet were still like blocks of ice from her night on the street. They would be the last to melt.

'You haven't told me why you were at Ash's place at the crack o' day,' Ryan said, as he tore a fragment from his sandwich. Bea had tried to persuade Ryan to have a hot breakfast bap, but he insisted on something that would last all day, if needed.

The news that she had been bursting to share sounded glib in the light of Declan's demise. Instead, she told them what she had found out about Kassab Enterprises. 'The websites on Declan's spreadsheet are all owned by Kassab. It's possible to get Kassab's bank accounts frozen and if the money is there, reimburse the people that his companies scammed. I've made an application to the High Court.'

Ryan looked approvingly at Bea and then whistled. 'Atta girl! Isn't she somethin', Ash?'

Bea blushed with embarrassment and pride. Ryan held her gaze and she felt the blush turn to crimson. She ducked her head to fiddle with a napkin.

'Is that why you got me out of bed at six in the morning?' Ash said.

'No. Not exactly.' Then Bea had to tell them about getting conned herself, and sleeping in Hartleys overnight.

'You should have stayed with me,' Ash said.

'Why didn't you stay with your parents?' Ryan said.

'I thought Ryan was already staying with you, until I got his message, and my parents are putting up my sister and her family, so there was no room. Anyway, I thought I would be okay there for a couple of nights. It kind of just happened. I was busy working and then it was too late to find anywhere. But last night…' She didn't know how to tell Ryan and Ash. They were looking at her with such concern, she felt tears prick behind her eyes. 'A security man found me and tried to rape me.'

Ryan leapt to his feet. 'I'll bloody top him.'

'It's okay. I got away.' Bea believed Ryan would tear the man limb from limb if she didn't stop him. His eyes flamed with fury.

'Cool it,' Ash said.

Ryan sat back down, but Bea could detect a twitch in his facial muscles.

'I was sitting on London Bridge when I had a revelation. Well, it seemed like one at the time. Now it seems a bit lame. I just thought if we could use the Suki Dee event to expose Kassab.'

Ryan looked thoughtful. 'Is that possible? It seems a bit of a longshot.'

'The clerk at the Courts of Justice said that the judge will consider the case as soon as possible. My sister is a lawyer and she believes we have a case.' They both looked a bit sceptical and Bea didn't blame them. She had been grasping at straws. 'I know,' she sighed. 'I still have to find some models and some designers willing to exhibit. I have nine days. You're right, it's impossible. I guess I'd better start looking for another job.'

'Why would you be doing that?' Ryan said. 'Wasn't you just a saying that you had nine days?'

'Yes, but –'

'Ah, that's not the girl I know. My girl doesn't give up on anything she sets her mind to.'

Bea breathed in his positivity. His belief in her was intoxicating.

'What's this event in aid of?' Ash said.

'We talked about Friends of the Earth and homeless charities, I don't think we made a final decision.'

Ash pushed away his plate. 'Okay. How about we make this all about Dec?'

Bea sat up in her seat. 'Go on.'

'You say you want to use the event to expose Kassab? Say

we found out who killed Dec. Everything points to it being a set-up. Dec has friends. People are angry that his murder hasn't been taken seriously. Homeless people don't matter. I could ask people who knew Dec to model at your show. I'll say 'Do it for Dec.' If you throw in something they could use – warm sleeping bags –'

'What about vouchers for charity shops?'

'Yeah, if they can do that. I reckon we could rustle up a few decent models. Dec was a popular guy.'

Bea felt a surge of energy. Maybe it wouldn't work, but she wasn't going to give up until there was no other choice. 'I'll phone Sav now. See what she's got.'

Ryan beamed. The anger had gone from his face. 'Okay. Ash and I will go and recruit some models. See you back at Ash's place?'

Every time Bea looked at Ryan, she felt as though he was holding her. It was the way he returned her gaze. As though they were the only two people in the room.

It was hard to leave Ryan and as Bea strode away, she kept glancing back to glimpse him again before he disappeared. She fumbled for her phone.

Sav picked up straightaway. 'Oh, thank goodness you called. When you didn't turn up yesterday I thought you had changed your mind. You haven't, have you?'

'No! I'm so sorry I didn't call to cancel. Is there any way I could meet you at your showroom today? This morning?'

Sav was waiting at the door of her showroom when Bea arrived an hour later. 'I hope you don't mind but I've invited a few friends to meet you.'

Bea bit her lip. She hated social events, especially with strangers; she must have gate crashed a Christmas party. Oh dear, her timing was bad. Maybe Sav had already been drinking Prosecco when Bea rang and that's why she sounded overexcited. Her heart sank. She'd thought it too good to be true.

'Sorry, it's bad timing. You're probably winding down for Christmas.'

'You must be joking. I've been working on the collection every day since we last met. Cancelled my holiday in Venice. Sorry, I'm babbling. That's why I was so upset when I thought… Never mind. You haven't, have you?' Sav clasped her hands to her breast.

Bea shook her head, unable to speak. Behind the Japanese screens was Sav's collection. *Please let it be magical.* She lowered her eyes – when she took her first peek she would try to be objective, to see it through Suki Dee's eyes. She was expecting too much. She couldn't accept anything less.

50

NINE SHOPPING DAYS TO CHRISTMAS

Bea gasped. She had walked into a gathering of incredibly stylish people. There was *nothing* in *Vogue* that had prepared her for this – it was a collection of such breadth, a burst of creative energy. Different. *So* different. A room of faces watched Bea. They were all trying to read her. What she thought really mattered.

'Did you? Are these all your –'

'No. Not all of them. I asked some other designers to contribute. We have very different styles but all of us work in recycled. I know you'll have lots of other designers to consider, but these talented artists are the best.'

The gathering clapped and Bea was unsure whether they were models or the designers.

'Let me introduce you to each of the designers and they can tell you about their collection,' Sav said, steering Bea towards a man dressed in a trouser and tunic ensemble. The textures of the materials and their cut was unique. Bea could imagine David Beckham wearing it. The style was very original.

'Everything has been sourced from the unwanted materials of a car factory,' he explained. 'Car seat covers, airbags, seat belts.' He pointed these out as three men dressed in similar apparel to him modelled the collection.

'This is Tara, she works mostly in silks.' Bea wondered whether Sav had stretched her brief – silk was not a typical recycled fabric.

'From discarded kimonos and saris,' Tara said as four beautiful young women modelled dresses, an amazing evening coat, and cute blouses and jackets. Truly glamorous. Bea wanted to buy everything for herself. She almost forgot that she was here to source a fashion show. Suki Dee had nothing to worry about; these designers were the best. It would be a spectacular show.

'There's more,' Sav laughed, nudging Bea on.

'I thought you would show me your collection first,' Bea said. Sav hadn't promoted herself at all; she had focused on the other designers that she had generously brought together.

'Oh, I will. Maybe save the best 'til last.' She winked at a red-headed girl who was waiting to show Bea some rainwear. 'I hope you don't think I've taken advantage of your offer, Bea, but it was too good an opportunity. These designers deserve to have a platform for their work. We're all passionate about recycling clothes and saving the planet. It's time to turn the tide from commercialisation and waste to reusing everything. We have more than enough resources – materials are all around us. If you saw the crap washed in by the tide on the beaches in Bali. Great piles of it. Or the shit in the sea when you go snorkelling. Oh, don't get me started!'

The redhead, Cybil, took her cue and invited a male and female model to join them. 'All of my rainwear is constructed from broken umbrellas. Janine is wearing a lined raincoat.' Janine flashed her tailored coat to show off the multicoloured lining. 'Simon is wearing one of the extra waterproof jackets.' Simon turned his palms to display the elasticated cuffs hidden beneath the sleeves and the combination of zip and buttons to keep the wearer dry. 'Zips and buttons sourced from used clothes, of course.'

There were accessories too. Handbags styled from can ring pulls, hats made from plastic bottles. Shoes woven from scraps of leather. Bea had no idea the scope of recycled fashion. And Sav must have worked day and night since Bea last saw her, because her collection was now complete. Sav's imagination and creativity bowled Bea over.

'This is more than I could have hoped for,' Bea said to the anxious faces waiting for her verdict. 'Hartleys will be proud to have you all exhibit at the Suki Dee fashion show. This is going to be BIG. We'll have national press coverage, fashion bloggers, and style magazines. Suki Dee followers too, of course.' She was breathless.

If the 'Do It for Dec' campaign worked they would have models. And – if her application to the High Court was successful, Suki Dee would have an exclusive exposé. Bea's hands pulsed and she had to clench her fists to stop herself from combusting. Yesterday, it seemed impossible, but today she had to tell Ryan and Ash. And Alastair! How would she wait until Monday?

'Thank you, Sav.' Bea hugged her saviour. 'And all of you! Thank you so much.'

Ryan and Ash were already at the flat when Bea arrived full of her news. She was so excited, she thought she would burst.

'Well?' Ryan said, grinning.

Bea did a little dance and then threw herself into his arms. 'It was amazing. You wouldn't believe. Oh, Ryan!'

He looked into her eyes with such love and tenderness.

The world stood still. No-one else existed. Just the two of them. She could feel a heart beating and didn't know if it was hers or Ryan's.

Ash cleared his throat. 'So, it's good news then?'

Ryan looked bemused as they parted. It was as though they had come out of a dark cinema to find themselves in the glaring light of day. Bea collected herself, 'Oh, yes. The best. Sav brought together what must be the best recycled fashion designers in the UK, if not the world. Honestly, they're much more edgy and interesting than Paco, Anastasia, or Lucille.'

'We'll have to take your word for that,' Ash said.

'We've got some news of our own,' Ryan said. His eyes caressed her, and Bea felt a magnetic field pulling them together. It was hard to sit in the same room and act cool.

'Go on,' she whispered.

Ryan smiled. 'They were all up for it. Legend, Bass, Phoebe, Sal, Hari, Dee –'

'They're doing it for Dec,' Ash interrupted.

'Oh, that's wonderful! We have a fashion show, and if my application to the High Court is successful, we have a wow factor too.'

'Brilliant. Job Done.' Ash rubbed his hands together. 'Much as I would like to celebrate with you, I've got things to do.'

'Yes, of course. We'll get out of your way. Thank you so much, Ash. And I'm sorry to have woken you up at the crack of dawn.'

'You mean before dawn. S'okay. I hadn't slept much. Not since Ryan phoned me from the police station last night.'

They fell silent as each of them remembered Declan.

Ryan rubbed Ash's arm. 'Thanks for everything.'

Alone with Ryan, Bea suddenly felt very shy.

'Well done, Bea. I knew you could do it.' His voice was low

and deep, as though he were whispering endearments. How she longed to touch him.

'I've nowhere to live,' Bea said. 'I'm homeless.' And then she laughed, because there was too much elation to hold it inside any longer.

'Come here.' Ryan put his arm around her. 'We'll keep each other warm.'

Bea slipped her arm around Ryan, beneath his jacket, and felt the warmth of his body. Never before had she felt at ease with a man. This thing with Ryan, whatever it was, had crept up on her. Being with him was effortless, like letting go and allowing the current to take her.

'You really don't have anywhere to stay tonight?' Ryan said.

'No. I don't even have a sleeping bag.'

'Shame your old flat's occupied.'

'I don't know whether the sale's been completed. I handed my keys to the estate agent. Hold on.' Bea phoned her sister. Her mum would be suspicious if she phoned on a Saturday.

'Hi, Lizzie, I can't talk for long as I'm late for a meeting. Just checking – when's completion date on the flat? The 17th. Are you sure? No reason, just wanted to make sure Mum had time to get the cleaners in. No, I'm all settled in my new place. Yes, see you at Christmas.'

Ryan gave the thumbs up.

'Molly has a spare key and my duvet.' Bea kicked herself for not thinking of using the empty flat before sleeping at Hartleys.

When they stepped into her flat and closed the door, it felt as though the air was charged with expectation. If there were rules, Bea didn't care. She tilted her face to Ryan and when his lips settled ever so slightly on hers, she pulled him to her. Nothing in the world mattered apart from being there, right now, with this wonderful man, who made her feel complete.

51

EIGHT SHOPPING DAYS TO CHRISTMAS

'I'll see you back here at six?' Bea said with a flicker of anxiety in her voice.

She still had a bruise on her forehead and Ryan was overwhelmed with love for her. He could understand Bea's mum wanting to keep her safe. If he could wrap her in cotton wool and make sure nothing bad ever happened to her he would.

'Where else would I go?' Ryan enjoyed teasing her, to see her frown as she thought through her responses, selecting the most appropriate.

'Um. The *Moby*? Ash's bedsit?'

'I'll be here, waiting to hear how Alastair has promoted you to Queen of Knickers.'

Bea's face disappeared behind a curtain of hair as she checked her messages. 'We've got a meeting with comms at two.' Her face lit up and it was as though she warmed Ryan's core. 'Now I have something to tell them! I can't wait to tell Alastair about the designers and models. Oh. Sonia's left a message from the Courts of Justice. She says that she has good news. Everything is working out. Except for Declan.' Her face clouded over. 'And your da. I'm so sorry, Ryan.'

He loved the way her face was so transparent. It amazed Ryan that her boss, Alastair, couldn't see right through her. Bea was a bit naïve, despite being superintelligent. Ryan wondered whether Alastair was expecting Bea to fall flat on her face. Well he was going to be disappointed, because his wonderful girl had pulled it off. He never had any doubt that she would. 'I hate to leave you, but you really should get off to work, Bea.'

'I will after I pop in to the Law Courts to see what Sonia has to say. If we can pull this off.' Her face sparkled, and Ryan wanted to kiss her.

'Now go.'

'What are you doing today? Will you be here when I get back?'

'There's something I have to do.' She gave him a questioning look. 'It's a surprise.' And her face lit up. He wanted to do something that made her smile every day for the rest of her life.

They had spent all of Sunday in bed together, telling each other stories about their lives. It was hard to be parted and if Bea didn't have her job to save, he would lead her back to the bedroom and lose another day, lost in the wonder of her, until the lengthening shadows reminded them that outside time passed, just as it always had.

Bea kissed him. A long, slow, and lingering kiss. 'Okay. But six o'clock right here.' His heart went with her as he watched her trip away in her high-heeled Jiminy shoes, her outfit a little rumpled after three days' wear. *Keep safe,* he thought.

Bea turned and blew him a kiss. 'Don't be late.'

When she was lost from his sight, Ryan set off on his mission. He smiled to himself as he imagined Bea's delight, the way her face transformed when she was excited. He could watch her face all day, it was so mobile and expressive. She thought that she was cunning the way she considered carefully before replying but her expressions gave her away. He could read each of her answers as she tried them out in her head and discarded them. Her lips would purse, her brow furrow, or she would tilt her head as though being witty, then scowl and raise her eyebrows as though about to ask a question. If only she would believe him when he told her that she was okay being herself. Being Bea.

'Morning,' an older man said as he passed by.

Ryan was surprised to find that he was already smiling and so waved a hand in greeting. This morning, the canal looked and felt different. He no longer felt homeless. There was a sadness in his soul; he had lost a dear friend. Declan didn't deserve to die like that. But, Ryan and Ash were not surprised when they heard the news. It was what they had feared from the day Declan went missing. He would never be forgotten. Maybe, if this fashion thing was all that Bea had cracked it up to be, he might have some sort of legacy. That would be something. Ryan whistled a nursey rhyme that Ma sang to him as a kid. It was called *On Saturday night I lost my wife,* and was a sad song. Ryan thought of Declan, and hoped that he, like the wife in the rhyme, was playing a tune with the stars around him.

In a few days' time Ryan would return to Ireland to make peace with Da and say sorry to Caitlin. When he had left Ireland, he wanted to return with something to show for himself, to prove to Da that he was his own man, that he didn't need his approval. He was still penniless but something inside him had changed. Being with Bea filled him up with love, the anger and resentment that had found a harbour in his heart had now been cast away. It was time to head home.

To forgive Da and to forgive himself for not being the son that Da wanted.

Ryan returned along the tow path, swinging a bag that contained his gift-wrapped package for Bea. He had spent some of the money that Caitlin sent, but Bea said that if he booked in advance, he could find a cheaper fare. Maybe he and Bea could visit the farm together. His cheeks ached from smiling. He was so happy, his heart so full of love, he felt as though he could fly.

Ahead of him were a couple of men; they seemed to be waiting for someone or something. Ryan prepared to greet them, to wish them a happy Christmas. But there was a darkness about them and Ryan felt uneasy. One of them looked in his direction and then the others. The muscles between his ribs contracted with fear. Ryan glanced behind him. He was not alone, two men were approaching. The space between the groups of men shortened and Ryan felt as though the air between them compressed. A magnetic field of intent. And he the prey. No, he was being paranoid, looking for trouble, because he couldn't quite believe how life had changed so miraculously. A smile within softened the tension in his body and he thought again about his gift for Bea. He had spent all morning trawling Camden Market and the shops but it was perfect.

As he got closer, he could see their faces and knew without a doubt he was about to get a beating. Before he could prepare himself, he was clubbed from behind. The pain was like nothing he had experienced before. It felt as though his skull had been cracked in two. He fell to the ground. Another blow would follow. He thought of the gift that Bea would never receive. How she would be waiting for him and he wouldn't show.

A dog was barking. Footsteps running.

'Ryan, mate. Don't go to sleep. Hang on in there. Quiet, Bear. It's going to be okay, someone's called an ambulance.'

52

EIGHT SHOPPING DAYS TO CHRISTMAS

'You can really do that? Freeze the accounts and reimburse the money to all of the people in my application?' Bea thought Sonia must have got something wrong. After all, she was only a clerk, maybe she had misunderstood.

'Absolutely. Judge Reynolds has been in the last couple of days and he looked at your case. He's had a few like this recently and has taken an interest in scammers. The accounts have already been frozen and the money should be reimbursed by the end of this week.'

'Everybody's? Mine? Ryan O'Marley's? Chloe Winters's?' Bea couldn't remember all of the names, but with Declan's help she had tracked down eight people who had been victims of Kassab. Although one of the eight had since died and another could not be traced.

'Yes. We'll need to know which bank accounts to pay the money into.'

Bea thought this through. 'Could you write cheques? We'd like to present them to the victims as a surprise.'

It gave her goose bumps when she imagined Suki Dee handing out these cheques to people who thought that they had lost everything. One of them was Ryan. He could go back to Ireland with his head held high, although she didn't want him to – not yet. Lying in bed, oblivious to the outside world or time of day, they had imagined all sorts of futures. Ryan had told her his childhood dream of building a treehouse. They talked about raising a gaggle of rosy-faced kids and living in the country, travelling around the world – a kind of gap year. It had been a game of make-believe, but Bea knew that she didn't want to be parted from Ryan. He shone a light on the parts of herself that she had thought best hidden. He made her feel whole. Ryan was solid and strong, and he was tender. A bright light twinkled in his eyes, as though the vibrancy within could not be contained. The lilt in his voice. The softness of his lips.

'I've checked and that should be okay, but we would need to deliver them in person.' Sonia returned from a back office, jolting Bea back to reality.

Thoughts of Ryan had inspired her and now she said, 'Would you come to a charity show on Christmas Eve?' Bea outlined the event.

Sonia clapped her hands together. 'Ooh, I hope it's me. I love Suki Dee but I expect Judge Reynolds will want to be involved.'

When information had been exchanged, forms signed, and other administrative processes followed, Bea left the Royal Courts of Justice filled with elation. Things could not get any better. Everything, absolutely everything, was in place for the stupendous event that Suki Dee and her team had dreamed of. The one that everybody – including Bea – thought impossible. *I am awesome. I am awesome.* This afternoon they would ask comms to send out a press release and make sure that national media were there to record the event. Maybe even *Hello!* magazine.

It was almost midday when Bea arrived at work. She would have time to brief Alastair ahead of the meeting at two. Before going up to the fifth floor, Bea made her way through the food hall to find Mr Delaney, the catering manager. It felt so Christmassy, she couldn't resist buying a mini hamper. Ryan would be outraged at the extravagance, but they had so much to celebrate.

As Bea left Mr Delaney's office, satisfied that all necessary arrangements had been made for catering, she came across one of the boys in black. He had been visiting his mate and was returning to the back stairwell via Salami Street. Bea fell into step alongside him. 'Did you hear the sad news?' she said.

'Dec? Yeah. I was gutted. He was a good bloke.'

Bea wished that she had known Declan properly. At least she would make sure that he was remembered and his murderers brought to justice.

'I'm going up to lingerie now,' the boy in black said.

Bea wished she knew his name, but was too embarrassed to ask, in case she should have known. They walked together, and Bea felt protected. Before she was attacked by the security gorilla, the network of underground streets had not held any threat.

On the fashion floor, they parted. 'Another order for your friend Suki Dee. Is she trying to buy up the whole store?'

Bea laughed. Since meeting Ryan and his friends, she felt more comfortable around the boys in black than the haughty sales girls.

Alastair was standing by Bea's desk when she arrived a bit breathless after climbing the stairs. He glowered at her. 'My office. Now.'

Of course, Alastair was still angry about the meeting she

missed. Once she had explained the amazing plans that were now in place he would be congratulating her. Bea suppressed a grin and followed Alastair to his little glass palace.

He clasped his hands together and Bea guessed it was going to be harsh. 'Stevens. I don't know where to start.'

'Then let me,' Bea said, sliding in to the chair opposite. 'I'm sorry that I missed our meeting, but when you hear what I have to say you will be –'

'No. Let me speak first.' He spread his fingers, stretched and reclasped them, as though restraining them from their natural tendency to dance upon his head. 'You're fired. Dismissed. With immediate effect.'

Bea's heart beat like an enormous bass. One, two, three thumps before she spoke. 'I expect you're angry that I missed our meeting. But if we had met on Friday as planned, I wouldn't have been able to tell you about the fabulous designers and their collections. Oh Alastair, we have everything now – even the extra special something that Suki was looking for.'

'Didn't you hear what I said? You are fired. It is over.' He said the words slowly as though Bea was an imbecile, incapable of understanding. 'Suki Dee and her team have been informed.'

'We can't do that, not now. Just let me tell you –'

'If you could hand over your ID card and pass. Personnel will be writing to you. I've been instructed to see that you are escorted from the premises.'

'Why?' Bea asked, although she knew the answer.

'For sleeping in Hartleys overnight. Misusing your authority and abusing the trust of your employer.'

Alastair did not take his eyes off Bea as he phoned for security.

'Let me leave on my own. Please, Alastair.' The thought of

seeing that man again shocked Bea more than losing her job. The devastation would come, maybe like when you were executed and carried on running without a head, or was that just chickens?

Bea blindly made her way out of the store. She didn't see the baubles and glitter, or smell the perfume. It could be the last time she walked through Hartleys, certainly as an employee. Her feet knew what to do and Bea let them carry her.

When the glass doors closed behind her for the last time, Bea was numb. Her blood cold; an icy void within. Two security guards were standing the other side of the glass, thankfully not the gorilla who had preyed on her. One of them held up her suitcase.

Sav and the other designers had worked so hard. Ash and Ryan had spread the word inviting their friends to turn up on Christmas Eve to model the collections. They would be expecting a meal. And the cheques. Judge Reynolds was going to oversee the presentations by Suki Dee.

Somehow, Bea travelled back to the flat, although she remembered nothing of the journey. The hope of seeing Ryan hanging around outside had kept her going. He wasn't there, but Bea waited, just in case. She didn't want to go into an empty flat. Snow began to fall. She could no longer feel her toes, and tears formed icicles on her lashes. And then she went inside to wait some more.

They must have left the lights on. It seemed so long ago that they had dragged themselves from the bed and the warm haze of making love and make-believe to face the world, too dizzy to notice that the lights were still on. Bea pushed open the door.

'Who's there?' A frightened voice.

'Mum?'

53

EIGHT SHOPPING DAYS TO CHRISTMAS

'Okay, the truth, Beatrice. You've been trying to pull the wool over my eyes, but I wasn't born yesterday.' Mum spoke in clichés when she was very angry or disappointed, as though parroting her own mother. 'When I saw your bedding on the floor, I knew I was right.'

Bea gulped. Did Mum know what she and Ryan had been doing in there? Blood rushed to her face.

'You don't have a new flat, do you?'

What was the point? It was all over now. She might as well move back in with Mum and find a job in the local supermarket. Bea shook her head.

'I thought as much. What are you going to do now?' Mum looked at her with the same disapproval as she had when Bea walked out of her GCSE history exam because it took place in the hall where the lighting was too bright and the invigilator kept tapping her pen.

'Go home with you?' she murmured. A door slammed in the building and Bea rushed to the window.

'Are you expecting someone?' Mum had her interrogation look.

'No. Yes.' She might as well come clean before Ryan arrived. 'My boyfriend. Ryan.'

'I see. I'm pleased that you have a friend, especially if he makes you happy. But, you can't stay here, Beatrice. Contracts have been exchanged, completion's tomorrow. Why didn't you tell me you had the lock changed? I had to collect a set of keys from the estate agent. There's a lot you haven't told me.'

Bea checked her watch, it was just after six. 'I know and I'm sorry. I will tell you, but I have to pop out for a few minutes. I promise I won't be long.'

Ryan wasn't there. The snow was settling and she had come down without a coat or shoes. He would turn up soon, she was sure of it. Reluctantly, Bea returned to the flat to face her mum.

'I bought some milk, teabags, and mugs, but we've got to leave the flat spotless.'

Bea watched Mum making their tea in what had once been her kitchen. It felt as though everything was being taken from her, just when she had dared to believe that the impossible could happen. Fortunately, she didn't mention the change of lock again which gave Bea a bit of time to make up a story.

'The train from Hampshire is about an hour and fifteen minutes. Dad will have to give you a lift to and from the station, so add on thirty minutes and then, the journey across London. How long will it take to get to Knightsbridge?' Mum handed Bea a mug of tea.

Bea sipped and then put it down. She didn't much like tea. 'It doesn't matter. I lost my job.'

'What do you mean – you lost your job?' Mum sounded furious but Bea didn't know if it was with her or with Hartleys.

It was too humiliating to tell Mum that she had been fired for sleeping in the store overnight, because she had been too proud to admit that she didn't have anywhere to live.

'What about the celebrity event? I thought your boss was relying on you to make a success of it. If they've set you up to fail then you have to stand up for yourself.' Bea could imagine Mum storming into Mr Evans's office to give him a piece of her mind, as she had at school when she thought Bea had been unfairly punished.

'I had everything set up. The design collections, the models, and an exclusive, live exposé on fraud with money being refunded to the victims. Suki Dee would have loved it. I did the impossible, Mum.'

Bea's mum smiled. 'When you set your mind to something, there's no stopping you.'

'Except there is, because the event's been cancelled and I've been fired.'

'Then it's time to set your mind to overcoming that hurdle.'

Why was Mum cheering her on now, when there was no hope? Now was the time to say, *I told you so* and bundle her in the car – to turn back time as if she had never come to London. This time Bea really was defeated. It would be hard to tell Sav and her friends that their efforts had been in vain. The cheques could be sent to the victims, she just had to put them in contact with the High Court. As for the models, let them turn up at Hartleys. Let Alastair deal with a dozen homeless people expecting a meal.

'I need a coffee. I'll be back in a few minutes.' Mum gave a concerned look and Bea, moved by this unexpected confidence in her, gave her mum's arm a gentle squeeze as she passed.

Please let Ryan be there. Please let Ryan be there. The words beat a rhythm as her shoes clicked on the stairs. But he wasn't.

The snow was settling, a covering one centimetre deep. Had he changed his mind? Had he realised that she was a fraud? Maybe she had done everything wrong, being so inexperienced with men. Why hadn't she googled first? Was it something you could learn from YouTube? Maybe not. *Oh Ryan, where are you?*

When Bea returned with frozen fingers, a red nose, and no coffee, Mum didn't say a word. She just waited. That same concerned look on her face.

'It's too late,' Bea said. 'The event's been cancelled.'

'Then you've got to uncancel it. Go and see this Suki woman and tell her what you've planned. Let *her* decide whether or not she wants it cancelled. Now, we've got to be making tracks. It's dark and it's snowing and I don't like driving in either.'

They loaded the car with the bedding and Bea's suitcase. Satisfied that the flat was ready for the cleaners, Mum locked up. Bea left a note for Ryan with Molly, who promised to look out for him. She scanned every face that they passed as they walked to the car. No Ryan.

54

SEVEN SHOPPING DAYS TO CHRISTMAS

The next morning, Mum sent Bea off into battle, armed with good advice and her belief that with Bea's determination, she could achieve anything.

It was a bit of a revelation, that Mum actually believed her capable of turning things around. 'It's not your competence that I doubt, you're a very smart girl and no one else has your determination.' At this Mum had exhaled, as though releasing twenty-odd years of frustration at Bea's stubbornness. 'But, that doesn't stop me worrying about you. You have a big heart and –' she hesitated and when Bea gave a weak smile of encouragement, continued '– I'm afraid that sometimes people take advantage of that.'

Just when Bea had resigned herself to moving back to Hampshire and giving up on her dreams, Mum was showing her the door, with war cries of encouragement. If only Bea shared Mum's confidence. As the train rumbled into London, all she could think about was Ryan. There had to be a good reason why he hadn't shown up last night. She had gone over and over the day they spent together in the flat, searching for a clue. Maybe she had misread him. It had felt as though they were perfectly attuned to one another, as though she had found her missing piece. Could she really have got it so wrong? If she had, then Bea would never put herself in that situation again. She had given herself completely, trusting him. Believing that she could truly be herself and that he would love her. Of course he had had second thoughts. Ryan would probably be in Battersea by now. As far away from Bea as he could walk – even run. But what if he hadn't just come to his senses? What if he was in trouble?

When Bea got off the train at King's Cross, she looked for Ryan amongst the homeless people huddled in sleeping bags. Sal wasn't there today; hopefully she was somewhere warm. Bea smiled when she recognised a couple of the warm hats that she had bought – one on a man who could have been in his forties, and another on a younger man. They would be perfect models for the car factory recycled collection. Then, Bea remembered, there wasn't going to be a fashion show, unless she persuaded Suki Dee otherwise. Neither of the men had seen Ryan in the past couple of days and suggested Bea check the homeless shelters. They even gave her directions to the ones that Ryan frequented for a meal.

Bea wandered along the tow path towards Fandangle's Food barge. If she tracked him down to a shelter and he was hiding from her it would be embarrassing, but Leila, Roots, or Mouse might know something.

The music Bea heard as she approached the *Fandangle* filled the little cabin with vibrations. A whiskered accordion player tapped his foot as he played an Irish jig.

'Can you play something a bit more contemporary?' Leila said and he paused.

They both looked up at Bea, who waited at the bottom of the steps. There were no other customers.

'I'm sorry, you're busy,' Bea said.

'I can spare a few minutes. You and Ryan are coming to our party tonight?'

'Oh, you've kind of answered my question,' Bea sighed.

'Give us a minute,' Leila said to the accordion player.

'I'll stretch my legs.' He took the steps up to the deck and Leila frowned at Bea.

'Sit down. You look a little pale. Is everything okay?'

Bea didn't tell Leila everything. Just that she had been expecting to see Ryan the previous evening and he hadn't turned up.

'Ah, is that all? You know Ryan, he never knows what day it is. When you find him, tell him that you've got to come to our party!'

Bea left Leila planning the evening's entertainment with her accordion player. Mouse was out, Bear too, as there was no barking from within *No Worries*.

Ash was no help when she phoned him. 'He's homeless,' Ash said. 'A wanderer. That's what he does. But I'll call you if he shows up here.'

Nobody else seemed worried that Ryan had gone missing. Maybe she was expecting too much from him. Bea had walked back to King's Cross Station without noticing. It was time to visit Suki Dee. She had memorised her address from the packages waiting for delivery, but her heart wasn't in it. She didn't know how she was going to get her to change her mind, and it was unlikely that Suki Dee would even meet with her.

What if Ryan *had* arrived at the flat after they left? Where would he go looking for her? Hartleys. Bea's heart kicked up a notch. He would be hanging around outside waiting for her. Ryan didn't know that she had been sacked. Of course that's where he would be. Her mind raced ahead of her as she took the same journey that she had five times a week for three years. She was outside Hartleys and Ryan was waiting, his eyes on the doors which she had once told him she favoured, as they were closest to the Tube. His face would light up when she arrived and he would pretend that he had only just got there. Bea was running through their conversation, when the train pulled into Knightsbridge. She ought to feel sad visiting Hartleys, knowing that her career was over, but when Bea pressed that bruise it didn't hurt. Humiliation and anger at the way the security guard had treated her, and embarrassment that she had been so naïve as to believe that she could get away with camping out in the store, but no sorrow. Her future was uncertain. She didn't know where she would live or what she would do, but it didn't matter. Because, there was a certainty inside her, a feeling of strength and self-belief. And any moment now, she would be meeting Ryan.

Bea circled the building, taking in everybody who loitered by the doors. 'Happy Christmas,' she trilled as she passed them by, expecting the next face to be Ryan's.

55

SEVEN SHOPPING DAYS TO CHRISTMAS

Although disappointingly, Ryan wasn't waiting for Bea outside Hartleys, the visit had been worthwhile, because now she was clutching the packages addressed to Suki Dee, thanks to her new friend, and was ringing the doorbell of an impressive four-storey house on the edge of Hyde Park.

'Deliveries to the side entrance.' A man answered the door and then shut it before Bea could introduce herself.

She had taken trouble with her appearance that morning, partly for Suki Dee's benefit but more for Ryan's. When she finally accepted that Ryan wasn't there, a feeling of dread crept over her. Declan's killer could have finished what he started. Ryan might already be dead. It was unbearable. She couldn't, wouldn't, dwell on that possibility. All of his friends said that there was nothing to worry about and they knew him better than Bea. But they didn't. They had just known him longer. Reasoning would not lighten the weight of dread that pressed like a vice on her heart. But, she had a delivery for Suki and this was her last chance to save the fashion event.

Not for Hartleys. Not even for her own future there; she no longer cared about being head of department. It seemed so trivial now. For Declan. For Ryan. For justice. For the people who had been swindled. For people who had no place to call home. And for the amazing fashion designers who were dedicated to saving the planet. Bea rapped on the back door.

The same man answered the back door and Bea had to bite her tongue. Maybe she did roll her eyes a little; it was hard not to when she could see through the hallway to the front door. Bea clung on to the parcels as the man tried to take them from her.

'Suki asked for them to be delivered in person,' she lied.

'Stay there.' He shut the door in her face. Again.

When the door opened a moment later it was by the young woman who had accompanied Suki Dee on her visit to Hartleys the day Bea had assisted with the fitting.

'Oh, it's you,' the woman said and she smiled, which was a good start. 'Suki didn't tell me that she was expecting you. I'm sure it's okay to leave the packages with me, as Suki has company.'

'I *could.*' Bea bit her lip. 'But, with it being so close to Christmas, if we haven't got it right…'

The woman had the same frightened look in her eyes as she had when Suki went into a meltdown in the Exclusive stylist suite. 'Yes. I see what you mean. Suki's wearing a new dress to a party tomorrow and if the undergarments aren't perfect… Maybe you'd better come in.'

Suki's housekeeper/maid/dresser – Bea wasn't sure of her title, but it seemed that she and Tom, the man who answered the door, did everything for Suki that needed doing – was called Heidi. Whilst they waited for Suki's visitors to leave, Heidi explained that Suki's partner, the actor Conran Holiday, was flying back from New York for the party and Suki wanted to look sensational.

When an hour had passed and several coffees had been consumed, Heidi said, 'Maybe I should interrupt Suki. You'll be wanting to get back to Hartleys and if Suki said she wanted you to wait, well, I'd better interrupt her.'

Bea followed Heidi up the stairs to the first floor. The house was uncluttered, expansive hallways and rooms, flooded with light from floor-to-ceiling windows, and views over Hyde Park.

'She's with a fashion editor from Russian *Vogue*,' Heidi explained as she knocked lightly on the door of another reception room.

Bea felt a frisson of excitement at the prospect of meeting a *Vogue* fashion editor. As she waited behind Heidi, Bea strained to hear the conversation. The fashion editor, a man with great poise and cheekbones to rival Johnny Depp, was talking in Russian. His eyes did not leave Suki Dee's, although she was dependent upon his translator to understand the meaning. Suki ignored their intrusion, as she watched each word fall from his lips.

Bea was able to follow most of what he said. 'Your feature will be in the November edition at the agreed rate. However, that is dependent upon us securing an exclusive for our glamour magazine.'

The interpreter said, 'Your feature will be in the November edition at the agreed rate. It is dependent upon us having an exclusive.'

Bea waited for the interpreter to finish the translation, but she didn't. Then, Suki noticed that Heidi wasn't alone. She dropped her kittenish pose and roared at Heidi, 'How dare you bring a visitor into a confidential meeting.'

'I'm sorry, Suki.' Heidi started to back out of the door, but Bea squeezed past her.

'Miss Licious, I'm sorry to interrupt but I've been asked to deliver these parcels in person.' Whatever happened next it couldn't make things worse than they already were.

Suki Dee looked as though she was about to erupt with rage. Heidi had disappeared, closing the door gently behind her.

'We have nearly finished here,' the fashion editor said, standing up. This was interpreted fully. He extended his hand to shake Suki Dee's.

'Excuse me whilst I show this intruder out,' Suki said, glaring at Bea. 'I'll deal with Heidi later,' she muttered.

'You didn't fully interpret the bit about the exclusive,' Bea said to the interpreter in Russian.

The interpreter blushed and said something to the editor. She spoke too quickly for Bea to follow the conversation but it seemed that she was defending her position. No doubt, she guessed that Suki would never have agreed to the terms he had suggested. Suki was watching this exchange with a questioning look on her brow.

Bea explained to Suki in English, 'The full interpretation should have been, "Your feature will be in the November edition at the agreed rate. However, that is dependent upon us securing an exclusive for our glamour magazine."'

Suki looked at the fashion editor for confirmation. He raised his palms and shrugged, as if it was nothing.

'Find out exactly what the deal is,' Suki said to Bea.

So, Bea acted as interpreter. Her Russian wasn't perfect, but she was able to pin down the key elements of the contract and no, Suki did not know that she was agreeing to pose naked for the glamour magazine. And the fashion editor had no intention of commenting on Suki's humanitarian work, although it seemed that the nature of that was still a bit vague. It ended with Suki and the beautiful Russian man shouting at each other, exchanging expletives in both English and Russian.

Then, when they had been shown out by Tom, Bea helped Heidi to calm Suki. No longer an unwanted intruder, Bea was a heroine.

She left Suki Dee's house two hours later with Suki's request that the event go ahead as planned. Bea told her about the exposé of the scammers and how those that had been duped of their life savings would be handed cheques by Suki Dee. It was everything that Suki had hoped for. She would launch her career as a goodwill ambassador for the homeless, an advocate for social justice, better access to health, housing, and work opportunities.

'You've got to help me in this role,' Suki implored Bea, clasping both of her hands. 'I can't do this without you. I'll put you on my payroll. Just say what you want. You can do all of the research, manage my publicity.'

It was all a bit overwhelming for Bea. 'Let's take one step at a time. First, you need to contact Hartleys to let them know you want to go ahead. As soon as I have the okay, I'll put everything in place for Christmas Eve.'

She stepped out of the front door and down the steps, her head in a whirl. Suki was just being dramatic; she would forget that she had offered Bea a job as soon as the event had passed. Her enthusiasm for improving the lives of homeless people would be discarded like yesterday's outfit. But the event was going to happen. If only she knew that Ryan was okay, her world would be complete. And then, as if in answer to her plea, Bea's phone rang. It was Mouse.

56

SEVEN SHOPPING DAYS TO CHRISTMAS

A nurse was blocking Ryan's view of the ward entrance as he went in search of a payphone, and so he didn't see Bea until her voice attracted his attention.

'Is there a Ryan O'Marley on this ward?'

Ryan had tormented himself thinking about Bea. She would have waited for him outside her flat and when he didn't show up she would think that he had done a runner. Surely, she must know that he would never do anything to hurt her. He didn't have a phone and even if he had, he didn't know how to reach her. Her voice was liquid gold infusing his soul and for a few seconds Ryan forgot the sickening pain in his head, back, and limbs. She didn't see him at first, and so Ryan took delight in observing this beautiful woman who was here because she loved him. It was the first time since Ma died that he felt cherished. Bea's love did his body more good than the drip he was dragging alongside him.

. . .

The bright lights and noise jarred Bea's already frayed nerves. Mouse told her that Ryan had been attacked and if he and Bear hadn't frightened the men off they would have killed him. When Mouse had left him at the hospital he was stable, but the doctors were concerned that he might have brain damage as a result of the head injury. She should have checked the hospitals when he didn't turn up instead of doubting him. *Please let him survive.* She would stand by him no matter what, even if she had to do everything for him for the rest of his life.

'Hey. I'm over here. Bea. Wait.'

Bea turned to see Ryan hobbling towards her. His poor face was scratched and bruised but he was there. In one piece. Looking like the most gorgeous man she had ever set eyes on. She caught her breath and everything around her faded – the bright lights, the rumbling trolley, a patient's plaintive cry. Everything was still. It was just her and Ryan. She wanted to hold him, to press him into her until his being was imprinted on her soul. But all she could do was look at him. There were no words.

'Would you like to use the relatives' room?' a nurse asked.

When they were sitting alone in a quiet room, they could finally talk. Ryan went first explaining how he had tortured himself worrying about what she would think when he didn't meet her as planned.

'Mouse phoned me. He's worried sick about you. We both thought you might have brain damage. Let me phone him back and tell him you're okay.' She couldn't stop smiling as she gave Mouse an update.

"He says that we're to stay with him on *No Worries* until you've fully recovered,' Bea said when she had hung up.

'It was the same men who killed Declan, wasn't it?' she said.

'Probably.'

'I have at least found a way to expose Kassab. A lot has happened to me too since we parted yesterday morning.'

Bea told Ryan about how she had lost her job and the event had been cancelled. Then she had to wait whilst he went through some of the emotions that she had in the past forty-eight hours, only Ryan flipped through them in seconds as Bea moved on to the happy ending. And then he hugged her, forgetting his injuries, and they both laughed as he yelped in pain.

'So, it's back on? That's fantastic! I've got a present for you, but it's in my locker.'

'Ooh, the surprise you spoke about when we said goodbye yesterday morning?'

'The very same. For my Princess Bea. It's a Christmas present but you can open it now.'

When they were back at Ryan's bed, he passed Bea a gift-wrapped package.

Inside were a pair of blue wellington boots patterned with yellow bees.

'I love them! How on earth did you find them?'

'I would like to pretend it was easy but it wasn't, it took hours. I was looking for a pair of glamorous snow boots but when I found these I knew that they were perfect.'

Bea tried them on. 'And they fit. But, these are an expensive brand. How did you…' She shouldn't have asked. Now she had spoilt it all by humiliating him. Why did she always say the wrong thing?

Ryan stood up. He looked sad.

'I'm sorry, Ryan, I didn't mean… I shouldn't have said…'

He pulled a piece of paper from his pocket. 'It's okay. I wanted to show you this. It's from my sister.'

Bea recognised the envelope as the one that she had

forwarded to him from Peacock Court. She read Caitlin's letter.

'You didn't spend your airfare on my present?'

'Not all of it. It's okay. I wanted to do something special for you.'

Bea read the letter a couple more times, committing it to memory, and then she handed it back. 'When will you be discharged?'

'The doctor's going to see me on her round this evening. They don't think I've fractured my skull or got brain damage but there are still some test results that they're waiting on.' He gently patted his head. 'This is pretty thick. Good job I'm a bit of a numbskull.'

The thought of what might have happened to Ryan if Mouse hadn't got to him in time overwhelmed Bea. 'I couldn't have... If you had...'

'Hey, I'm alright.' Ryan took her hand in his. 'I'll be out in time for your Christmas extravaganza.'

57

CHRISTMAS EVE

'Can I keep the shoes?' An elegant lady in a silk dress waved a pair of cerulean blue shoes at Bea. They were perfect, as they matched the blue in the patterned dress, one of the refashioned kimonos.

Bea wondered whether Alastair had sneaked in some professional models and looked more closely at the woman before her.

'Don't recognise me, do you?' Of course, it was Sal but her hair, which was usually hidden beneath a jaunty hat, had been cut into a choppy bob that fell in waves around her face. Her mousy hair had blonde highlights and her face was made up.

'You look gorgeous,' Bea said.

Sal winked and did a little wiggle before slinking off in her killer heels. If Sal wanted the shoes, Bea would see if she could keep them. Maybe she just wanted a reminder that she was a beautiful woman.

Heidi poked her head around the dressing room door. 'Sal needs to be interviewed by the film crew and then they should be ready for the fashion show. Where are the cheques for Suki? There's a big turnout. Oh, this is so exciting!'

Bea had it all under control. The past week she had worked like a demon but everything had come together and today felt like the best day of her life. Her friends and family were out there waiting for the fashion show: Suki and the other designers, Leila, Roots, Mouse, Ash, Ryan of course, and Mum and Dad. Bea had a couple of surprises for them all. Bringing those to fruition had really tested her tenacity and resourcefulness, but she had done it. Today, Bea didn't need a mantra to convince herself of her worth. She had done what she thought was impossible.

'Tell them we will be ready to go in thirty minutes,' Bea said as Sal slinked behind Heidi practicing her catwalk poses.

There was a standing ovation for the recycled fashion designers who came to the stage to take their bow. The event was being covered by a news documentary team but there were also photographers from celebrity and fashion magazines. Sav and her friends posed with their arms around one another. And then Sav waved at Bea, inviting her to join them on the stage.

'Go on,' Ryan said, sensing Bea's reluctance to be in the limelight.

Standing in the centre of the designers whilst the audience continued to whoop and clap, Bea felt as though her heart was too big to contain. The cameras eventually stopped clicking and the designers left the stage for Suki Dee.

'You have a visitor waiting in the Exclusive stylist suite. She said that you wanted to greet her personally,' Pippa said.

Suki Dee would be addressing the audience for thirty minutes and then it would be time to present the cheques.

There was no time to be nervous, she just had to go down there and meet her.

The young woman waiting in the Exclusive stylist suite was with Mr Evans of all people.

'Miss Stevens, you have excelled yourself. Hartleys are proud to host this worthy event and I am proud to have you on my staff team. In fact, I have a proposal for you, so don't go rushing off this evening until after you've seen me. Now, this young lady is waiting to meet you and I believe you will be wanted back on stage in a few minutes.'

Bea took in what Evans was saying but all of the while her eyes were on the girl, Caitlin. She looked so much like Ryan, Bea wanted to hug her.

Evans took his leave and the girls faced one another.

'I came as soon as I could, in fact my plane only landed a couple of hours ago.' Caitlin looked as though she might cry. 'I can't wait to see him. Does he know that I'm here?'

'No.' Bea had a lump in her throat. Ryan didn't know Caitlin was here, or that his da had died some months ago. 'He'll be overjoyed to see you.' That was an understatement. Bea knew that Ryan adored his sister and that he had been hurting ever since he read her letter. 'Come on. You can watch the rest of the show from the wings and then I'll take you to him.'

Suki was in full flow and Bea admired her acting ability; she knew how to play for the camera. There was complete silence as Suki spoke of the plight of people who lost their life savings as a result of scammers. Bea had done her research and Suki spoke confidently as though she had spent her entire life fighting for social justice. Behind her, a screen showed a film that had been prepared earlier – interviews with some of the people scammed telling their stories.

'Wait here. Look, you can see him there in the front row. He's sitting next to my parents.' Bea squeezed Caitlin's hand.

The film was coming to an end, and Bea could see a few people wiping tears from their eyes.

The spotlight was back on Suki Dee. 'But that's not the end of the story,' she said. 'Some of you may have known Declan Connor.' There was a murmur across the audience. 'In fact, he worked here at Hartleys for a while as a delivery boy.'

The boys in black called out, 'Yay, Declan.' And Bea imagined Declan high fiving them.

'The models here today were friends of Declan; he was a popular man. It was my request that they participated in this event to *Do It for Dec.*' Suki paused to wait for the applause to die down. 'Declan Connor started what I have finished. He tracked down the scammers that defrauded the people in this film.' There was more applause and whooping. 'It was Declan's courage and determination that resulted in him being cruelly murdered.' Now there was complete hush.

'On 14th November, Declan Connor arranged to meet with the scammers – representatives from Kassab Enterprises. The outfit that fronted each and every one of the scams that you have just heard about.' There was a grumbling as people turned to their neighbour to express their disgust. 'Declan was injected with a lethal dose of heroin and dumped in a disused railway station.' In the second row, Ash had covered his face. Bea wondered whether Suki Dee's sensationalising of Declan's murder was perhaps insensitive to his loved ones – Ryan and Ash. Declan had grown up in care, he didn't have a family. In a way all of the people here today who were 'doing it for Dec' were his family. He would have been proud of them.

'But it wasn't Kassab himself that delivered this blow.' The tension in the room was palpable. Even Ryan didn't know what Bea had uncovered with the High Court when they reviewed Kassab Enterprises' bank statements. Judge Reynolds had gone the extra mile. He was in the audience somewhere with Sonia. Bea made a mental note to introduce Sonia to Suki Dee when it was time for refreshments.

'The men who murdered Declan worked for Hussein Kassab. Why this senseless killing? Because he was close to exposing Kassab for being a scammer. Today, we are here to see justice done for Declan and for the people who were victims of fraud. With the assistance of the High Court I froze the bank accounts of Kassab Enterprises and now I have a few more surprises.'

Suki Dee called each of the fraud victims to the stage, one by one, and handed them a cheque. Finally, she called the name Ryan O'Marley. Ryan hadn't been included in the film and didn't know that he too would get his money back. As he leaned back to find Bea in the wings, his face changed to one of disbelief. He had seen Caitlin.

The next part was unscripted. Ryan threw open his arms and Caitlin ran to him. As they hugged and cried the audience cheered, enjoying the drama without understanding what was going on.

Suki Dee improvised and asked Ryan to tell his story, which he did, with Caitlin wiping away her tears.

'And so, this is the first time you have seen your sister since you left Ireland nearly two years ago?' Now Ryan was crying too.

58

LATER

Ryan was overwhelmed. Bea had kept her secrets well – Caitlin's visit and evidence to link Kassab to Declan's murder. She was an amazing woman as he had repeatedly told her parents. Now, he was sitting in the Exclusive stylist suite away from the cameras with his little sister.

When they had finished hugging each other and crying, which took some time, Ryan said, 'I'm sorry I didn't come home. You know why now, but if I'd received your letter sooner I would have. How is Da?'

Caitlin took his hands in hers. 'I'm sorry, Ryan, he passed away three months ago. He wasn't in too much pain, not until the end, and then he had morphine.'

'Did he ask for me?'

Caitlin looked remorseful and Ryan knew that she was filtering what to say before she spoke. 'Yes. I told you in my letter, he complained that neither Sean nor I shaved him properly not like you.'

'I bet Sean curses me.'

'No,' Caitlin laughed. 'But there was one time that he broke a mug and Da went crazy, said it was one that you made for him.'

'The one I painted at school?'

'I think so. I always thought it was Ma's mug but when it got smashed, Mother of God.' Caitlin threw up her hands. 'You'd have thought it was our best china.'

Ryan had forgotten about the mug that he painted at school. How he had been desperate for Da to come home so that he could present him with his gift. Why hadn't he shown any appreciation at the time? His rejection had made Ryan feel worthless, as though there was nothing that he could do to make the bugger love him. And now this. His throat tightened.

'I should have been at his funeral. I am so sorry, Caitlin.'

'Come here, you eejit.' Caitlin hugged him tight.

'How are things with the farm? I hope Sean's not regretting taking it on.'

'It's a challenge, for sure, but we're not quitters. Da left you money in his will.'

Ryan hadn't expected anything, but it was good of Da to think of him.

'He and Ma agreed years ago that one of us would inherit the farm and the other a lump sum from the sale of the farthest meadow.'

This was news to Ryan. When Da said that he wouldn't inherit the farm, he thought that meant he wouldn't get anything. So much had been misunderstood between them. He felt Ma's loving presence, as though she was smiling on him. Da would be with her now and Ryan hoped that he was at peace and that Ma had forgiven them both for wasting so much time fighting. The farthest meadow had been left for nature to do its thing, because they couldn't afford to do anything else with it. Ryan had thought Da was being stubborn when he refused to sell the land to bring in some extra income. Now he understood. Da was keeping it for him.

'But you'll need the meadow for the herd,' Ryan said.

'It's already been sold. We got a tidy sum for it – seventy-five thousand pounds, no lie.'

Seventy-five thousand pounds. Ryan felt as though he was dreaming. This morning he was a homeless pauper and now he had choices.

As if on cue Bea joined them. She looked from one to the other trying to read their faces. Ryan explained about his da and his unexpected inheritance.

'I've got some news of my own,' Bea said. 'I've been offered head of luxury accessories.'

'Yay!' Ryan punched the air. 'Congratulations, Bea.'

'I haven't decided yet whether I want the job. I would have been over the moon a few weeks ago, but so much has changed.'

Ryan watched her beautiful face as happiness, doubt, and then resolve flitted across it.

'*I've* changed. Maybe I haven't changed so much as got to know myself better. I love fashion but I'm not good with customers. I can't pretend to be somebody that I'm not. Suki Dee has offered me a job too, helping her to build her humanitarian profile.'

'So, what are you going to do?' Caitlin asked.

'I have an idea but I need to talk to Evans and Suki. I want to buy and sell recycled fashion for Hartleys, both in the store and through the internet, but not on the shop floor dealing with customers face to face. I'm no good at that. I want a percentage of all sales to go to a trust fund for homeless people – one that helps them to get social justice. It could be in memory of Declan. Maybe I could be self-employed but work for Hartleys and Suki Dee.'

'Wow. Did you just think that up?' Ryan said.

'Kind of. But in a way the idea has been taking shape ever since you came up with that thing about finding a shoe to fit.'

Caitlin made a face and Ryan and Bea smiled sharing the memory.

'You made me realise that I had been trying to meet other people's expectations instead of figuring out what was best for me.'

'Sounds like my big brother,' Caitlin said. 'I miss his wise words. Now, brother of mine, what about you? Are you going to buy a little cottage in Ireland, somewhere near the farm? Please say you're coming home. At least for Christmas.'

'There's nothing I'd love more than to spend Christmas with you and Sean on the farm.'

'And then?' Bea and Caitlin said together.

'And then I'm coming back.'

Bea let out her breath and Ryan hugged to himself the knowledge that she loved him. He didn't need the money to feel rich. Bea had enriched his life more than he would have thought possible.

'I'm going to put my carpentry skills to good use. Mouse and I are going to renovate houseboats. How would you like to live on the canal, Bea?'

Joy and then suspicion flitted across her face. 'Please don't tell me you're thinking of the *Moby*?'

'We could rename her the *Queen Bee*.'

'No,' Bea said. 'Just *Bea*.'

MORE INFORMATION

If you enjoyed reading Just Bea a review would be much appreciated as it will help other readers discover this story. A rating and just a few words would be great.

If you would like to find out more about me and my books you can find me at

www.abrakdeborah.wordpress.com

Sign up to my readers list to receive a quarterly newsletter with additional stories about the characters in my books, behind the scenes information, book release dates and more.

You can also follow me on:

Twitter: @DeborahKlee

Facebook: https://www.facebook.com/DKleeAuthor

ACKNOWLEDGMENTS

I am immensely grateful for the help and support of friends, family, experts, professionals, and other creatives in the writing and publication of this book.

I will start at the beginning of this book's journey by thanking Sue Chotipong, who worked for many years as a buyer at Harrods of Knightsbridge. Sue took me on a tour of Harrods revealing its hidden depths and shared fascinating stories about the store's history, its customers, and staff.

The other inspiration for this book came from talking to homeless people on the street. Everyone has a story. This book is dedicated to all of you.

I am privileged to be a member of The Frinton Writers' Group. A group of talented novel writers and friends. Thank you for your encouragement, support, and insightful critiques: Anita Belli, Gerald Hornsby, Ellie Holmes, Lesley Kara, Janet Bridger, Janine Swann, Peter Best, and Catherine Rendall.

I was fortunate to be supported by three excellent editors: Anna Barrett, Ellie Holmes and Beth Attwood. Thank you for the time and commitment you invested in this book and in me as a writer.

Asya Blue is responsible for the beautiful cover design. Thank you Asya for listening to my vague ideas and turning them into something wonderful.

OTHER BOOKS BY DEBORAH KLÉE

THE BORROWED BOY

A borrowed boy, a borrowed name and living on borrowed time.

What do you put on a bucket list when you haven't done anything with your life? No interesting job, no lovers, no family, no friends. Believing she has only weeks left to live, Angie Winkle vows to make the most of every minute.

Going back to Jaywick Sands, is top of her bucket list. Experiencing life as a grandmother is not, but the universe has other plans and when four-year-old Danny is separated from his mum on the tube, Angie goes to his rescue. She tries to return him to his mum but things do not go exactly as planned and the two of them embark on a life changing journey.

Set in Jaywick Sands, once an idyllic Essex holiday village

in the 70s, but now a shantytown of displaced Londoners, this is a story about hidden communities and our need to belong.

Reviews from readers of The Borrowed Boy:

★★★★★ Engaging characters, good pacing, an absorbing story, an almost palpable sense of place, and a heart-warming ending.
★★★★★ This book has the feel-good factor. Lovely well written characters with depth. Great story line. A great read for on the beach or a cosy weekend at home.
★★★★★ An accomplished book that touches on a myriad of emotions whilst delivering an exciting plot that keeps you turning the pages.
★★★★★ This is one of those books that you start reading and can't put down. Full of warmth, humour and characters that you care about. This a thrilling book full of twists and turns where you're routing for our unlikely hero Angie Winkle.
★★★★★ A lovely story, told with heart and humour and one which will hold you rapt until the end.
★★★★★ This is a novel that will tug at your heart strings. There is a dark undercurrent too, but that only makes it more interesting and exciting to read. I also loved the humour threaded through. It is a book of light and shade, but ultimately a life-affirming story. Highly recommended.

Available from Amazon:
UK: https://amzn.to/2CZJ6yL
USA: https://amzn.to/2CZIEAz
Other: https://bit.ly/2HZ6m2V
And all good bookstores

Printed in Great Britain
by Amazon

23138537R00212